KING

OF

CORIUM

USA TODAY BESTSELLING AUTHORS

C. HALLMAN
& J. L. BECK

1

QUINTON

*I*t's funny how one day all can be normal in your life, and then the next, the rug is ripped away, and you're left fumbling, trying to regain your footing. A year ago, I was a different person. Happy, normal, and content with my life. I couldn't think of one thing I would've changed about my life, but now, if I could, I'd change it all.

Every-fucking-thing.

It wasn't like my father had sheltered me from our namesake or the violent and dangerous things we did. The blood running in my veins was mafia blood; my father had bled for our name, and I know I will do the same someday.

Growing up, I didn't think there would ever be a time when that would change or that I would want to escape the life I was born into and hide from the rest of the world, but that day came one year ago, and since then, everything's been headed in a downward spiral.

The happiness inside me shattered and evaporated into thin air, making me the vile pit of anger and hate. I didn't need this pathetic university, but it was this or sitting in that giant house, a reminder of everything I wanted to leave behind looming over my head. At least now, I might be able to escape my mother's constant worrying and my father's watchful eyes.

"Ready?" I ask, glancing over at Ren.

He shrugs, his hands still tucked perfectly into the pockets of his black jeans. Even with all the money his family has, he still chooses to wear the least expensive clothing. Ren is modest at best, never showing or bragging about what he has. It seems like he cares about nothing, but the truth is, he simply doesn't give a shit about material things. The single most important thing in the world to him isn't even a thing, but a person. His sister.

Sometimes, I think the only reason I've been so close to my sisters is because I see how Ren is with Luna. My father once told me it's because of how they grew up, and that they only had each other for so long, which is why he's so protective over her.

Ren has always been her protector, and I doubt that will ever change.

"If you want my honest opinion, I'd rather jump off a cliff, but..." His voice trails off.

You and me both, I want to say, but I keep the words to myself. The last thing I need is what I've said getting back to my father and him thinking I'm suicidal. Then I really won't have a choice in coming or going.

"If you didn't want to go, you didn't have to. I'm sure your father would've allowed you to take some time off or do something else."

Ren understands my life more than anyone else ever will, but that doesn't mean he knows what it's like to have a father who never takes no for an answer or to be dealt the blow that we were just dealt.

"Believe me, I made the best choice." I speak through my teeth, staring off into the nothingness.

It wasn't like I was going to a normal university, where I'd be bored out of my mind.

No, Corium University is where high-profile criminals around the world send their children. While normal parents send their kids off to state universities, expecting them to get a decent education and good job, our parents ship their children off to Corium, a school that will teach them how to become better criminals.

I don't need training or guidance, but I want to go anyway. Which is why, for the unforeseen future, cold-ass Alaska will be my home. I want as many miles as I can get between my family and me. I can only hope that the more miles I put between us, the less the pulsing ache in my chest will bleed.

The sound of the helicopter propellers slicing through the air invades my ears, bringing me back to the present. I look up just in time to see my father's plane—which brought us to this small Alaskan airport—taking off in the distance. The private plane dropped us here, and the school's helicopter will take us to the university.

The wind whips through my hair, and I shield my eyes as rock and dust debris swirl around us. Ren is standing beside me as still as a statue. We've been best friends since his parents adopted him and his sister, Luna, when they were kids. Most people think we're cousins, but I've always seen him as my brother.

It's a little ironic that most people don't even know my actual cousin because my uncle chose to keep his only daughter hidden from the world.

Shoving my hands deep into the pockets of my jacket, I exhale and start toward the helicopter. I don't have to look back to know Ren is following me. We agreed to do this together. Well, more like I told him he had to come with me. Surprisingly, it didn't take much convincing. I figured he would fight me since leaving meant being away from Luna, but unlike me, Ren will travel home to visit his parents and sister. He'll call and talk to them.

Whereas I'll do everything I can to pretend mine don't exist while still doing my best to maintain a relationship with my sister, Scarlet.

I drop into my seat, and Ren takes the seat beside me as the roar of the engine fills the space.

It's only a short flight to the secluded area that used to be an old military base before recently being turned into a high-tech university. The place is so classified there are no pictures of it anywhere online. My father, of course, helped with the funding. Yet another reminder that going here is nothing more than a false sense of escapism. Still, to me, it is better than nothing.

I let my eyes fall closed with a sigh, the weight on my chest already lessening with each breath I take. The darkness inside me, however, swirls, building slowly. For months, night-mares have plagued me, making it hard for me to sleep at night. I let out a yawn and sink my head back into the head-rest. I try not to think of how fucked up my life has become in the past year, how much of a lie it's all been, or worse, how much I've lost, *we've* lost. Shoving it all to the back of my mind, I allow myself to shut down. I must doze off because a short while later, I blink my eyes open and find Ren leaning across my seat to look out the small window at something off in the distance.

"How long have I been out?" I yell over the loud roar of the engine, shifting forward in my seat.

"Long enough for me to realize just how in the middle of nowhere this place is. If you wanted to commit murder and get away with it, this would be the place to do it."

"What are you talking about?" I ask, brow furrowed.

Ren points out the window, and I lean forward to see what the hell he's looking at. I scan the area below us. Hundreds of miles of trees stretch from where we are and in every direction. There are no roads, no houses, just nothingness until I notice what looks to be an old fortress, half-built into the side of a snow-covered mountain.

From the little bit of research I was able to do on this place, I know it used to be a castle, left behind from when the Russians owned this land before the United States took it over in the late 1800s. I never could've guessed it was this isolated, though. Then again, that's probably for the better if you're housing the offspring of thousands of criminals.

"Whose idea was it to build a fucking university out here?" I ask the question out loud without realizing it.

"I'm pretty sure someone who wants to torture us. It's the only sign of life I've seen this whole flight."

My father told me the place was secluded, but I would never have anticipated this. Ren is right; we're in the middle of nowhere. Most colleges are huge structures, elaborate and expensive-looking, drawing the attention of every graduating student like a beacon, but this place looks like an abandoned castle. Of course, that's by design. A single road seemingly appears out of nowhere and winds up the mountainside, and a large stone wall separates the outside from the inside.

"We're preparing to land." The pilot's voice comes over the intercom system.

"You ready?" Ren asks.

I turn in my seat, the finality of it all finally sinking in. I'm finally free, or at least a little bit free. I grin, knowing that at this place, my darkest desires and needs can be brought to light. Here I won't have to hide the pain. I won't have to pretend to exist. Anyone who gets in my way will become a target.

I suck a ragged breath into my lungs, my chest suddenly feeling lighter.

"I'm ready, but I doubt this place is ready for us."

"Probably not." Ren gives me an equally dark smile.

The lower we get, the better the view of the university becomes. I realize how massive the place is when we finally land and exit the helicopter. The structures that seemed so small are larger than they appeared so high up. My heart starts to race in my chest, the sound thundering in my ears.

From the helipad, we walk down a small path that leads into a tunnel, and the fact that this place was rebuilt to be a military base becomes readily apparent. After a short walk, we end up at an enormous door that looks as if it could withstand a direct bomb blast. Several checkpoints and guardhouses lead up to the entrance, and everyone gives us a chin nod as we walk by.

Rumor has it, the government had big plans for this place. Using and expanding on the underground tunnels already built, they were ready to move their troops in. They were less than happy when the founding members bought it right out from under their noses.

Nobody moves an inch from their posts or asks us for identification. I suppose when your father is who he is, you get special treatment. Not only is my father one of the most powerful criminals, he also pours a lot of money into this school.

"So is this a university, or are we walking into some secret society shit?" Ren nudges me with his shoulder.

"Both."

Either way, a lot of money was put into this place to make it secure. Which, of course, makes it perfect for the type of activities that occur deep underground here.

It would be difficult to even get a satellite to focus here. Not that the government would do that. This place probably doesn't exist to them... *anymore.*

A guard escorts us to the entryway through the large bomb-proof doors. Just inside are an identical set of metal doors with the university's crest edged into it.

The double doors ahead of us open automatically, and Ren and I glance at each other. It's not an awestruck look that we give each other, but more of a what the hell have we got ourselves into. My father provided us with information for our room and class schedule before we left, so there's no need for us to stop anywhere or ask where to go next. We move deeper into the building, walking down the long corridor. The floors are polished marble, and the dim lighting gives the place a unique feel—like we're being marched off to integration instead of our dorms.

Ahead are three elevators. Ren pushes the button, and the doors open immediately. We step inside, and I press the glowing C button, which is the level our room is on.

As the elevator doors open with a bing, Ren nudges me with his shoulder, holding his phone out to me. I look down and see there's a map on the screen.

"At the end of this hall, we turn right, and our room should be on the left-hand side."

I shrug. "I studied the map before we left. I've got most of this place mapped out in my mind."

Ren shakes his head. He knows I like to be prepared.

We were each given a key card to get into our room before we left, and it was space we decided to share. We were both given the opportunity to have our own small one-bedroom apartment but decided against it. Ren isn't the boyfriend type, so all I had to worry about was a random hookup here or there.

Neither of us is interested in anything other than mindless sex.

As we walk down the hall, I notice a few other students in the corridor, but none I recognize by face. As we pass them, I can feel their eyes on us, and I hate it. Hate feeling like they can see right through me, like they know me simply because of who my father is. Everyone knows my name and who my father is, but they don't *know* me. No one here knows me, the real me, and it's going to stay that way.

There might be tons of high-profile criminal offspring in this place, but no one is more powerful than my father, and if that doesn't scare them, then I certainly will.

2

ASPEN

*M*y back aches, my ass is sore from sitting for so long, and my limbs are stiff. I'm dying to get out of this car and get a good stretch in. Shifting around in the seat, I try my best to get comfortable, but the worn-out seat doesn't get any softer.

We've been on the road for almost five hours without a single stop, not that there is any place to stop or that we are even technically on a road. I haven't seen any signs of life, at least not human-wise, since we left Takotna, and most of the time, I'm not sure how the driver knows where we are, let alone where we are going.

I wonder if he's been out here before. According to their welcome packet, most people fly into Corium, but of course when I called to get a seat, there was no room on any of their helicopters, leaving me no choice but to make the grueling trip to the secluded university by car.

The Jeep bounces heavily, and the seat belt digs into my shoulder as we drive over a fallen tree unannounced. I glare at the back of the driver's head, who didn't even tell me his name. The middle-aged local with black, uncombed hair and a full bushy beard seems to be just as happy to make the trip as I am. At least he's getting paid.

"Sorry about that, Miss," the driver grunts from the driver's seat.

Wow, that's the most he's said to me since we got in the vehicle. Since he's opened the lines of communication, I figure this is a good time to make sure we're still on track.

"It's okay. Are we almost there?"

"Twenty-five miles to go," he answers, and I sink back in my seat. Twenty-five miles driving on a dirt road through the forest can take a good forty minutes, maybe even longer. That thought barely leaves my mind when the Jeep comes to an abrupt stop, and I sling forward in my seat at the press of the brakes.

Confused, I look around, scanning the area for any sign of civilization or another reason we would stop so carelessly. All I see are trees—trees, trees, and more trees. He certainly didn't stop because of a tree in the road, not when he just drove over one less than a mile back.

"Out of gas, I need to refill the tank, or we're not gonna make it to the base," the driver explains before unbuckling and opening his door. He's been calling Corium University the base, which doesn't surprise me since most people have no idea what that place really is.

Not wanting to miss the opportunity to stretch my legs, I

follow his lead and climb out of the Jeep. My legs protest at first, but as soon as I pull my arms above my head and lengthen my limbs, my muscles thank me.

A shiver skates down my spine at the nippy breeze that blows through the trees. It's much colder here than I'm used to in North Woods, but the fresh air and tranquil landscape make up for it.

Now that I'm up and moving around, I realize that my bladder is pretty full, and I wonder if I should find a tree to relieve myself or wait. Then I think about the bumpy ride and the fact that I really don't know how much longer it's going to be.

"Um, I'm going to go pee. Please don't leave without me," I joke, well, half-joke. A part of me wonders if he would leave without me.

The driver comes around the vehicle, gas can in hand, and a frown on his face. "Hurry up then," he snaps. For a moment, I contemplate holding it and climbing back into the seat, but then he continues, "Well, go piss. I'm not stopping again until we arrive at the base."

I'm not sure why he's being so rude, but I ignore his nasty tone, spin around, and speed walk out into the forest to find a spot that's far enough away to be out of sight but not too far that I risk getting lost. Quickly, I undo my jeans and pull them down along with my panties.

Cool air washes over my naked skin as I squat down behind a large tree and relieve myself. When I'm done, I dig an old tissue from my pocket and wipe before straightening back up.

I turn to walk back to the car but freeze before I can take a single step. Not even ten feet behind me is the driver... staring straight at me. A mischievous grin dances on his lips as his gaze darkens. His pants are undone, and his hand is wrapped around his dick, his piss spraying onto the ground.

That pervert was watching me. Fear slithers up my spine like the wind slices through the leaves surrounding us. I'm alone, out in the middle of nowhere, with a man I don't know. A man who just watched me while I was peeing. He could easily overpower me and take whatever he wanted, and not a single soul would hear my screams. Running enters my mind, but where the fuck do I run to? I have no idea where I am, and there is no way I would survive a night out here on my own.

So I do the only thing I know how to do. I steel my spine, puff out my chest, and look him straight in the eyes. "Was that necessary?"

"What? I had to take a leak too," he says innocently, tucking himself back into his pants.

My stomach churns, and my breakfast is threatening to make an appearance as the realization sets in that not only did this asshole just see me half naked but I'm also going to have to get back into the Jeep with him. This feels all kinds of wrong, and I wonder how my parents would feel if they knew how messed up the man who's delivering me to Corium is.

I'm back in the Jeep and buckled up in no time, wishing I had even more clothes on besides the jeans and thick sweater I'm wearing. Then again, it probably wouldn't matter how much I'm wearing. I'd still feel exposed in his presence.

Fuck. He's such an asshole for making me feel this way.

I spend the rest of the drive even more uncomfortable than I was before. Now, it's not only my body that is protesting but my mind as well. All my instincts are telling me to stay away from this man, yet I'm inside this all-terrain Jeep with nowhere else to go. It's this man or the wilderness, and neither looks like good odds.

After a while, the trees become thinner, and the dirt road becomes a little less bumpy as the terrain opens up. The forest thins out as we get closer to the side of the mountain. The peak is covered in snow, reminding me I'm far away from home.

I know we must be close, but I don't see the university nestled into the mountain as we approach. Instead, the first thing I see is a large gray wall. The road we are on leads us straight to it, and as far as I can see, there isn't a way around it.

An enormous metal gate comes into view, and I can't help but sigh in relief. We're here, and once I'm out of this car, I never have to see this bastard again.

The tires have barely stopped rolling over the gravel, and he throws the Jeep into park. "Out," he orders.

Baffled, I stare at him for a long second. "You're supposed to take me to Corium. This is just..." I wave at the structure in front of us. "A gate."

"This is as far as I go." Impatience bleeds through his words. "Trunk is unlocked. Get your shit."

I have half a mind to tell him to at least get my suitcases out since I gave him a free show earlier, but I bite my tongue, not wanting to poke the bear.

Getting out, I suck a huge breath of fresh air into my lungs. It seems to have dropped at least twenty degrees since we stopped earlier. My lungs prick as the icy air fills them, making my whole body shudder, the cold temperature seeping into my skin.

I work quickly to get both suitcases and my backpack from the trunk. Not even a second after I close the back does the Jeep take off, reversing down the mountainside before he whips it around and starts back down the mountain. The tires toss dirt up into the air and onto me. *Fuck!* I cough and bury my face into the crook of my elbow until the billowing cloud of dust settles. It's like the world hates me and wants to see how much more I can take.

With my backpack slung over my shoulder, I pull my suitcases behind me and walk up to the gate. Only when I'm a foot away do I notice the school crest etched into the metal. The letters C and U for Corium University are on each side, with a skull and a dagger pierced through it. On the top is the word refugium, and below peccatorum.

Lifting my hand, I bring it to the ice-cold metal and run my fingertips over the words.

Refugium peccatorum—Refuge of sinners.

I don't know who came up with the name, but I can't think of a more appropriate denomination for this place. We are our parents' children, after all.

"Name?" A booming voice comes out of nowhere, breaking through the silence forcefully. I'm so startled that I jump back.

My heel catches on the bottom of my suitcase, and I go tumbling to the ground.

Dumbfounded, I sit on the freezing gravel and stare up at the gate.

"What's your name, kid?" The same voice speaks again, and this time, I notice the slight distortion like it's coming from a speaker. I follow the sound and pinpoint it's coming from the top corner of the gate. Only then do I notice the small gray camera staring back at me.

"Aspen Mather," I announce, dusting my hands off on my jeans.

The man on the other side doesn't answer, but a moment later, a loud buzzing noise fills the space, and the gate slowly swings open.

I scramble to my feet and grab my suitcases. The gate inches open, revealing yet another road. And to make matters worse, it's all uphill.

Ugh, is this day ever going to end?

Grinding my molars together, I start my hike up the mountain, dragging my heavy suitcases behind. My arms ache with the effort, but at least my butt isn't sore anymore. After a while, the above-ground part of the university comes into view, which from the outside is nothing more than an old castle.

By the time I finally arrive at the entrance, the sun is setting, and my legs are on fire. I already know I'm going to be sore as hell tomorrow. I basically just ran a marathon, my chest is heaving, and a thin sheen of sweat covers my forehead even in these unruly temperatures. The only plus side is I'm not cold anymore.

The building in front of me has no windows, and there is only one large wooden door. I start looking for some kind of doorbell, but before I can find anything, the door opens on its own. I quickly realize that the wood was only a façade, and the actual door is made out of metal thick enough to stop a semi-truck.

"Took you long enough," the man who appears on the other side sneers. He's dressed in military clothing, and I recognize the voice as the same from the gate at the bottom of the hill.

"Sorry, I'll try to be faster next time," I say under my breath as I stomp past him.

The space opens up to a great room with a polished floor, the school crest inlaid in the tile. A strange smell lingers in the air, like an old dusty basement mixed with floor wax. At the end of the large space, several statues and very large paintings are displayed. Above, in bold gold letters, it reads *FOUNDING MEMBERS*.

I recognize one of the faces as Julian Moretti, another of Lucian Black, Adrian Doubeck, Nicolo Diavolo, and then there is Xander Rossi... the picture of him alone sends a shiver running down my spine. Not only is he one of the most ruthless people I know, but he also holds a very personal grudge against my family.

To the right and left of the shrine of powerful criminals are more doors. My escort leads me to the one labeled freshman and sophomores. Through the door, we enter into a long hallway that seems to go on forever. The lighting is dim, making it difficult to see.

We walk for a minute or so before stopping in front of a large elevator. The guy pulls out a folded map and hands it to me. I let go of my suitcase—he never offered me help with—and take the map from him.

"You're at level C, room 3001. Good luck." Before I can ask one of the twelve questions on my mind, the guy turns and all but runs away. I let out a defeated sigh. Well, I guess I'm on my own again.

Pushing the elevator button, I wait for it to arrive. The bags in my hand and on my shoulder are becoming increasingly difficult to bear, and I can't wait to get rid of all of them and finally rest. This has been the longest trip on the face of the earth, and I need a hot shower and some sleep so I can start over tomorrow.

The elevator opens with a bing, and I step into the surprisingly large space. The panel only has four buttons, A, B, C, and T. I press the C and watch the doors slide closed.

I knew that most of this school—including the dorms—were underground, but I didn't know how far underground until now. The elevator keeps descending until I wonder when we're going to reach the center of the earth.

Then it stops so abruptly that I'm knocked off balance and have to lean against the wall to steady myself or risk falling over. The doors slide open, and I step out of the elevator and into yet another hallway.

As I look at the map, my room appears to be at the end of

the corridor. Which might not be that bad of a thing. I count each step, the only thought on my mind being the bed inside my room and the mattress I'm going to fall into when I get there.

I'm so fucking tired. I don't even care that my stomach is growling, demanding food. I have to sleep. I'm too tired to even lift a fork, let alone walk around this maze to find the cafeteria.

My legs ache with protest, but I push onward until I'm standing right in front of the supposed door to my dorm. I look up from the polished marble and see three large, bright red letters painted on the wood. The sight of them makes my heart sink into my stomach.

RAT

I should have known there would be no escaping what happened. Everyone knows who I am now. This place is going to be even worse than high school was. There, people just stopped talking to me and stayed out of my way. Avoiding me like I was the plague. The writing on the door tells me I won't be so easily dismissed here. I shake my head and look down at the door handle.

Pulling the key card from my pocket, I swipe it, and the door clicks open. Hesitantly, I step into the room I'm going to call my home for the next year.

I scan the space, my gaze ping-pongs around the small space. The first thing I notice is the dust and mildew smell. The second is the large brown stain on the ceiling. The third is the bed. I'm grateful to have a place to sleep, but somehow, I feel like this is a joke.

I'm almost certain no one has lived in this room for a while. It's probably been condemned, looking at its condition, but right now, all I can think about is the bed. How pitiful is it that at this point, I'm willing to sleep anywhere? Pulling my luggage inside, I shut the door behind me and lean my back against it, briefly closing my eyes.

You can do this. A small voice whispers in my mind, giving me enough strength to believe I can do this.

I don't know how yet, but I will get through this year. Pushing off the door, I start undressing and lay my clothes out over my suitcase. I pull my pajamas out of my backpack and quickly get dressed for bed. The mattress is bare, but a large bag on top of the bed holds a comforter, a pillow, and sheets.

I'm too exhausted from traveling to put any effort into anything else, so I spread the sheets out over the mattress and crawl on top of them. I don't even bother turning the light off. I simply cover myself with the comforter and tuck the pillow under my head.

I'm out cold the next minute, and all I can think is I hope tomorrow will be a better day.

Spoiler alert—it won't be.

3

QUINTON

As usual, I'm wide awake by four o'clock even though I didn't fall asleep until well after midnight. Sleeping a few hours a night isn't abnormal for me. Ever since I can remember, I've had a hard time falling asleep. The events of the past year have only intensified my insomnia.

Rolling out of bed, I ignore the tired feeling lingering at the back of my mind and get dressed in a pair of gym shorts and a black hoodie.

I quietly walk out of the bedroom and into the kitchen, grabbing a bottle of water from the fully stocked fridge. Ren is a light sleeper. I don't want to wake him because if I do, he'll follow me, and I don't need him tailing me everywhere I go.

On silent feet, I leave the small apartment without incident and find my way to the in-house gym. I love mornings because at this hour, everyone is still asleep, and I don't have to worry about anyone watching me or force myself to put a mask on to cover up the pain. I can just be me.

The sound of my Nikes bounces off the walls of the corridor. Ahead, a single girl who keeps her head low enough that I can't see her face scurries past me, turning into one of the rooms on the left.

The building houses all three hundred students attending this school. Guys and girls are not separated here by dorms. I guess when the parents are a bunch of criminals, the school administration doesn't worry about the students' virtues. Not that separation would stop sex regardless. I suppose it might help, though.

I turn the corner at the end of the corridor and locate the gym. Using my key card, I wait for the door to open automatically, and I step inside. I half expect to find someone as dedicated to their fitness as me at this hour but am pleasantly surprised to find the space unoccupied.

Wasting no time, I hop on a treadmill and start my four-mile run. I use the time to clear my head and focus on my tasks for the day. Here, the tasks are limited to attending classes, but after that, who knows what could happen. I'm only here to get away from my father, not to train, or because I need knowledge on what my parents do or who they are. This place is more or less a babysitter for me until I decide I'm ready to face what happened. And honestly, I'm not fucking sure when that will be.

By the time I'm finished with my run, beads of sweat are dripping down my face.

My heartbeat is pulsing in my ears, and the burning in my muscles is invigorating. Running gives me a high that carries me through the day. I move on from running and onto weights and then pull-ups. My muscles are burning, and I feel rejuvenated as I pull my shirt off and use it to wipe away the sweat from my face.

I check my phone and realize I've been gone for two hours. I'm sure Ren could figure out where I'd run off to if he wakes up, so I'm not in a hurry to get back to the room.

Chugging the rest of my water, I toss the bottle in the garbage and leave the gym.

I've studied the map, but the best way to get acquainted with your surroundings is to become familiar with them, which means walking every inch of this place.

The long corridor is mostly empty except for a few people who keep their heads low. I bet it's because they don't want to start trouble, or they want to go unnoticed by me. Little do they know, I notice everything and everyone. Ducking your head and pretending you don't exist isn't going to protect you. Let's be honest: people always go for the quiet ones first.

My steps come to a screeching halt when I reach the last door at the end of the hallway. Large red letters are painted into the wood, spelling out the word: RAT. It doesn't even take me a fraction of a second to figure out who resides inside that room.

Aspen Mather.

The thought of her name makes me clench my fists, and in the back of my mind, a memory sprouts.

All eyes are on us as we enter the large banquet hall. As always, when my father enters a crowd, people move out of the way, making room for us to walk through without anyone being too close. He's like a king to all these people.

Like a flock of birds, my sister and I trail a step behind him on either side and behind us are two more guards. I glance over at Adela, who is walking with her head slightly bowed, her eyes on the ground, just like she is supposed to do when we're in public.

Very few people know that my sisters have my father wrapped around their little fingers, and when we are in the safety of our home, they are anything but meek and obedient. This is for show and nothing more.

As the head of the Rossi empire, my father has a certain image to uphold, one that shows no mercy. He is known to be ruthless and cruel—which he is with his enemies—but never with his wife and children. Showing in public that he has a soft spot for his daughters would be seen by many as a weakness because, in our world, women are still only seen as a means to an end.

Maybe that will change in our generation, but in my father's reign, we have to play by the rules of the kingdom.

"Xander, it's good to see you, old friend." A man I don't know steps up to greet us.

"Clyde, it's been a few years." My father stops to shake the man's hand, and I take my place right next to him, my sister on the other side. Someday, this will be us, shaking hands, making deals, and spilling blood.

"You remember my son, Quinton," he introduces me, but not Adela.

"Of course, yes." He gives me a nod, swallowing as he looks at me. I'm only sixteen, but I'm already taller than most people here. "I brought my daughter as well. Aspen, say hello to my friend, Xander."

A small figure pops out from behind the man. She's so tiny. I didn't even see her standing behind her father until she stepped around.

"Hi," she greets my father so quietly, I almost don't hear her at all. A shy, almost scared smile appears on her glossy lips.

Then her gaze falls onto me. Her hazel eyes narrow as she studies me with interest. It's nothing I'm not used to. The gawking and licking of their lips, wanting to be the next queen of the kingdom. They all know that in a few years, my father's legacy—the money and enemies—will become mine. The allure of danger and the idea that I might protect them from it have them fawning over me.

This meek little mouse doesn't look at me like that, though. She's interested but unsure. I let my eyes roam down the length of her body.

She's wearing a baby-blue dress that hugs her barely-there curves. My eyes linger on her breasts a little too long, wondering if she is wearing a push-up bra or if that's her real size. When I snap out of my boob-induced trance, I look up to find her glaring daggers at me like she is about to deliver a swift kick to my balls.

Surprisingly, when I glance at her dad, he looks pleased.

How odd. Normally, I would get the opposite reaction.

Girls like it when I look at them, and their dads don't.

I snap out of the memory, my jaw tightening to the point of pain. I should've known then that something was off about them. I was just too young and stupid to realize it at the time. Funny, even then, Aspen was a snake slithering through the grass, and if she is smart, she will stay the hell out of my way, especially since there is no one here to protect her from me.

4

ASPEN

I groan into the quiet room and roll over on the mattress to face the brick wall. The bed frame squeaks with the movement. It's all I've heard all night as I tossed and turned on this antique bed, trying to find a comfortable position. I wonder if anyone else's bed is as horrible as this one. Something tells me no, but how would I know? It's not like I had a very welcoming greeting. Not with the word RAT written across my door for the entire dorm to see.

Even though we're who knows how many feet underground, it's like I can feel the cold Alaskan air seeping into the brick. I tighten my hold on the thin sheet I've cocooned myself in, wondering if I'll ever get warm again.

Every single aspect of this place makes me want to scream. I hate it here.

The bed, this room, this entire fucking place can get tossed in a dumpster and set on fire. Rolling over once more, I scream my mounting frustration into the small pillow and slam my fist down onto the mattress. I don't know why my parents insisted I come here.

I could've gone to any university; my grades are stellar, my GPA perfect. I'm smart as hell, and until a year ago, I was popular too. Now I'm a nobody, a crux that everyone stays as far away from as they can get. Tears form in my eyes, my anger rising with each breath I take, the more I think about how much I've lost.

Why did he have to do it?

I know for a fact when my father chose to work with the feds, he did so out of selfishness. He thought he could protect himself, maybe get less time in prison. The smart move would've been to never sell illegal guns in the first place, but what did I know?

In his plea, he gave up info on the Rossi family. One thing my father failed to realize was that Xander was a smarter criminal, and he was able to spin it all around and pin everything on my father. Everything he did, every ounce of information he gave away, was for nothing. In the end, it hurt not only himself but my mother and I also got dragged down with him.

Now he was off serving time in prison, and my mother and I were taking the fallout. I've lost every friend I ever had. No one wants to be seen with me.

My father might be the rat, but through association, I am as well. In the criminal underground, a rat is the worst thing you can be. People who are enemies will work together to bring you down because a rat is a loose end, and loose ends can bring empires to their knees.

Sighing, I stare up at the ceiling, wondering what I'm going to have to do to survive this place. Xander has become more ruthless and cruel since my father's imprisonment. He hasn't sent anyone to hurt my mother or me yet. But he is the reason no one wants anything to do with us. Frankly, he doesn't have to do much anyway, not with the shitstorm my father left behind.

People want us dead simply because of my father's choices. By talking to the feds, he hurt more than the Rossis; he hurt everyone involved in the deals he made, and that's a lot of fucking people.

A lot of criminals have it out for me, and here, they could easily get to me. Why my mom sent me here out of all places is still a mystery, but she didn't give me a choice in the matter.

I have no doubt in my mind that Quinton, Xander's son, is here. We'd met a few times in passing at fundraisers and such, never conversing unless it was forced. Even though our fathers worked together, we ran in different circles. Quinton was set to become the heir to the Rossi empire, and I was going to go to college and become a doctor. It's cliché, but it's the truth. I knew what kind of person my father was, so I wanted to be the opposite. I thought becoming a doctor would balance the scale. I would help people, save lives instead of ending them. At least, that's what I had planned.

I wanted nothing to do with this life while he was born and

bred into it. I could only imagine the number of people he had already killed, the blood on his hands. The thought makes me shiver, and I force myself to think about something else.

Rolling off the squeaky bed, I gasp as my bare feet touch the cold floor. Yet another reason to hate this place. The constant cold is going to take a while to get used to. I grab my cell phone off the nightstand and cross the room, which is smaller than the one I have back home. I'm pretty sure they gave me someone's old closet. I try to ignore the negatives and think a little more positively.

It's only one year. If I can stay off Q's radar, then I'll be fine. Even if I have to walk through fire every day here, so long as I don't draw the attention of the beast's son, I should be fine.

Looking down at my phone, I check the time. *7:30.* Panic bubbles to the surface as the realization of what that time means. I'm late. I'm supposed to attend the freshmen orientation in the atrium near the cafeteria.

Shit!

I can't seem to make my feet move fast enough as I scurry around the room, rummaging through my suitcases for clothing. I pull on a pair of black leggings and a light sweater, then slip my feet into some running shoes. I was so tired last night I didn't have time to look over my schedule or the school map, which I'm regretting now as I stare down at the half-crumpled paper. God knows if I get lost, the last thing I'm going to do is ask someone for help.

They'll most likely lead me to the nearest cliff's edge anyway.

I find the cafeteria on the map and make a roadmap of where I need to go and what I have to pass to get there. Since it's in another building altogether, I'll have to exit the dorms and go through another set of double doors. The atrium is right outside the cafeteria. It's not that long of a walk or hard to find, but if I've learned anything, the easiest things can become the hardest in an instant.

I'll keep my head low, my mouth shut, and I'll be just fine. I mean, it's not like the teachers will let another student hurt me, right? I don't even want to think of the answer to that question. I pull my long, unruly blond hair into a bun. I used to be the girl who did her hair and makeup every day and ironed her clothes. That ship has since sailed. To do my hair or makeup would draw unwanted attention.

Making sure I have my key card and phone in hand, I leave the protection of my room and slip out into the hall. I'm not surprised to find the corridor empty and quiet, especially when all the freshmen are probably at the orientation. Still, even if it makes me late, it makes me feel safer to be alone.

I take a look at the map again and force my feet to move me in the right direction. Before I know it, I've reached the end of the hall. I look down to double-check that I'm going the right way and look up just as I'm colliding with another person. The impact knocks the air out of my lungs, and I stumble backward, clinging to the wall for support.

The person—a guy with short blond hair and menacing eyes, shoves past me, slamming his shoulder purposely into mine. The fucking audacity, I swear. All I can do is grit my teeth and keep myself standing up straight.

"Rat." He snickers under his breath.

The guy beside him chuckles, and they walk away happily while I stand there trying to gather my wits. I should be used to the name-calling, the snide comments, and the hate, but I'm not. I don't think a person ever gets used to being hated. They just simply learn to deal with it. Ahead is the entrance to the atrium.

My heart gallops in my chest, and I suck a ragged breath into my lungs.

Sweat clings to my palms like a second skin, and worry ignites in my gut. I really, really don't want to continue down this hallway. I could turn right and go into the cafeteria, but that would be considered skipping, and I don't want to do that until I really need to.

The double doors ahead are like staring at the gates of hell. All I can do is hope that no one notices me once inside, which is doubtful, but a girl can hope. With no other options, I suck a ragged breath into my lungs and hold it as I grab the handle and open the door. A low hum of chatter fills my ears as soon as the door is open. The room is already packed with students, and I have to force myself to walk inside and maneuver against the back wall with my head down, with my eyes on my feet, and every step I take so that I don't do something stupid and trip, drawing all the attention in the room to me.

Slowly, as if my lungs are balloons, I let the air inside of them out and breathe in even slower. I can feel my panic rising, pricking at my senses, making me want to run out of this room and back to the dorms.

"Snitch," someone whispers into my ear, but I don't dare look up or back to see who it was. I don't care what they say about me or what names they call me. I'll persevere.

"Dirty fucking rat," another person says, this time a little louder. I force my feet to move faster and only stop once I find an empty spot against the wall. It takes me a second to look up, but when I do, I feel intimidated.

Rows upon rows of students sit before me. Instinct takes over, and my eyes scan the room. I hate myself for doing it, but I'm only looking for one criminal's son in this room right now. The muscles in my stomach tighten, and I nibble on my bottom lip nervously while scanning over each head.

He's here. I know it. There's no reason he wouldn't be. My anxiety mounts with each person who isn't him until the moment I spot him, and the bile in my stomach rises up into my throat. Someone walks onto the stage, but all my attention is on the dark-haired man with piercing blue eyes. I'm not fascinated with him, by any means.

Yes, he's attractive in a sort of dark and mysterious way, but my main objective isn't attraction. I'd just like to know where my enemy is at all times.

I drag my attention away from Quinton and to the stage where a man in a dark suit is speaking. His jacket is off, and his hair is an unruly mess on top of his head. Even from a distance, I can see the tattoos on his hands.

At first glance, I don't recognize him, but then the dots connect in my mind.

Lucas Diavolo.

It makes sense. The Rossi family and Diavolos have been known to have ties. It's no surprise that Lucas is here, most likely doing all the spying he can for Xander. It's just another reminder that no one here will help me. That I'm not as safe as my mother told me I would be.

"The rules here are really simple. Don't kill each other and don't get yourself sent to my office. Do the work and learn all you can. You have an opportunity that some could only dream of having." I almost scoff at the words that roll off Lucas's tongue.

Like the opportunity to kill is something special. Ha. I'm sure most of the people in this room have already done that five times over by now.

Lucas continues to talk, and my eyes gravitate back toward Quinton. I'm thankful he can't see me even though I'm sure he can feel my eyes on him.

I recognize the guy sitting next to him as his best friend, Ren. The two I need to watch out for most because where one is, the other isn't very far behind.

My stomach rumbles loudly, the sound interrupting my thoughts and gathering the attention of the person beside me. Out of the corner of my eye, I see the girl whispering something into the ear of the person beside her.

I'm not going to wait for this to implode in my face. Gritting my teeth, I push off the wall and start toward the exit. This time, I don't drop my eyes to my feet, which is a mistake I regret to have made when someone puts their foot out in front of me, and I trip over it.

"Fucking rat." The person who tripped me snickers. "Nobody wants you here."

It's a miracle I keep myself from face planting on the floor, but somehow, I do. Stopping in my tracks, I turn and sneer at the asshole, who, thankfully, is no one that I recognize. His arrogant smirk makes me want to punch him in the face, but I wouldn't even consider it.

Turning back around, I continue my walk to the exit and breathe a silent sigh of relief once I step through the double doors and back out into the corridor.

Ahead is the cafeteria, just on the other side of a pair of double doors. I can hear the clanking of silverware and the buzzing of conversation from where I stand. A group of girls stands outside the doors. I can feel their eyes on me and practically hear their whispers.

Again, I find my heart galloping in my chest.

Do I really want to go in there? The way I see it, I don't have a lot of options; it's either this or I starve. Briefly, I wonder how long I could go without food. The answer isn't something I believe, especially not with the hunger I'm feeling at this moment. A second passes, and I don't even want to admit the amount of mental fortitude it takes for me to cross the space and enter the cafeteria. My stomach churns, and my hands become clammy. I really hate it here. I hate it so much.

I catch the door as two guys stroll out. I don't bother looking up and trudge forward like I'm heading into battle instead of getting breakfast. I look up once I'm inside, the bright lights making me squint, and I'm a little amazed at the size of the space. There are lots of tables with bench seating. To think a year ago, I would've been thinking about where I was going to sit in this room. Now the only thing I want to do is eat my food and escape to my bedroom.

Following the line of other students, I walk up to the food bar and grab a tray. All of the food is served buffet-style, but the cook puts the food on your tray. There's an array of items from biscuits and gravy to avocado toast and eggs.

The smell of bacon wafts into my nose, and my mouth waters at the scent. I scoot down the line and look up at the person on the other side, serving the bacon.

I know something is up as soon as our eyes meet. The man's face is stone cold, carrying no expression whatsoever.

"Can I please have some bacon?" I ask, wondering if maybe that's why he hasn't put any on my tray yet, but another student meanders up beside me, nudging her tray forward.

"Get out of the way. You're holding up the line," she sneers, but I ignore her comment. Like I don't exist at all, he places two strips of bacon on her tray. My mouth hangs open for half a second at his dismissal before I snap it shut. I blink slowly, my anger rising with every tick of the clock.

I'm already hungry, and now there is food in front of me, but this motherfucker wants to play games with me. I don't think so.

"What's the deal?" I growl.

I can feel eyes on me, and I'm doing the one thing I don't want to do: drawing attention. But how the hell am I going to eat if they don't serve me food? The guy on the other side of the buffet shrugs.

"If you want something to eat, we can serve you eggs, toast, and fruit." I'm completely baffled by what this man has just said and damn near slam my tray down in frustration.

"Why?" I ask.

I already know why, but I have to ask anyway just to make myself feel better. For the first time, I truly feel singled out, but this is different because the staff is in on it too.

"I don't make the rules. Do you want the food or not?"

My lip curls, and I have half a mind to tell him no but nod my head instead. I'm too fucking hungry not to eat. So long bacon, at least I got to smell you. He places the food on my tray along with a glass of milk, and I scan my card at the end of the line. I find a table without a person at it and sit down to enjoy my bland meal. How shitty is it that I don't even get to decide what I eat? I wonder what they'll try to choose for me next? Actually, no. I don't want to think about that right now.

I eat my entire meal in less than ten bites but am still hungry. I look back up at the line. If I hadn't been so humiliated while getting my food, I might consider getting seconds, but I'm done with today and done with the people I've encountered.

Hell, I'm done with this school. I'm done with everything. I'm angry and annoyed and just really want to go home.

I take my tray up to the dishwasher and then leave the cafeteria. I've only just started down the corridor toward my dorm when my heart falls into my stomach, and the food I just ate threatens to come back up. Fear zings down my spine when someone grabs the back of my hoodie and tugs me backward.

Reaching for anything that might provide me some type of balance, my fingers are met with air. My throat constricts. This isn't going to end well.

A second later, my back collides with the front of a very firm chest. I stand there for half a second before I turn around and am forced to crane my neck back to look up at the two men crowding me.

"I was wondering when we would see you." Ren Petrov chuckles. "Seems the rat found us faster than I expected."

My gaze ping-pongs between Q, who is standing as still as a statue, his penetrating gaze piercing my soul, and Ren, who is smirking like someone told him a hilarious joke.

The two of them are like Adonis, both equally as gorgeous as they are dangerous. I try not to notice how attractive Q is with his sharp jawline, piercing blue eyes, and unruly black hair. His clothing hugs his chiseled body, and I take a step back, trying to put some distance between the three of us. I told myself I would stay under the radar, protect myself, and keep my mouth shut. The problem is, everything has started to compound, and the reason for all my problems, or at least a part of my problems, is standing right in front of me.

"Don't you have anything better to do than torment me? My life's shit as it is, and I don't need the two of you heaping more onto it with your bullying antics."

I've never been the type to sit down and shut up, but something tells me right now should've been one of those instances. Too bad, at this moment, there's no one to stop me or tell me that I'm basically signing my own death certificate. The objective was to steer clear of him and his family, not put a bright red X on my back.

"Excuse me?" Q blinks, his gaze turning feral in a flash.

All I can hear is the swooshing of blood in my ears. Q takes a step toward me, and instantly, I'm in a trance, a rabbit caught in a trap. I'm not sure where the courage comes from to say what I do next, but it's something I'll come to regret. I know it.

"You heard me. I'm the one being called a rat, the one with a father in prison. Your life is still perfect, as it always has been and will continue to be," I growl, my own anger over the past year rivaling any sanity inside me.

Q's perfectly sculpted lip curls in disgust, and I notice the way his body tenses and his fist clench at his side. I should be scared, and on the inside, I'm all kinds of terrified, but I also feel powerful. I feel like, for once, I'm being heard and seen. He takes a threatening step toward me, that single step eats away all the remaining space between us, and I can feel the rage rolling off him. It's threatening to swallow me whole, and at this point, I kind of wish it would. Ren must see something I don't because he slides between us, grabbing Q by the shoulders while pushing him backward.

"She's a rat. Don't let anything she says bother you," Ren says while leading him away from me. My legs are like Jell-O, and how I've managed to remain standing this long is a mystery. The promise of violence and pain reflects in Q's eyes and back at me, and somehow, I know I just made the biggest mistake of my life.

5

QUINTON

Until five minutes ago, I had no intention of messing with her. I knew she would be here and that our paths might cross, but that didn't matter because I never put the blame for what happened on her. My hate was solely reserved for her father and the people involved in the attack on my family back home.

All that went to shit, and the rage shifted the moment her spiteful words met my ear. *"Your life is still perfect, as it always has been and will be."*

She had no fucking idea, not a clue as to what the past year has been like for my family and me. What her father did was merely the icing on the cake. If she wants to play the innocent card and pretend she's done nothing, then she's in for a rude awakening.

"She's a rat. Don't let anything she says bother you." Ren's voice takes on a calming tone, and I become hyperaware of his hands on my shoulders. I peer over his shoulder, my gaze going to the spot where Aspen was standing just moments ago.

She's gone now, but her presence still lingers. Her words still swirl in my head. My anger toward her plateaus and my muscles burn, the need to expel the hate and rage burning like a blazing fire across my skin. I already know no amount of time at the gym is going to help. It's only going to be a drop of water on a hot stone.

No, I need a new way to calm the storm inside me, and that way is going to involve Aspen Mather.

A smirk forms on my lips as I imagine all the things I can do to her, the ways I can make her pay and cause her pain. I'd never considered myself a sadist, but the feelings she brings out in me are making me second-guess myself. I know I'm going to enjoy every minute of bringing her to her knees.

"What the hell are you smiling about?" Ren asks, dropping his hands and taking a step back. He looks as confused as I feel.

"I think I just found a new hobby."

Ren raises his eyebrow. "Yeah? What's that?"

I ignore his second question since it's obvious. "I'm going to head to the administration office and get some info on Aspen. I want to know what classes she's taking."

I don't say it out loud, but I actually want to know everything about her. The more I know, the easier it's going to be to hurt her where it counts.

Ren doesn't even question my request. He knows me well enough to know that when I get fixated on something, nothing will get in my way. Whether Aspen likes it or not, making her life a living hell just became my newest obsession.

"How about I get you her class schedule, and you go to PE? A little workout is going to do more for you than trying to charm the panties off some secretary, especially when you look as pissed off as a grizzly bear."

I pin him with a stern look. "We both know I won't have to charm anyone. They'll give it to me out of fear and simply because I ask them to."

"True, but sometimes you catch more flies with honey. Plus, my class isn't for another hour. Let me do the panty snatching, and you can do the scheming."

"Fine." I nod. "I'll see you after lunch."

Ren slaps his hand on my shoulder and leans into my side. "Don't kill the girl. You know the rule. Can't end her while we're here."

"Killing her is the last thing I want to do. That would give her an easy way out. What I have planned will make her afraid to step foot out of her dorm room."

"I like the way you think." He grins and saunters away.

I do my best to shake off the lingering rage and head to PE. The building that houses the main recreation center is closer to the surface. I take the elevator up with a few other students and make my way to the large gym. The inside is the size of a football field, the ceiling high and slightly bowed, making it look more like a hangar than an actual gym. The only thing giving away what this place is meant for is the field markings on the ground and the various sports equipment scattered around.

I walk up to the small crowd of congregating students, trying to figure out what everyone's doing. It's then that I notice the floor mats, and I catch sight of the teacher handing out hand wraps. He's about my height but bulkier with black buzzed hair and olive skin. He's of Asian descent, but when he talks, it's without an accent.

"Welcome to class. I'll be your instructor for today. First thing you need to know about me: I hate repeating myself. So pay attention the first time because I won't show you twice. You can call me Quan. We're gonna start with basic hand-to-hand combat. Most of you are probably well versed in it, but I need to see where everyone is at, so we're going to start out slow."

All I can do is roll my eyes. I don't need this class. There's nothing he can teach me that I don't already know. I'm about to turn on my heels and walk out, but then as fate would have it, I spot *her* sitting on the ground with her back against the wall.

Aspen.

Sparks of excitement form in my chest as I take in her small frame just as she's pushing herself to stand. She tucks a loose strand of blond hair behind her ear, her gaze trained on the instructor. She hasn't noticed me yet, so I slowly move closer to her, making sure to stay hidden behind a few other students.

Quan continues talking, but I drown the sound of his voice out and give Aspen my full attention. I study her delicate face, map each curve of her body, twitch of her muscles, and hair on her head. The more I know about my enemy, the better.

"All right, everyone, find a partner." Quan's voice booms through the space, and students start to pair up immediately.

None of the guys even glance my way. Everyone is keeping their distance from me. One petite but brave girl actually gathers up the courage to walk up to me. Her blond hair is knotted into a tight bun at the top of her head. Her icy-blue gaze sizes me up.

"Want to partner up, big guy?" she asks with a heavy Russian accent.

"Any other time, I'd love to, but today, I have someone else who needs an ass-kicking." I look past the nameless girl and over to where Aspen is standing. She still hasn't noticed me, even though she is actively looking for a partner.

Russian girl walks away without another word while I stalk closer to my prey. Much like me, people don't want to partner up with her, though for entirely different reasons. They all know what her father did, and if criminals hate one thing, it's a fucking rat.

"Need a partner?" I ask casually, walking up to her side.

At my voice, she spins around so fast that I think she might give herself whiplash. Her already large eyes go even wider as she gapes at me. She's a good foot shorter than me and has to crane her neck back to look up at me.

She blinks slowly like she's digesting what I've said.

"That would hardly be fair. You are twice my size."

"Did you just call me fat?" I can't help but smirk.

"Funny." She rolls her eyes at me like she has no idea the amount of danger she is in. Earlier, she put on a show, and now she has to face the consequences.

Folding her arms over her chest, she scans the room, realizing that everyone has found a partner, and we are the only two left.

"I guess you're stuck with me." I can practically hear her swallow.

Her sass evaporates as she frantically looks for a way out. Her eyebrows pinch together, and fear overtakes her features. I'm not sure if she wasn't scared until this moment or if she's simply good at hiding it. Either way, her mask has slipped, and I can see the panic starting to set in.

"Let's go, you two," Quan calls over to us. Everyone else is already practicing the moves he demonstrated, and we are the only two people standing around doing nothing. "Start fighting."

Aspen gives the instructor a pleading look as if he could save her from me. To drive it home, he actually turns away from us, giving us his back.

"You heard the man, no more standing around." I snicker, and then I'm on her.

I've never fought anyone smaller than me, so when I tackle her to the ground, I do so with much more force than necessary. The thin mat isn't much of a buffer to her small body as she falls onto it, so the air passes her lips on a wheeze. She grunts clearly in pain and squeezes her eyes shut. I almost feel sorry... almost.

A soft whimper passes her lips, and she tries to roll away from me, but we both know things aren't going to end that easily. I climb on top of her and straddle her hips. Her eyes fly open, and her hands finally start moving. She tries to push me off, but I easily snatch her wrists and pin them to the mat. If she thought I would let what she said and what her family did slide, she's stupider than I thought.

"What the hell are you doing?"

"Hand-to-hand combat." I wink.

"This is not what we are supposed to practice." She sneaks a peek around the room, and I follow her gaze. No one is paying us any attention. Quan still has his back to us, ignoring what is happening like the rest of the class.

"I don't think anyone cares what I'm doing to you."

Leaning in, I put most of my body weight on her, immobilizing her completely. With my chest pressed against hers, I can feel her heart banging against my skin furiously.

Her blond hair fans against the floor, and her cheeks have turned a soft shade of pink. Her chest rises and falls so rapidly I can see her pulse in her throat.

Lowering my head even more, I brush my lips against her ear. Fear laced with her unique flowery scents invades my nose, and I fight the urge to take a deeper breath. Her entire body trembles, and my cock stirs to life.

"Let me make it clear to you since you obviously haven't figured it out yet. You're at the bottom of the pole. You're the dirt beneath the feet of everyone else here. You mean nothing to anyone. I bet I could pull your leggings down right now, fuck you on this mat, and not a single person would stop me, no matter how much you screamed. Care to prove me wrong?"

My threat sends her into a struggle, and she tries pathetically to push me off, but all she does is rub herself against my already half stiffened dick.

I chuckle into her hair, and that's when she does something I didn't see coming.

She turns her head toward me, so her cheek is pressed against mine and her lips are on my neck. Her hot breath fans out over my skin, chasing a shiver down my spine.

For a moment, I think she's going to fucking kiss me. However, instead of the softness of her lips, I get the sharp bite of her teeth.

She bit me, and not just a little bit. The bitch bites me... hard.

"Fuck," I hiss, startled by the unexpected pain. I shove away from her, giving her enough time to buck me off and roll away from me.

Stunned, I get up on my knees and bring my hand to the side of my neck to touch the tender spot.

She really fucking bit me.

I watch her get up, and I already know her next move. She's going to make a run for it. It's what weak prey that can't fight back do. She doesn't get a single step in before I snatch her ankle and pull her back down onto the mat. Her body lands on the floor with a thud, and she lets out a yelp. She kicks at me with her free foot, but I evade her attack with ease.

Grabbing her from behind, I pull her body flush to my chest and hook my arm around her throat, putting her in a choke-hold. She fights me in earnest now, elbowing me in the ribs and even trying to throw her head back, probably hoping to connect with my face. None of her moves faze me. All that matters in this instance is control.

Ignoring my surroundings and her struggling, I tighten my grip on her. Like a boa constrictor, I pull her in, closer with each breath she takes.

Her ass grinds against my crotch while she fights harder to get away, and both of her hands claw at my arms shackled around her. Her sharp nails pierce my skin, eliciting a hiss from me. I already know she's going to leave more than that bite mark on me.

Once more, I tighten my hold on her, drawing a defeated whimper from her lips. One moment, her whole body is stiff, fighting against me with all her might, and the next, she goes completely lax in my hold.

Her head lolls back and onto my shoulder, and her arms fall uselessly to her side.

The room goes eerily quiet, and when I look up, I notice the whole class has stopped fighting. All eyes are on me, holding a passed-out Aspen in my arms.

My first instinct is to release her altogether and let her unconscious body fall to the mat, but something has me pausing. I drop my arm from her throat but continue holding her, supporting her weight fully. The concept has an allure I didn't know I was craving. I don't know why, but I like cradling her to my chest when she is passed out and can't defend herself—not that she has a chance against me even when fully conscious.

An odd sense of calmness washes over me. There is something about having this kind of control over her. I'm not only holding her body in my arms; I'm holding her entire life in the palm of my hands.

For the past year, everything around me has been chaos. I couldn't protect the people I love... I was so helpless. I had no power over anything, but right now, at this very moment, I'm in charge. I, and only I, decide what happens next.

The only question is, what am I going to choose?

6

ASPEN

A sharp sting to my cheek drags me from the darkness of my mind. My eyes are already fluttering open when someone slaps my face again.

This time, it's hard enough for my head to jerk to the side.

What the hell? It takes me a moment to make sense of what's happening.

My vision focuses on Quinton's face, who is scowling at someone to my right. Following his glare, I find Quan—the instructor—kneeling on the ground beside me. His hand is raised, hovering inches from my face. Then I notice Q's fingers wrapped around Quan's wrist like he just stopped him from slapping me a third time.

I must have hit my head because there is no way I'm reading this situation right.

Quinton shoves the instructor's hand away, and the man

who is supposed to be teaching us scrambles to his feet like he's scared of his student.

"She needs to be taken to medical to be checked out," Quan says.

"She's fine," Quinton answers like he's in charge.

"Yeah, but I still have to bring her ass to medical. Liability and shit. I'm not losing my job over something small."

"All right, fine. I'll take her," Q offers.

"No," I croak, trying to sit up. My throat feels like someone shoved crushed glass down it. "I don't need to go to medical. I'm okay." I'm really not, but the idea of being alone with Quinton has me pushing through my lightheadedness. I can't imagine what he would get away with if we were alone after what just happened in a room full of people. My best bet is to put as much distance between us as I can.

"Nonsense. I'll be happy to take you." Q winks at me.

Asshole.

"I said no." I push myself up to stand, still a little disoriented. I wobble on my feet, and Q has the audacity to grab my arm. Almost like he's being a good Samaritan helping me off the ground and not the one that just choked me to unconsciousness. I pull my arm from his grip as soon as I'm on my feet, but the quick movement has my head spinning and making me sway from side to side like a leaf in a storm.

Quinton wraps his arm around my back and pulls me into his side to stabilize me. Whatever game he's playing, I want out of it.

"Yup, definitely taking her," Quinton announces.

I want to protest and ask the teacher to keep me here, but I already know he'll do anything Quinton asks. I press my lips into a thin line and swallow down the words I want to say. Like I'm a child, Q escorts me from the gym and into one of the empty corridors.

"I've got it from here," I snap at him as soon as we're alone, trying to shrug him off.

"I don't think so. You need to go to see a doctor and get your head checked, and I need to have the nurse look at my neck where a feral cat bit me and my arms where that same animal scratched me."

"The only animal here is you. All I did was protect myself," I growl, wanting to sink my nails into his face.

"Are you sure about that? I could have sworn you were rubbing your ass into my crotch like a cat in heat."

"You're delusional."

"And you're feisty," he counters. "Kinda gets my cock hard a little, but not as much as you passed out. I like you better when you're not talking or moving. Kind of like a doll I can play with." I can't believe I ever said he was attractive in any way. I knew that darkness lurked inside of men like him, but I never anticipated it would be directed at me.

"You know they make blow-up dolls for guys like you who can't get a girl to like them. I think they even have a hole to stick your dick in." I don't know why I keep antagonizing him. Maybe he would leave me alone if I just kept my mouth closed. Then again, I'm done being shit on and treated like crap by my peers.

"I'd rather stick my dick in something warm." His arm is still wrapped around my back, and when he pulls me closer, I grind my teeth together and press my feet into the floor, trying to get him to release me.

"I hear the pie in the cafeteria is served warm."

"Do you ever shut up?" He shakes his head. "Talking will be the downfall of your entire family. Your father didn't know when to shut up, and as it turns out, you don't either."

I can't help but wince at his words. Pain slices through me at the reminder of everything my family has already lost, and I have no witty comeback to that.

"Are you sure this is the way to the medical building?" I ask when I realize we've been walking down this corridor for a while.

Quinton doesn't answer, but he picks up his pace, making it hard for my shorter legs to keep up. An uneasy feeling builds in my gut, and I force my legs to stop walking, digging my heels once again into the ground.

I lean back into Q's hold, turn my head, and look up at him. The lights are dimmed in the halls, making it hard for me to make out his features, but what I do see will haunt my dreams for the next week. The way he's looking at me right now—like I'm his prey, instead of a human with feelings and needs—makes me shiver. The darkness in his gaze mounts and his lips curl up at the sides, his features turning villainous.

"You're not taking me to medical, are you?" I try to hide how afraid I am of the answer, but the low shudder in my words gives my fear away.

"Smart and funny. You'd be the total package if it weren't for your fucking mouth. Maybe if I find a better use for it, you won't be so unbearable to be around."

I don't know why, but I feel the need to apologize. Perhaps it'll make him change his mind about wherever it is he's leading me. "Look, I'm sorry. About what I said this morning."

He tightens his hold on me, his fingers digging into my flesh with bruising force, and he forces me to take a step forward, basically dragging me alongside him.

"I don't give a fuck about what you said this morning. I don't want your apology. That won't save you from me." He releases me and shoves me back against the wall, and pain radiates down my spine upon impact. His huge frame cages me in, leaving me no escape. I can feel the heat from his body rolling off him and into me.

I shiver at the coldness in his gaze, and the tiny hairs on the back of my neck stand on end at his next sentence. "What I want are your screams, your tears. I want you weak and immobile. I want you begging me to stop while I take and take until there's nothing left to take."

I was certain I had felt real, true fear before now, like back in the gym when he choked me, but nothing compares to this moment.

"Please, Quinton, just let me go. I'll leave you alone. I'll stay out of your way. I won't come back to PE. It'll be like I was never here. Like I never existed at all." I'm full-on rambling now, grasping at straws for anything that might get me out of this situation.

Quinton tips his head back and laughs like I just told him a joke. The sound bounces off the walls and echoes back into my ears. It's as menacing as it is mocking.

I choose then to make a run for it. I might not be strong enough to fight him, but if I get a head start, I can outrun him. Adrenaline spikes in my veins, and I dart under his arm, putting every last bit of energy I have into escaping him.

"I don't think so, Aspen." His voice caresses my ear a moment before his hand circles my wrist. A scream catches in my throat as he whirls me around, shoving me against the wall and wrapping his hand firmly around the slender column of my neck.

"Don't. You don't want to do this," I croak, barely getting the words out as his grip tightens. He leans into me—the hard ridges of his body fit mine so perfectly. I let out a wheezed gasp when his hard cock presses against my stomach.

"That's the problem. I do want to do this. I want to do this more than anything." The air in my chest rattles, and I'm afraid of what will happen next.

I squeeze my eyes shut, preparing to sink deep into my mind, when suddenly, Quinton's grip on my throat disappears.

"What do you think you're doing?" A young, feminine voice meets my ears. I blink my eyes open, turning in the direction of the voice.

About twenty feet away stands a woman with bright blue hair, black-rimmed glasses, and a scowl on her face that could rival Quinton's. She appears young but not young enough to be a student. She adjusts her cardigan and continues staring at us.

"Well..." She taps her foot on the floor impatiently, awaiting an answer. My tongue is stuck to the roof of my mouth, so even if I wanted to say something, I couldn't.

"We were just talking, weren't we...?" Quinton's jaw clenches at the effort it takes for him to expel the words.

"I'm sure that's what you were doing. Why don't you get out of here, and I'll pretend I didn't see or hear the entire conversation?"

Leaning into my ear, he whispers, "You got lucky this time. Next time, you're mine."

My throat constricts, and I don't dare look at Quinton. I'm afraid of what I'll see if I do. His searing body heat fades as he takes a step back and then another, putting enough space between us to where I can finally breathe. The heady scent of man and woodsy cologne drift away, and I continue staring at the woman, my heart thumping against my ribs, threatening to break free.

Quinton's footsteps disappear into the distance, and I let out a heaving breath, nearly collapsing against the wall. I wasn't even aware of how tightly strung every inch of my body was until now. I guess fear will do that to you.

"Come, let's go into the library. I'll make you a cup of hot cocoa, and you can calm down a little," the young woman offers.

"Who are you?" I ask, my voice cracking.

"I'm Brittney, the librarian." *The library.* Just the thought has me calming down slightly. I push off the wall, my limbs shaking as I take a hesitant step toward her. I don't want to call her my savior, but in a way, she saved me. "You look a little shaken up," she states the obvious, and I turn to look over my shoulder to see if Quinton actually left or if he's hiding somewhere behind me.

I want to go into the library and wait it out a bit before trying to head back to my dorm, but not one single teacher or student has been kind to me since I arrived. This woman, even if she is the librarian, could be just as mean and hateful as the others. This could be a trick, *or it couldn't.*

I don't have a lot of options, but I do know whatever this teacher could do to me is small in comparison to what would happen if Q got a hold of me right now. I start walking toward her, and the closer I get, the more I realize she is standing in the archway of two massive double doors. Once I'm close enough, she whirls around on her heels and walks into the library.

Following her, I stop at the entrance to stare inside. As soon as I do, I realize that this is one of the tunnels that connects to the castle part. The ceilings are much higher and bowed, giving the space an airy feel. Numerous glass windows on the right side of the room let ample light in. My feet move all on their own, and I enter deeper into the room. The space is warm and inviting, with hanging chandeliers that I'm sure look magical at night.

I don't want to admit how much I already love this place.

Tables are situated on both sides of the room while rows upon rows of books lie ahead of me. In the center of the room is the circulation desk, where Brittney, the librarian, is headed. A bookworm's heaven, that's what this library is. The tiniest of smiles tugs at my lips, but I sink my teeth into my lip to stop the smile from showing.

Like a timid mouse, I trail her. She walks behind the circulation desk, and I approach slowly, half expecting her to start laughing in my face or something.

"There's a sitting area over there. Go sit, and I'll bring you your drink."

"You don't have to." I try to make my voice sound strong, but it comes out wispy.

She lifts one of her dark brows and pins me with a do-as-you're-told stare. I decide to listen and walk around the desk and into the open space. There are leather couches and chairs, and the space is boxed in with bookshelves, making it the perfect place to sit and read your favorite book. I sink down onto one of the leather couches; the smell of books, leather, and chocolate permeates the air.

I stare off into space, not ready to digest what almost happened.

"Here," Brittney says, handing me the mug. Her voice startles me, and I jump in my seat, my hand going to my chest.

I sputter to get, "*Thank you*," out and take the mug from her, staring down into it.

"You're welcome," she says, and I watch out of the corner of my eye as she takes a seat on a big comfy-looking chair across from me. Hesitantly, I bring the mug to my lips and take a sip of the steaming hot liquid. "Now, normally, I don't allow students to eat or drink in the library, but for you, I'll bend the rules a little bit."

I look up from the mug, the steam billowing out of it, and find Brittney is smiling, and though it looks like a genuine smile, I can't be sure. While she seems nice, I don't want to owe anyone any favors or dig myself a deeper hole. Her threat to Quinton still hangs in the air, and I know if she truly heard and saw what happened, she has the power to tell someone, and that could make my time here a lot harder. I need to end this, need to tell her I'm okay, that he wasn't hurting me or bothering me. I should've said something in the hall, but I was too afraid, too shocked that someone had stopped him.

The other option would be to confide in her, to tell her the truth, but that seems like a bad idea, one that could blow up in my face. I decide to go with the first idea for now.

"Whatever you saw or heard..." I start, but she waves her hand out in front of her, stopping me in my tracks.

"When you want to talk about it, we can talk about it, but for right now, feel free to sit here and enjoy your drink."

"I just want you to know he wasn't hurting me or anything," I continue. The lie rolls off my tongue so easily, it's scary.

She leans forward in the chair and pushes her black glasses up the bridge of her nose. Her gaze is pensive as she studies me. The light catches on something silver, and it's then that I notice the ring in her nose. "As I said, we can talk about it later."

She doesn't let on if she believes me or not. She simply ends the conversation and moves on, almost like she is giving me an out. Giving me a chance to talk to her when I'm ready to speak the truth. "Why don't you tell me what your name is?"

I gulp down some more of the hot cocoa, cursing myself as

it burns a path of fire down my throat. "Aspen," I wheeze, half choking.

Brittney laughs. "It's called *hot* cocoa for a reason. It's hot, or it would be called lukewarm cocoa. You sip it, not gulp it."

This time, I return the smile and lower the cup from my mouth slowly. "Sorry. I'm kind of ashamed I didn't make it here sooner. I love books, and this library is like a bookworm's haven." I peer around the room, drinking in the grandness of it.

She sighs. "I wish more students felt the same, but they don't."

"They're stupid," I deadpan. "I could live here." It's a joke, well, kind of. This library is already a place I could see myself coming to daily.

Silence settles around us, and I sip on my warm drink, letting it calm me from the inside out. For a brief speck in time, I forget about Quinton, about my father being in prison, about my crumbling life. I let it all fall to the wayside and relax in the comfort surrounding me.

I frown once I reach the bottom of my cup and look up at Brittney, who has been watching me the whole time.

"Thank you so much for...the cocoa, and..." I trail off. I'm not really ready to explain what was going on out in the hall.

"No worries, and I want you to know you're welcome back here anytime. In fact, I'm already looking forward to seeing you again."

I can't help but smile, especially since she's the first teacher to talk to me—the first person to treat me like a human in this twisted place. I hand her the mug and push off the leather sofa.

My legs feel like Jell-O, and I'm exhausted, both mentally and physically. I can only hope that when I walk out of here, Quinton isn't waiting for me.

"Thank you, Brittney. I'll definitely be back, and next time, I'm bringing a book."

"I'm looking forward to it." She smiles, and I can feel her eyes on me as I walk out of the library. And just like that, I think I've found the one haven I'll have at Corium.

As soon as I step out into the hall, I pull out my phone and check the map to figure out where the hell I'm going. I make it to my afternoon class just in time, which, by some miracle, goes by without an incident.

When I finally get done for the day, all I want to do is sprint to my dorm and lock myself in. But the corridor is crowded with people trying to get into their room. Then my stomach growls, reminding me that I haven't eaten anything since breakfast. I ignore the grumbling and use my key card to get in my room. I'll sacrifice dinner tonight if that means I don't have to worry about running into Quinton again.

7

QUINTON

It didn't take me long to figure out who the blue-haired lady was. I'm not sure how the quirky woman in her late twenties ended up at this place, but something tells me she's going to be trouble, at least where Aspen is concerned.

It was pure luck that she slipped through my fingers the other day.

I could've forced the librarian's hand. It was, after all, my word against hers, and knowing who my father is and how much money he invested in this place made it certain she would shut her mouth in risk of losing her job, but something about making Aspen feel like she had escaped me added to the thrill. It heightened the stakes of the game.

It was fucked up, but fucking with her was a high I never wanted to come down from.

A knock echoes through the apartment, and I don't bother

moving off the couch to get the door. Ren is already across the room, ready to host our first gathering with a couple of other guys we know. I've been spending way too much time studying Aspen's social media, which is seriously lacking. She hasn't made a single post in months, and even before that, it was nothing I could use against her.

"I brought beer," Nash yells as he walks through the open door.

"Thank fuck!" I shove off the couch and slide my phone into my pocket. Nash's father is a close colleague of my father's, but he's not the same caliber of criminal. Except for some petty theft, the guy's never killed or hurt anyone. No, his crimes include money laundering, fraud, and bribes. I can see why his father sent him here, though. Not only does he want him to form connections, but it's clear that Nash needs some assistance in becoming a better criminal, which is exactly what this place is for. You can't protect your empire if you don't know how.

Ren closes the door, and a moment later, it opens again. Matteo comes walking in like he owns the place.

"Sure, come right in, make yourself at fucking home," Ren says, sarcasm dripping from his voice. Matteo, who is a bear of a man, simply shrugs. He's as tall as I am and as muscled as both Ren and I combined. He grunts and walks right past Ren.

Matteo is the son of Dick Valentine, an assassin who works for my father. Like me, I doubt he's here for training. I don't know anything about Matteo's and Dick's relationship, so I can't say why he's here, but his father's been preparing him to be a trained killer since he was a kid. Nothing at this school can teach him more than his own father has.

After Ren passes me a beer, he twists the cap off his. I gladly accept it, twist the cap off, and swallow down half the beer in two gulps.

Nash plops down at the tiny dining room table, provided so kindly by the university. "Does anyone else agree the pickings for girls here are fucking slim? I thought college was supposed to be hot college coeds fucking each other. Every girl here wants to scratch my eyes out."

"The Russian girl seems to be up for a good time," I say between sips of beer.

"No thanks. She is batshit crazy like her mother. I'd rather jerk off than worry about her killing me in my sleep."

Matteo shrugs, his dark gaze emotionless. "What about Aspen Mather?"

The mere mention of her name sends a shiver down my spine. I almost want her to be a secret, my secret that no one else knows about, that I get to torment and touch whenever I please.

"I wouldn't touch that bitch if you paid me to."

"You don't need money, asshole, so nobody's paying you to touch her." I snort and take a drink of my beer, trying not to think about how territorial that statement sounded. The truth is, Aspen doesn't mean shit to me, not in the sense that I actually care about her, but strangely enough, I don't want anyone else interested in her either.

"Her father's caused a shit load of problems for people. I

can't tell you how many offers my father's had slide across his desk to kill him," Matteo admits casually.

Nash takes a long pull from his beer before speaking. "I heard she helped her father, made friends with people, became quite a socialite for her daddy. Spied on people and shit."

A socialite? I lean my head back and listen to them talk. I've seen Aspen at a few fundraisers, but she never looked like she was there to make friends with anyone. I always got the impression she hated being there.

Ren chimes into the conversation. "Even if she didn't help him, she's a rat simply by association. You know the shit her dad did to Quinton's family. The apple never falls far from the tree. She can't be trusted."

"It's shaken shit up, that's for sure. I've heard rumors that people had to move, go into hiding, and don't even mention the shit load of money lost because of that prick. In my opinion, she deserves whatever penance she gets," Matteo explains with an odd tone, almost like he wants to be the one dealing out the penance. Too bad for him that someone else will... *me.* Matteo better not get in my way.

He continues talking, saying something that makes both Ren and Nash laugh. For a moment, I space out. Whatever it is he's saying turns into background noise.

It isn't until the subject changes that the grip on my beer bottle tightens, and my own frustrations bubble to the surface.

"The booze they have here sucks..."

"I need a sleazy strip club and a hooker who will do whatever I want for fifty bucks..."

"I just want a fucking double cheeseburger..."

Sitting here listening to everyone else's so-called problems makes me snap. Their complaints are superficial.

They don't have the first fucking clue what it's like to lose, to be lost and never found. The beer slips from my hands and crashes to the floor. Brown liquid sputters out the top, reminding me how close to breaking, to succumbing to the pressure, I am. Who knows what the hell I'll do if I don't walk away right now, but I don't want to find out.

Ignoring the spilled beer, I turn, storming off in the direction of my bedroom to be alone with my thoughts.

"Q, what the fuck?" Ren's concerned voice fills my ears, and a second later, his hand clamps down on my shoulder.

I shrug off his hand and whirl around on him, pinning him with a glare. "I'm done socializing for the night. Leave me the fuck alone."

The warning in my tone is clear, and Ren's brows shoot up, shock etched into his features. Taking a step back, he raises his hands, and I turn away, walking the rest of the way to my room. Once inside, I close the door behind me and lock it.

It's so stupid, especially when a door isn't going to stop Ren from coming in here. A part of me knows one of the reasons he came with me is because he's afraid of me snapping. Afraid of me shutting down and never resurfacing.

As soon as my ass hits the mattress, my cell phone starts to ring. It's a FaceTime call from Scarlet. My fingers itch to hit decline, but a sliver of guilt cuts through me. If I don't talk to her, she'll be upset, and I care way too much about my baby sister to ignore her call. Plus, I'm the one who left her to deal with all the problems at home. The least I can do is maintain my relationship with her. I owe her this much.

Without thinking further on it, I hit the answer key, and on cue, her smiling face reflects back at me, and I force myself to smile.

"For once, I wish you would smile with a real smile. You look so angry all the time."

"I do not, and if I do, I don't mean to."

Scarlet's pink lips form into a pout. "I miss you already."

"I miss you too. It won't be long till winter break. I'll fly home to see you." I shudder at the thought. I want to see my sister more than anything, but my parents are a different matter. I can't stomach a visit with them right now. It's all too soon, too much.

"I know, but it's so far away. I wish you were here. Mom and Dad are driving me insane. They're like two mother hens, always checking in on me and asking me if I'm okay."

I hate the sadness that reflects in her eyes and back at me. Sometimes, I feel like Scar is all I have left, and I'm all she has. We have to stick together even though I'm miles and miles away.

"You can call me whenever you want, even if it's just to talk. I'm still here for you." The light in her eyes brightens and what I've said seems to cheer her up a little bit. The door behind her creaks open, and Mom pops her head inside the room. As soon as she sees me on the screen, she closes the door.

Scar looks over her shoulder at the door that's now closed.

She shakes her head and then returns her attention to me. "Mom's really upset, and Dad, you know he's good at masking his emotions, but even he can't hide that he is miserable. I know they miss you, though, and they want to talk to you."

I can feel my blood pressure rise at the mention of them wanting to talk to me. It's not my fault that I left with so many things unsaid.

"I'm not talking to either of them, not after what they did, and all the secrets they're keeping." It's hard to hide my anger from Scar, but I manage to keep my voice even and the venom out of my words.

"All they want to do is talk," Scarlet replies.

"And I'm not ready yet," I snap, but regret it the moment I do. Scarlet frowns, her brows pinching together like she's been scolded. "Look, I'm sorry, Scar. I didn't mean to snap at you, but I'm not ready yet." My voice becomes gentler, and that eases some of the tension from Scarlet's face.

"I understand. I just miss being normal." I hate how depressed she sounds and that there isn't a damn thing I can do about it.

"Things won't ever be the way they were before, but each day they can get better." I don't care what happens to me or how I feel. The only thing that matters to me is that Scarlet is happy, healthy, and content with life. I won't fail her.

A knock echoes through the phone, and she peers over her shoulder once more. "I've got to go, but I'll call again soon. Behave yourself, brother." She smiles, and then the screen goes dark, the call ending before I can say goodbye.

I toss my phone down on the mattress and lay back, staring up at the ceiling. I'm spiraling again, and every day I get closer to losing the last remaining shreds of my control. I need something to anchor me, something I can control.

No, not something, someone. The enemy. Aspen. I need to have her under my control again, at my mercy, because as sick as it is, as wrong as it is, it's the only time I feel like my old self. The only time I feel in control of my life.

8

ASPEN

*T*he days start to blend in this hell hole. The only reprieve is that I've somehow stayed off Quinton's radar. I've managed to go an entire week without having a single run-in with him. Granted, I did skip PE class this morning, so I wouldn't have to see him.

Between the fear of being caught by him and being alone and singled out everywhere I go, I'm a mess. Even the teachers seem to dislike me. I'm trapped in this place with nowhere else to go. Not to mention, I haven't been able to reach my mom. Every time I try to Skype her, she's *busy*. All I want to do is vent to her about this place, not that she would care. She advocated the most for me to go here.

I shelve the pity party I'm setting up in my mind for later and gather up all my clothes in the laundry bag provided to me when I arrived. I have to go down to the lower level to drop my laundry off for cleaning. Apparently, the students here are too high class to operate a washer and dryer. I scoff at the nonsense and heft the bag over my shoulder.

Yeah, most of us grew up wealthy, but this is still a university. People should at least know how to do their own laundry.

My only clean clothes are what I'm wearing—a pair of sweats, a T-shirt, and an oversized sweatshirt. I've pushed off going downstairs to do laundry for so long that I literally have nothing else to wear. I generally procrastinate doing anything that means me walking through the dorms or anywhere else, for that matter.

I actually played with the idea of no longer attending classes altogether, thinking if I fail, they'll surely send me back home. But what then? We lost most of our money when my dad was convicted. The only assets we got to keep were the house and my trust fund. I don't even know how much this place costs to attend, but I doubt they will refund my tuition.

Wanting to get this over with quickly, I speed walk down the hall, hoping to pass people before they even realize it's me. I succeed most of the way. Only a few shoulder bumps, insults, and dirty looks are hurled at me as I make my way downstairs.

Luckily, there is no line when I walk up to the desk. The maid who takes the laundry looks up from the book in her hand with a smile. That smile is immediately wiped off her face when she recognizes who I am.

They must have a fucking picture of me posted in the employee break room or something. How does every freaking person know me?

"I'm sorry, Miss. I can't take your laundry," she tells me, a sad frown on her lips. At least she isn't actively mocking me. "I'm sorry," she repeats, and I can tell her apology is real, which means it's not her. Someone is telling her not to help me. As defeated as I feel, I'm not going to let it bother me. I know how to use a washer and dryer.

"I understand. Can you point me in the direction of a washer I can use?"

Her head lowers, and her shoulders sink. "Students are not allowed to use the washers."

I'm so flabbergasted, I almost drop my bag. "What do you mean?"

"I can't let you into the laundry room. It's off-limits to students."

"But you also can't do my laundry?" I clarify, and she shakes her head. "So, how am I supposed to wash my clothes?"

She sighs and gives me a tiny shrug. I know it's not her doing, but it's hard not to let my anger out at the person in front of me.

"Thanks for nothing," I sneer and storm off.

I basically run back to my room with the bag of clothes bouncing off my shoulder. My arm already hurts from holding it at an odd angle for so long, but I welcome the pain. I let it fuel my anger.

Swiping my key card, I shove open my room long enough to throw the bag inside, then slam the door back shut and head to the administration building.

By the time I make it to the headmaster's office, my vigor is slowly diminishing, but I know I have to do this. I have to stand up for myself at some point. What better time than now?

"Can I help you?" the secretary at the front desk asks with a fake smile painted on her bright red lips.

"I need to talk to someone."

"Someone?" she parrots back at me.

No, not someone, the man in control.

"I want to talk to Mr. Diavolo," I say, keeping my voice strong.

"Are you sure about that?"

"Yes," I answer before I change my mind.

"All right, dear." She pushes some buttons on the phone and waves her hand toward the door beside her desk.

Taking one deep, calming breath, I head toward the head-master's office and push open the heavy wooden door. I find him sitting at his desk, his feet propped up, and he leans back in his leather chair. His eyes are glued to a large TV screen that is made to look like a window into a forest. Soft sounds of nature play in the background.

"What can I do for you?" he asks, sounding bored. He doesn't even look up at me until I start talking.

"I get it, you hate me. Everyone does. But I need clean clothes, and since the laundry services refuse to do my laundry, I'll do it myself, but you need to at least give me access to wash them."

"You have a bathroom. Wash your clothes in the sink."

"My sink is broken, and the janitor won't fix it."

He simply shrugs, like he couldn't care less about the condition of my room. "That seems like a personal problem. I'm sure you can figure it out."

"You know I pay the same tuition as everyone else, right? You can't just take stuff away from me."

Slamming his palms onto the table, he sits up so fast I barely see him move. Startled, I jump back a foot, bumping into a side table behind me.

"Let's make one thing very clear, you do not come in here making demands. I don't give two shits about your comfort or how you wash your fucking clothes. Be glad we gave you a room in the dorms at all because there is a nice little shack with no running water or heat at the surface. Would you rather stay there?"

I shake my head furiously, in the universal sign of no, my tongue suddenly heavy in my mouth. The tranquil sound of the forest scene coming from the TV is drowned out by the heavy thud of my pounding heart in my ears.

"If that's all, you can get the fuck out now." He's halfway through the sentence, but I'm already heading for the door. I can't get away from him fast enough, and coming here was definitely a mistake.

In defeat, I walk back to the dorms, drowning out any snide comments from people I pass. Back in my room, I pick up the bag of clothes and dump them out on my bed. I'll have to somehow wash them in the shower later using my shampoo, but for now, I pick the cleanest of my clothes and change into them.

The shirt is now wrinkled, and the smell is less than pleasant. I drown myself in perfume and run the comb through my hair until I look and smell halfway presentable. Grabbing my bag on the way out, I head to my history class, which I missed last week thanks to Quinton.

Surprisingly, I find the classroom right away, and thankfully, I arrive a little early. I take a seat furthest in the back, tucked into the corner of the room. Maybe no one will notice me.

I actually make it through most of the class without anyone bothering me. Professor Brush goes over the Cold War, espionage, and other tactical warfare. It isn't until he touches the subject of treason that I become the center of attention.

"You probably know that officially Julius and Ethel Rosenberg were the only two people executed for treason, after being found guilty of conspiracy to commit espionage. Of course, many more people were put to death, but your high school history books don't have that information. Lucky for you, ours do. Open your books and take a look at page sixty-nine."

I unlock my computer and flip the e-book to the page in question. My stomach flips when I see the image. It's a naked woman, strung up by her arms in the center of the room. Her lifeless body bloodied and beaten.

"The Rosenberg execution by electric chair might have been called inhumane, but their deaths had nothing on some of the lesser-known traitors. As you can see from the image, Clara Morris suffered for days before she died a slow and painful death."

"You mean Mather?" someone whispers, and a wave of

chuckles moves through the class. The professor continues as though nothing happened at all.

"As I was saying, Clara was raped and tortured for an entire week until she finally died. Videos of her punishment were distributed across the dark web to let everyone know what happens to those who betray their own."

"Maybe we should do this to Aspen," another guy says, not even bothering to whisper it. I keep my eyes trained on the screen in front of me and ignore more laughter erupting in the classroom.

"Are you even listening, Mather?" A balled-up piece of paper hits me in the side of the head, making me look up.

"Was that really necessary?" I glare at the guy who clearly hates my guts.

"No talking in class, Aspen," Professor Brush warns.

I know talking back will only make things worse, but my stupid mouth moves on its own. "Are you serious? Everyone else is talking. He threw something at me." I point at the guy and immediately hear the word snitch mumbled by a few people.

The professor's eyes turn murderous, and the tone of his voice is menacing. "Marcel was just trying to get your attention since you are clearly distracted," he defends the guy. "Everyone else is contributing to the class material. You are not."

"I know a way she could *contribute*..."

The laughter feels like nails on a chalkboard to me. It doesn't only hurt my ears, it hurts my soul, and I know I can't spend another minute in this room without losing my shit.

Without looking up, I gather everything in front of me, shove it in my bag, and storm out of the class. The door falls shut behind me, and I break out into a run as soon as my feet hit the marble floor. Fuck this class. Fuck all of them.

I push my legs to run faster, feeling as if I'm not getting away from these people quick enough. I round the corner to the elevators and run full force into someone. Bouncing back, I land on my ass with a hard thud. Pain shoots up my back, making me groan in pain. In the process, my bag slips from my hand and goes flying across the corridor.

"What the fuck are you doing?" an angry voice booms from above me. My head snaps up, and I find Quinton and Ren staring down at me.

Of—fucking—course.

9

QUINTON

My chest tingles where her small body crashed into mine. Using my palm, I rub the spot and glare down at Aspen, who is sitting on her ass in front of us.

"Do you always run around corners without looking?" I question.

She doesn't answer with words, simply shakes her head and starts gathering the contents of her bag. She is on her knees crawling over the floor, and my eyes zero in on her apple-shaped ass. My cock twitches against my zipper, and I hate how her body makes me feel. I hate not being in control of my lust.

She is just about to pick up one of her books when Ren kicks it away from her grasp and in front of my feet.

"Very mature," she murmurs and glares up at him.

"Let's go, Ren," I growl and purposely step on her book. Some pages tear beneath the sole of my shoe, and a shocked gasp falls from Aspen's lips. Her eyes go wide, and she scurries

over to my feet, grabbing the book as if it's some precious artifact. She is kneeling inches in front of my feet but not paying
me the slightest attention. All she's worried about is her stupid
little book, and I fucking hate it.

I hate that she is ignoring me.

I hate that my dick is getting hard just from looking at her.

I hate everything about Aspen Mather.

"Yeah, let's go. We have better things to do." Ren nods and
walks past me. I fall in step with him, leaving Aspen behind to
gather her things.

Wanting her gone from my mind, I walk faster in hopes that
distance between us will also distance my thoughts, but like a
cancer, the image of her kneeling in front of me is only growing.

"Fuck!" I call out more to myself than anyone else.

"What?" Ren asks, totally clueless about the battle going on
in my head.

"Nothing," I snap. "I'm skipping this class. Have something
else I have to take care of."

"Okay," Ren says, drawing out the a.

Spinning around, I walk back the way I came from and take
the elevator down to the dorms. The door slides open with a
bing, and I make my way down the corridor, opposite to where I
usually go.

The word rat is still painted on her door. It doesn't look like
anyone ever tried to clean it off. Raising my hand, I rap my
knuckles against the door, glad that it doesn't have a peephole since
I'm certain she wouldn't open if she knew I was on the other side.

As soon as I see the doorknob turn, I push the door open and shove my way into the room.

"What the hell—" Aspen yells, stumbling back.

Smirking, I step inside and close the door behind me, shutting us in together in the small space that is her room. I can already breathe a little easier, my mind slowly winding down as I take in her trembling body in front of me.

Now, I have her full attention, and here, I'm in control.

"What do you want?" she asks, squaring up her shoulders like she isn't scared, but the slight shaking of her voice gives her away. She is afraid all right, and she probably should be.

"Just coming to check on you." I shrug. "You seemed upset in the hallway."

"Fuck you. What do you really want?"

She wants the truth? Fine. "I really want to choke you out again, so I can do with your body whatever I want to without you fighting or talking."

Her breath hitches, and all the blood drains from her face. Slowly, she starts backing away from me until her legs hit the edge of her bed, and she is forced to stop.

"There is seriously something wrong with you."

"Probably, yeah." I take a step toward her. "You don't seem too fond of that idea... so maybe I could be satisfied with something else."

"Like what?"

I haven't actually thought that far yet, so it takes me a moment to come up with something. What would satisfy me? I want to control her, I want her to submit to me, but I know she won't just give it up to me no matter how scared she is.

I have to start small, give a little—so I can take a lot.

"I want you to let me touch you."

"No." She shakes her head before I even finish speaking. "I'm not having sex with you."

"Who said anything about sex? Get your mind out of the gutter, Aspen."

"Whatever it is you want, the answer is no."

"Take your shirt off and go lie on your bed."

Wrapping her arms around herself like that could protect her from me, she shakes her head furiously.

"Do it yourself, or I'll do it for you." I let the threat hang in the air while I look around. Her dorm room is smaller than my closet, and the walls look like this place should be condemned. Ignoring the condition of her living space, I walk into the attached bathroom.

There is a shower in the corner, a toilet, and a sink with a small shelf over it. Fuck, this place is more dreadful than a prison cell.

"When I get back in that room, you better be on the bed with your shirt off," I yell over my shoulder as I sift through the toiletries on the shelf. When I find what I'm looking for, I grab the small bottle and waltz back into her room.

A triumphant smile tugs on my lips, seeing her sprawled out on the mattress in only her leggings and bra. She is flat on her stomach, her arms lying next to her body, and her face turned away from me.

I'm surprised by her position since turning her back to me makes her more vulnerable, but I'm not complaining.

Slipping out of my boots, I leave them sitting next to the door and get on the bed with her. The mattress gives way with a screeching sound as I move over her and straddle her thighs. When I settle on top of her, the metal springs dig into my knees, and I try to shift, rubbing my crotch against her ass in the process. Her entire body is stiff, her hands balled up in tiny fists next to her.

Unclasping her bra, I let it fall open, and it slides to the side, exposing every inch of her delicate back. Flipping the top off the lotion bottle in my hand, I squeeze a generous amount into the palm of my hand and drop the bottle to the ground.

With my free hand, I move her hair away from her shoulders, letting it fall around her head like a halo. Her shoulders are shaking, and I'm not sure if it's because she is cold, angry, or scared.

I rub my palms together, making sure I don't spill any lotion before placing both hands flat on her back. She sucks in a sharp breath at first contact but doesn't protest as I start rubbing the vanilla-scented lotion into her skin.

It takes about five minutes of massaging her back before she relaxes the tiniest bit. I run my thumbs down her spine and my whole hand up, wondering how much force it would take to break the bones below her skin. I pay special attention to her shoulders, which are so tight they make my fingers hurt.

"Why are you doing this?" She suddenly breaks the silence.

"No talking," I warn. "Just relax."

She doesn't listen, of course. Even though she doesn't say another word, her body never fully relaxes. I keep massaging her back, shoulders, and even her arms until all the lotion has soaked into her skin, and my hands are dried up.

This entire time, my cock has been as stiff as her shoulders, and I know it won't take much for me to come right now. Placing my hands beside her body, I shift my weight off her.

"Turn around," I order, and to my utter shock, she complies.

She rolls her body onto her back awkwardly, her hands clutching to the bra covering her chest. When she is all the way turned, I push myself up, settling back onto her thighs.

"Lose the bra," I demand while flicking open the button on my jeans in a hurry. Her eyes lower to where my hands are already undoing the zipper, and she can undoubtedly see the bulge hiding beneath.

"I told you, I'm not doing this with you. Just—"

I cut her off midsentence by wrapping a hand around her throat. Suddenly, not caring about the bra anymore, her hands fly up to clutch onto my wrist. I'm not choking her, my grip simply holding her in place, but the threat is there.

"Submit to me... drop your arms and let me do whatever I want to you."

"No." She shakes her head as much as I allow it.

"Why do you have to be so fucking stubborn?"

If looks could kill, her death stare would send me straight to the gates of hell. She won't give in unless I'm offering her something.

"Submit to me, and I'll leave you alone for a few days." I

glance down at the thin and scratchy-looking blanket. "And maybe even get you a new blanket and pillow."

She studies my face, probably watching for any signs that I'm lying, but I'm actually telling the truth. If it gets me my way, I'll do it.

"You know I'll stand by my word. Just give me what I want. It can be our little secret; no one has to know you gave in to me. Your pride won't be harmed."

"It's not my pride I'm worried about." Her voice is low, and somehow, she seems even smaller as she drops her hands from my wrist and places them next to her body.

Her chest rises and falls rapidly as I release her throat and pull away the bra completely. I cup her breast in my palm and run my thumbs over her rosy nipples, making her shiver.

As if the universe is making fun of us, her tits fit into my hands like they were made for me. How can we fit together so well physically when there is no way we could ever belong with each other?

We're enemies, and that will never, ever change.

Shaking the thought away, I straighten up and free my throbbing cock.

"Last week, you marked me." I point at the faint red oval on my neck where she embedded her fucking teeth into my skin. "It's my turn to mark you, and lucky for you, my mark doesn't hurt."

I wrap my fingers around my aching length and start stroking. Her eyes are glued to my cock, as if she's never seen one in her life. Her innocent act turns me on even more, and it doesn't take me long before I feel the tingle in the base of my spine.

Fisting my cock with one hand, I grab her hip with my free one, imagining what it would be like to have her tight cunt swallowing my dick and not my hand. My pumps become furious, and I throw my head back with a grunt when my balls draw together.

And then I explode. Ropes of sticky cum shoot out of my cock in spurts, landing all over her stomach and chest. My orgasm seems to go on forever, and only when the last aftershock has rippled through my system do I open my eyes and look at what I've done.

She is gaping at me like she is in a trance, mesmerized by what I just did. Like shiny paint, my cum is splattered all over her creamy white skin.

Letting go of my cock, I use both hands to rub my cum into her, massaging her breasts and stomach like I did her back earlier.

"You marked me; now I've marked you. We're even."

She blinks slowly like she is not sure this is even real. I don't bother telling her that it is. Instead, I climb off the bed and tuck myself back into my pants. I clean my hands on a towel hanging over the chair in her room, and then slip on my boots before heading out the door.

"See you in a few days," I say, right before I close the door behind me. If I'm going to stand by my word, I have to get away now.

10

ASPEN

You know that saying, you can only avoid something for so long? While Quinton stayed true to his word and left me alone for the past two days, I can't exactly avoid the rest of the student body, who also happens to hate me as much as he does.

I was sure he was going to hurt me that night. When he told me to get on the bed, I hid my face so he wouldn't see how scared I really was. I figured he was gonna torture me like the woman from the book. Images of him with a knife in his hand, carving into my skin like I'm nothing more than a piece of meat, ran through my mind.

Not in a million years did I think he would give me a fucking back rub. I still don't understand what that was all about. If he wanted to jerk off on my boobs, he could have forced me to do it right away. There was no reason to massage me like that unless all he wanted to do was play mind games.

While I'm still trying my best to figure Quinton out, there is no question where I stand with the rest of the school. At every turn, people are messing with me.

This morning, someone tossed their orange juice at me and called me trash. Because apparently, rats and trash go hand in hand. Every day, I have to fight to get through the corridor. No matter what time of day, I always find myself pressed against the wall, my fellow students pushing and shoving me around like a doll.

Relieved that my classes are done for the day, I head back to my dorm room to grab my library books. I've not even reached the door when I notice something hanging on the doorknob. My stomach sinks, my mind immediately going to the worst case, that someone is probably pranking me or trying to humiliate me in some way.

I approach the bag like I would approach a bomb threat. As I inch closer, I realize it's a bag like the one my bedding came in. Hooking my fingertip on the edge of the opening, I slowly pull on it so I can peek inside.

All I see is a rolled-up comforter, but I doubt that's all that's in there. This has to be a trick. Something is definitely going to jump out of the bag any minute now.

When a few seconds pass and nothing happens, I start to feel stupid for standing around. Using all my courage, I finally snatch the bag off the doorknob and push into the room. Turning over the bag, I dump the contents on the floor in front of me and watch as a pillow and the rolled-up blanket unfold.

Strangely, they look normal... clean, like someone grabbed them from the laundry room and put them in the bag.

Grabbing the corner of the blanket, I bring it to my nose. The fresh scent of laundry detergent fills my nostrils.

Mmm, smells normal too.

Could it be? Is there a chance that Q actually got me a blanket? That he followed through on his bargain.

I inspect the inside of the empty bag and every inch of the blanket one more time before I decide it must be so. I don't know how or why, but I'm not going to complain about it. For the first time in a long time, I feel glee, and I'm almost afraid to allow myself to enjoy this moment because I know at any second things will change. Still, I take a moment to revel in the joy, and with a smile on my lips, I switch out the old sheets and scratchy blanket and replace it with the fluffy new one.

If Brittney wasn't waiting for me, and I didn't have books to return, I would cuddle up in the bed right now. The newfound comfort calling out to me like a siren.

No, I can't. I have shit to do. While gathering my books, my eyes land on my computer, and I decide to try to Skype my mom real quick before I leave.

Maybe she'll finally answer one of my phone calls. I've been trying to Skype with her since I arrived, but she never answers, and I'm getting really tired of putting effort into it, but who else do I have to call? No one, that's who.

Flipping the laptop open, I pull up Skype and click on my mom's name. The weird ringtone that sounds like an alien invasion is rolling in fills the room. After three rings, the sound suddenly breaks off, and my mom's face fills the screen.

"Mom?" The word comes out like a question. That's how surprised I am that she actually picked up.

"Aspen, honey. How have you been?" My mother's face is painted on perfectly, like a rare canvas, and her blond hair is styled like always.

She looks the same even though I know it's fake.

"Terrible," I admit, not sparing her my truth. "This place is the worst. I hate everything about this school." I try not to come off whiny, but it's so hard. She has no idea what I'm going through here.

"You're overexaggerating." She rolls her eyes at me.

"No, I'm understating it. This is a nightmare. Everyone, and I mean *everyone,* hates me. I can't walk around without people bumping into me on purpose, shoving me into walls, and tossing their breakfast on me. On top of it, I have no place to wash my clothes, and Quinton Rossi is here. Living here, tormenting me."

"He can't touch you," she says, examining her fingernails.

"He can, and he has."

"You don't look hurt," she points out, downplaying everything I say.

"He choked me out in gym class the other day." For a fraction of a second, my mom's eyes widen, and worry flickers through them.

"He probably didn't mean to." She recovers quickly. "Besides, that's better than being dead, don't you think?"

"Anything is better than being dead, but at this point, I don't think it's safe or even smart for me to stay here." I don't even want to try to explain to her what I think might happen next.

Quinton has no boundaries—he's the jaguar, and this is his jungle. I don't and never will stand a chance against him.

Uncertainty pools in my mother's blue eyes, eyes I remember looking up to as a little girl. Over the years, my relationship with her has become more and more strained. It only got worse when we lost everything, and when Dad went to prison, it became nonexistent.

"Mom, you have to believe me. I'm trying. I'm really, really trying. I've been staying out of everyone's way, keeping my head down, but they're all out to get me. Even the teachers hate me."

My mom's uncertainty turns into fear. Seeing her like this makes my stomach twist and knot in a different kind of way. A way that tells me I'm in more danger than I ever thought.

"Listen to me, Aspen. Out here, you're as good as dead. People are after your father, people who want him, and by extension, us, dead. So, while I understand people might be shitty there, anything is better than being out here. I promise you that."

All I can do is shake my head. She has no idea what I'm experiencing, the fear I feel every night when I close my eyes, and the second that I wake. Some nights, I wonder if this will be the last time I close my eyes.

"I really hate it here." I play with the idea of telling her what happened last night, what Q did to me, but the fact of the matter is, he could've done much worse.

In our world, women are often treated less than men. Many daughters get married off or sold to the highest bidder as soon as they turn eighteen. A fate that I luckily escaped.

Her pink lips press into a thin line. "It's time to grow up. We all have to do things we hate sometimes. Look at your father; he went to prison, sacrificed it all for us."

I roll my eyes. "Everything he did was his own fault."

"You're safe there."

"Even with the enemy's son hot on my heels? He hates me, and so does everyone else. I'm afraid that one night something bad will happen." I hate saying the words out loud, but it's the truth, and it makes me wonder, am I really safer here than out there?

"The school has strict rules, one that even the Rossis can't break. *No one dies.* He can't touch you. Please just trust me. There is no safer place than that school."

"I wish I could believe that."

"I'm sorry, Aspen. I have to go, but I'll call you in a few days to check in, okay?"

"Okay," I agree even though all I want to do is throw the stupid laptop across the room, get on a plane, and fly home.

"Goodbye," she says, and the call ends before I can reply.

The screen goes black, and I shut the laptop a little harder than necessary. I don't allow myself a second to wallow in self-pity. Instead, I gather up my stuff once more and head out for the library. It's the only place I can escape, where people leave me alone. It's where I can sink into my work and read. Where I don't have to worry about anyone humiliating me or pushing me around.

My haven.

AFTER SPENDING the rest of the afternoon in the library, I return to my dorm just after dinner. I stopped by the cafeteria on my way back and picked up a prepackaged sandwich. It's expired by a couple of days, but it's all they'll allow me to have. Most days, I have to beg for food, which makes me feel like complete shit, and when they do give me something, it's already expired, like my milk from breakfast the other day. I opened it to eat with some cereal and almost hurled at the smell. After that, I felt it was safer to drink water.

As soon as I reach my door, I know something is off, and the tiny hairs on the back of my neck stand on end. The door is cracked, and I'm certain I shut it before I left. Slowly, I approach the door, waiting for something or someone to jump out. After a minute of waiting, and when I don't hear laughter or move-ment, I shove the door open with my foot and flick the light switch on.

No one jumps out or starts screaming, so I walk inside and shut the door behind me. A knot of worry tightens in my gut. I should've expected that someone would eventually try to sabo-tage my room. After all, it is the only place I can escape from all of them.

Placing my backpack on the floor and my books on the desk, I scan the room, looking for anything that might be missing or out of place.

Whoever it was came in here with an agenda; they wouldn't risk breaking into my room without a purpose.

My gaze passes over the nightstand and then the bed, where I notice something red on the all-white comforter. Pulling the comforter back, I let out a shriek of terror because on my mattress is a dead rat, with a knife stabbed through its body.

My appetite evaporates into thin air, and all I can do is stand there staring at the dead animal and blood on my white sheets. I ball my hands into tight fists, anger overtaking the fear. I don't need to think very hard to know who did this.

Quinton. He did this to mess with me, to hurt me. By giving me the blankets, he gave me a false sense of hope. He made me think that if I let him do what he wanted, he would help me, but what he really wanted was to hurt me, to make me look like an idiot.

Lava burns through my veins, and I rip the sheets from the bed and angrily toss them out into the hallway. Tears sting my eyes, but I blink them back, refusing to let a single one drop. I will not cry because of him. I will not show him how weak I am because that's what he wants. Exhausted both mentally and physically, I curl up on the floor in the fetal position and stare at the door, wondering how I can get even with someone who is bigger than this university, bigger than my father, and far more dangerous than anyone I know.

If he wants a game, then he's going to get one. It might be

me versus everyone else, but if what my mother said is true—that no one can kill me here—then I'm at least safe from that. No matter what I do to get even, he can't kill me.

I let my eyes fall closed with that thought in my mind. I have to find a way to take back my life.

11

QUINTON

Staring up at the ceiling from where I'm sprawled on my bed, I wonder how many days a few actually is? I've stayed away from Aspen for three days now, and the urge to go and find her is growing by the minute. I'm just not sure what I'll do to her yet. All I know is that I need her in my grasp.

My phone vibrates in my pocket, interrupting my inner dialogue. Pulling the small device out, I find Scarlet's smiling face lighting up the screen. I swipe to answer the video chat, and the live feed of Scarlet in her room pops up.

"Hi!" She greets me like seeing me is the most exciting thing that's happened to her all day.

"Hey, what are you up to?" I ask, making conversation.

"Oh, the usual, being wild and rowdy. Got blackout drunk last night and had a bunch of guys over... I think they were bikers." She taps her finger on her chin and scrunches her nose like she is thinking.

"Yeah, right." I snort. "I'm sure the guards let them right in."

"Oh, they party with us, and we had a stripper popping out from a cake!"

"Your imagination knows no bounds. You should write a book or something."

"Hmm, maybe I will. Have to make it through high school first, though."

"You'll be fine. You'll probably graduate way early." Scarlet is only fifteen, but she's skipped two grades already, and I wouldn't be surprised if she started studying here before I was done. The idea of having my little sister here with me both excites and terrifies me.

"Yeah, you're right. I totally will. What about you? How is school going? How is Ren? Did you guys make friends yet? Are the teachers nice?" She goes on, bombarding me with questions.

"Calm down. I'll tell you everything." I lean back against the headboard and start telling her about the school, what the classes are like, down to what the cafeteria serves. I don't mention Aspen, and I'm not planning on doing so in the future.

"Q, you should really talk to Mom—"

"No." I shake my head. "I'll talk to her when she is ready to tell me the truth about my birth mother."

"Q..." Scar gives me her best puppy dog eyes, and I already know I'm going to give in. "Don't make her suffer because you are stubborn. You know she can't go against Dad's wishes. He doesn't want you to know. Please, Q. Mom is really hurting, and I hate seeing her like that."

"All right, stop with the guilt trip and get her on the phone." The words have barely left my mouth when Scarlet is already up and running out of her room. I have to look away from the screen since the video is bouncing up and down, making my brain hurt.

"Mom! Mom! It's Q," Scar announces in excitement. "He wants to talk to you."

Scar shoves the phone into Mom's hand, and her face fills the screen. Her mass of strawberry blond hair is tied into a bun on top of her head, and her blue eyes clash with mine. I'm reminded instantly why I chose not to talk to them yet.

Just looking at her—the only mother I've ever known—is like pouring salt into an open wound.

"Quinton," she whispers, almost like she can't believe I'm here.

"Mom." In my eyes, she is my mom and always will be; even if we don't share DNA, we share more important stuff. Love. Memories—laughter, sadness, happiness, and pain.

Her pink lips form a smile. "How are you? How is school?"

"Everything is going good." I try not to sound as tense as I feel.

She nods. "That's good. Everything here is mostly the same." She pauses before adding, "Your father and I miss you."

"I doubt he does," I bite out. If he missed me that much, he wouldn't have sent me away without telling me the truth.

"He does... and I... since you left, I feel like I've lost two children." Her blue eyes get all misty, and it's like a knife plunges into my chest at the image on the screen before me.

Fuck, now I feel like shit, and on top of that, guilty. I've been putting off talking to either of them, the anger and sadness still as fresh as the day I found out the truth, well, the partial truth.

"I'm sorry. I should've called and talked to you sooner. I don't want you to worry about me. I just..." I trail off. Suddenly, avoiding her seems like nothing more than a tantrum. I was so fucking selfish to make her suffer just because of what my father did.

"It's fine. I know you are grieving too, and then the other thing on top of that. It couldn't have been easy to have your whole world turned upside down. I just want you to know it never mattered to me. I loved you all the same, and you will always be mine in my eyes."

"You'll always be my mom," I murmur and look away from the camera, getting uncomfortable with the onslaught of emotions. "Can we talk about something else now?" I clear my throat, which feels constricted somehow.

"Yes." Mom laughs, and the sound is like a warm blanket on a dark, chilly night.

"Tell me about classes. Are you learning anything?"

I give her the same washed-out response I gave Scarlet, which seems to satisfy her just the same. After a few more minutes of talking, my arm is already getting stiff from holding the phone in front of my face.

"I'm glad we got to talk. I really miss you, Q."

"I miss you too, Mom. Talk soon." She blows me a kiss, and I roll my eyes right before ending the video chat with a smile on my face. I already feel better, lighter now that I've talked to my mom. I could kick my own ass for not doing it sooner.

Tucking my phone back in my pocket, I'm about to head out the door when it opens. Ren appears on the other side, grinning at me from ear to ear.

"Did I just hear your mom's voice in here?"

"Yeah, I talked to her." I walk past him into our shared living space.

"I'm glad you did. How are they doing? How is Scarlet?"

"Well. She was even joking around with me today like she used to."

"Good, I know she must be having a hard time with you gone. So many changes."

"Yes, but she is resilient and strong." Sometimes, I think she is stronger than me, but I don't say that out loud. "Wanna head to lunch?"

"Yeah, sure." Ren nods to the door, and we head out together.

When we reach the cafeteria, it's packed. I know the school has about three hundred students. I feel like every single one is here. After we get our food, there isn't a free table in sight, but as soon as we walk close to one, four guys grab their trays and get up to make room for us.

"Sometimes, being who you are has perks," Ren points out as we sit down.

"I can't deny that," I say, picking up my fork.

I'm about to dig in when a voice cutting through the crowd makes me pause. I scan the room, and my eyes land on the petite girl with her blond hair pulled into a loose ponytail. I can't make out what she is saying over the chatter in the cafeteria, but I can hear its high-pitched parts.

She is flailing her arms around like she is yelling at the person behind the counter. Suddenly, she spins and stomps away like she is about to tackle someone. Her face is flush, anger etched into her features, and her hands are balled up into tiny fists, ready to throw a punch.

Some guy shoulders her on the way, and I tighten the grip on my fork. She doesn't even acknowledge the guy, simply steadies herself and keeps walking. She is almost at the door when yet another person rams a shoulder into her. This time, it's a girl with short brown hair. She turns her nose up at Aspen, daring her to say something.

Aspen turns away from the girl and starts walking around her. That's when her furious glare lands on me. I've never seen her eyes filled with so much hate and anger. Like a volcano ready to erupt, she stomps toward me like some kind of shield-maiden ready for battle.

"Are you happy now?" she yells once she's closer. There is so much venom in her voice, she barely sounds like herself.

She stops right in front of the table, and before I can even comprehend what is happening, she swipes my tray off the table. I'm only vaguely aware of the shocked gasps of people around me as I watch the tray together with my plate, drink, and dessert fly through the air and land with a loud crash on the ground beside us.

The whole cafeteria goes quiet, the only sound Aspen's

ragged breathing. "I. Fucking. Hate. You." Each word drips from her lips with venomous rage. Her chest heaves, and she gives me one last withering look before she walks away. I watch her, stunned by the whole situation. No one shoulders past her this time. Instead, they step out of her way like she has some kind of disease they are worried they'll catch.

"Does she have a fucking death wish?"

I hear Ren's question, but I can't manage a response. Dazed, I look around the room.

All eyes are on me. The same shock I feel reflects back at me wherever I turn. Still holding the fork, I gape down at the now empty table, then at the mess on the floor. Some of the staff are already starting to clean up the spilled food and broken plate. Trying their best to fix everything and make it look like it never happened, but I know better than anyone that there are things you can't fix. I stare at the broken pieces of the plate as a memory weasels its way out of my mind.

Sitting on Adela's bed, I cradle the picture frame between my hands like it's a priceless artifact. Her smiling face beams back at me. At that time, she didn't have a care in the world. Her big blue eyes were so full of life, her smile jubilant, her hair soft.

She had her whole life ahead of her, and now she is gone. Dead. My beautiful sister is gone. The room still smells of her, and maybe that's why I like sitting in here. It makes me feel closer to her. Like she's not really gone.

My grip on the picture frame tightens. It's been two weeks, and my parents still haven't made an announcement. No one even knows she's gone besides us. Three days after she passed, we had a tiny private funeral for which I'm thankful for. I'm glad it was just us and not hundreds of people who really didn't give a shit anyway. I didn't want their pity or pretend apologies. People only cared when it benefited them, and someone would ultimately use the gathering as a way to form an alliance or strike a deal.

I'm glad he didn't let that happen, but I still don't understand why he's keeping it a secret. I guess I shouldn't be surprised knowing that he has been keeping all kinds of truths hidden. But not acknowledging that she's gone enrages me more than anything.

Did she matter so little to him? Does he not want to honor her memory?

So many unanswered questions are running through my mind, and the worst of it all, I don't think I will ever get answers to them.

Placing the picture back on the bedside table, I get up, ready to leave the room when a loud crashing sound comes from downstairs. One minute, the house is completely silent; the next, all hell breaks loose.

Men are yelling, shots are fired, my sister and mother are screaming, and I panic and run out into the hallway, needing to get to them. I can't lose anyone else. I'll die before I do.

I don't make it but one step out of Adela's room before I'm tackled to the ground and pushed to the floor face-first.

"Get the fuck off me!" I throw back my elbow at my attacker, but he doesn't budge.

My face is turned toward the open door, a knee pressed into my back as I'm helplessly forced to watch four men in tactical gear enter my dead sister's room. The letters FBI are written on the back of their bulletproof vests.

What the hell are the feds doing here?

That question disappears into thin air as the four men start to tear apart Adela's room.

"No! Leave her stuff alone!" I yell over the noise, but no one is listening. They tear off her bedsheets and flip over her mattress, knocking down the picture frame in the process. Carelessly, they walk all over her stuff, not looking where their heavy boots are landing. I can feel tears building in my eyes. My anger is so profound it's all I can feel.

I might be my father's son, but I have a heart, and it beats proudly for my family. One of them steps on her picture, the glass crunching beneath his foot, and the sound penetrates my heart. In a haze of despair and fury, I watch as they destroy her room. Tainting all of her stuff... the only thing I have left of her.

"Hey, you okay?" Ren's voice drags me back to reality. I shake away the memory, but I can't shake away the feelings it brought on. The loss of control, the pain, the agony of watching the last memories you have of someone being ripped to pieces.

Pain echoes through my chest with every beat of my heart. *Will I ever be okay?*

I think of Aspen, and that only intensifies my rage. I know it's not her fault, that it's her father's, but that doesn't change anything, not in my mind.

To me, she's the enemy, and the stunt she just pulled put a bright red X on her back. Aspen will suffer the consequences of her actions because not only will I not be seen as weak in front of my peers. I won't let her think for a second that she has a chance at winning control over her life back.

12

ASPEN

I'm so fucking hungry, I could cry. I'm not particularly fond of only eating what's left from the day before, but expired food is better than no food. When the guy behind the counter told me there were no leftovers, and I couldn't get anything, I lost it.

The mixture of painful hunger, lack of sleep, burning anger, and humiliation was too toxic to be held in. My only regret is letting it out on Q. Not that he didn't deserve it, but I know making a scene in front of the entire school will cost me. He will not let that go. He's going to retaliate, and I'm not sure if I'm ready for it.

Ignoring the emptiness in my stomach, I pull the hood from my sweatshirt over my head and go to the only place at this university I actually feel safe.

As soon as I enter the large doors leading into the library, I relax a little. Pulling off the hood, I walk around and glance between every aisle until I find Brittney. I finally spot her in the fiction section with her nose deep inside a book.

"Checking out the romance books again?"

My voice drags her out of whatever universe she was visiting, and her eyes snap up to me.

"Oh, hi!" She closes the book in front of her abruptly and quickly shoves it on the shelves. "Just doing a routine quality check. It's part of my job," she says innocently.

"Sure, it is." I laugh, feeling a little lighter already. Brittney has become a friend, my only friend, making the library the only place I'm actually welcome. My smile fades at the thought of how lonely I really am. Even though I have Brittney, I only see her at the place she works. She probably wouldn't even be my friend if she didn't work here.

"What's the matter? You look a little pale." Brittney walks over, concern etched into her face. She pats my shoulder as if she actually cares.

"Oh, it's nothing. I just haven't eaten anything today." *Or yesterday*, I add in my mind.

"Well, you are in luck then. Because I brought lunch, and there is plenty for both of us."

"Are you sure? I don't want to—"

"I told you, there is plenty for both of us," she interrupts. "Now, let's go and get you fed before you fall over. You're already skinny as hell."

Taking my arm, she basically drags me across the library and into her office. "You just sit." She pushes me into the chair and disappears into another room that's attached. I hear the bing of the microwave, and then the wonderful scent of savory aroma fills the air. I have to muffle a moan. My stomach is growling so loud, I'm surprised Brittney can't hear it from the other room.

A moment later, she reappears, carrying two full plates in her hands. "Here you go, dear." She places a plate in front of me and hands me a fork. I try not to eat like a savage, but it's hard not to shovel food into my mouth like I haven't eaten in days.

To make it less awkward, I try to make some small talk between large bites.

"Have you worked here for a long time?"

"This is only my second year, but this year is much more fun since I actually have a student coming to the library." She giggles.

"How old are you?" I ask while shoving pieces of marinated chicken into my mouth.

"How old do you think I am?" She retorts, spearing a piece of romaine lettuce on her fork. I tilt my head to the side and examine her face. Other than some fine lines around her eyes, nothing else shows her age.

"If I had to guess, I'd say late twenties?"

"Your guess is correct." She beams, and her smile is contagious enough that it makes me smile too. I've only known Brittney a short while, but she gives me a different vibe than any of the other staff I've come across here. Each person has been hateful and dismissive, including the damn headmaster. I can't help but wonder how she ended up working here, and while I know it's a bit rude to ask, I can't help myself.

"Sorry if this question comes off as stepping over the line between student and teacher, but how did you end up getting a job here? You don't seem like a criminal. I mean, maybe you are, but you're good at hiding it."

Brittney lets out a low laugh, and her cheeks flush red. I can't tell if I've embarrassed her or if I've done something wrong.

"Well, it's kind of a long story... and a little personal." Her cheeks are bright red now, and she's looking at me like she isn't sure if she should tell me.

"I totally understand if you don't want to tell me. I was just curious."

Brittney shakes her head. "No, no. It's okay, it's just..." Her eyes skirt away for a moment before coming back to meet mine, and then she lets out a breath. "I went through a bit of a wild phase in my college days. I was dating a computer geek at the time, and he showed me everything he knew about hacking and getting into stuff I had no business getting into."

My mouth pops open, and I won't lie. I'm kind of shocked by her response.

"He taught you how to hack into people's computers?" I want to tell her how cool that is, but I don't since I get the feeling this story isn't going in a good direction.

She nods. "Phoenix taught me everything."

"His name was Phoenix?

"Yes, I always loved his name too. His username was Firebird." She giggles, and a spark I've never seen before flashes over her eyes but vanishes faster than it appeared.

"He seemed like such a normal guy. Everything started innocently, like a game, but then the game turned serious. I got really good at it, and the worst part was I enjoyed it." I can hear the shame in her voice and become even more engrossed as she continues her story. "Being college students, we had little money, so I started hacking. At first, it was for small amounts and nothing heinous, just here and there, but like anything, it spiraled out of control. Before I realized what I was doing, he had me hacking into the CIA database."

"Wow, that's... well, that's crazy."

"I know, and I almost went to prison for it, but I was able to cut a deal with Julian Moretti. He came to me and basically said if I do my hacking for him exclusively, he would help keep me out of prison. Of course, I did it. Prison wouldn't have looked good on me." She laughs. "He set me up with this job, and whenever he needs something hacked, I'm his girl."

"I had no idea. In fact, I doubt anyone would have ever suspected you to be a hacker."

"It's the quiet ones you gotta watch out for." She winks, and we both break out into laughter. Just talking to another human has made me feel so much better, and by the time we're finished eating, I feel completely content.

"So, what happened to Phoenix and you?"

"Well... as it turns out, he was more than the sweet computer geek I thought he was. The deal with Moretti included making sure Phoenix ended up in prison, but he escaped when they were transferring him, which is one of the reasons I'm here."

"Oh."

"Yes, *oh* is right. Phoenix is looking for me, but I doubt he'll find me here." Brittney shrugs. "It's not a bad deal, though. This place is still way better than prison, and I've made a pretty awesome friend here."

"I've made a pretty awesome friend too." I smile. This place would almost be bearable if it wasn't for Quinton.

"Now, what's your story?" she asks, her question catching me off guard. Am I ready to tell her about my father? I'm sure she already knows, so what am I really hiding?

"I don't really have one. My father was an arms dealer; he's in prison now, which I'm sure you've heard." I try not to sound as disgusted as I feel while speaking about the revolving door of hate sent my way every day because of him. I wasn't the one who turned my back on the Rossi family. I didn't stab the knife into their backs, yet I'm paying the same consequence as my father...maybe worse.

"There are rumors spoken between staff, but I'm not a believer of that nonsense. I judge a person based upon what I know about them and how they treat me. I don't care what someone else thinks about you. As long as you're good to me, then I'm okay with you."

That explains why she didn't turn her back on me that night in the hall. She had heard the rumors and knew what people said, yet she formed her own opinion of me by spending time with me. It was something I wished more of the staff here would do. I wasn't a bad person, and I wasn't *the rat* either.

"Thank you for not judging me and assuming I was a shitty

person right off the bat. Every day since I arrived here has been hell, and the only reprieve I have is this place."

"You're welcome in the library whenever. I'm always here, doing something. I hardly sleep at night anymore."

Night... oh, god. I look out the window and realize it's now dark. How did the time pass by so fast?

"Shit, I need to get back to my room. I have to shower, do some studying, and then get to bed." I scramble from my chair but pause before taking another step. "Thank you for dinner and for hanging out with me and sharing a little about yourself."

"Please, it's not a big deal. I enjoy spending time with you. It's nice to have students use the library, even if there aren't as many as I'd prefer."

I smile and say, "I'll be back tomorrow."

"Already looking forward to it."

I give her a tiny wave before I turn and start walking toward the exit leading back into the underground part of the school.

The large hallway is empty, which I'm normally thankful for, but today there is something in the air that doesn't sit well with me. A shiver skates down my spine, almost as if the universe is trying to warn me about something.

I should have fucking listened.

I take the elevator down to the lower level, my irrational fear never leaving me. The door slides open with a ping, and I half expect someone to jump into the small space. When nothing happens, I step out and look both ways down the hall.

Empty. Heading toward my room, I run my palms over the

front of my shirt nervously. My heart races, but I don't know why. Maybe I should go back to the library? No, that's ridiculous. I'm fine. Instead of letting my fear win, I push on like the foolish girl I am. Shaking the sixth sense away, I ignore all the signs... until it's too late.

"Look who we have here," Matteo's voice booms from behind me. I spin around, ready to start running, but two guys grab me. "Aspen Mather... I've been waiting a long time to get my hands on you."

Trying to pull free only makes them tighten their hold on me, and when I turn my head to glare at them, I realize I know both. One is Marcel from history class, and the other is Nash, one of Quinton's friends.

"What do you want?" I grit through clenched teeth. Marcel is on one side, and Nash is on my other. Their meaty fingers are digging into my arms painfully, but I force myself not to react.

"You owe me a blow job, you know?"

"I don't owe you anything."

"But you do. If it wasn't for you, I would have gotten my dick wet that night at the Belmonte fundraiser. Or have you forgotten about that?"

I couldn't forget it if I wanted to.

"Stop!" As soon as I step out of the lady's room, I hear a high-pitched voice coming from somewhere down the hall. It's only one word, but I can tell whoever said it is scared. I spin around to find its origin, but the hall is empty.

For a moment, I just stand there, listening, wondering if my mind is playing tricks on me. I'm just about ready to head back to the ball-room when I hear the same voice again.

"I said no!"

This time, I'm able to pinpoint where the voice is coming from better, and I set off in the direction of it. Right behind a large column, I find a small corridor. My blood boils when I see a large figure pressing a much smaller one against the wall. His back is so broad, I can't really see the girl he is cornering until I step closer.

"Hey! Let her go," I demand, anger making me braver than I probably should be.

The large figure spins around to face me, his dark eyes wild with rage. "We're just talking. Get lost."

"Let her go," I repeat. When the words don't seem to register in his small mind, I continue, "I'll go and call security if you don't."

"Fucking snitch," the guy growls and stomps past me.

I rush toward the girl leaning against the wall. Her head is bowed, her chest heaving, and she wraps her arms around her torso like she is trying to hold herself together.

"Hey, are you okay?" I ask, gently rubbing her upper arm. She looks up, her eyes brimming with fear.

"Thank you," she whispers, and only then do I realize who she is.

"Adela?" I've only met her once before, but I remember her to be Xander Rossi's oldest daughter. "We need to tell your dad. He'll make sure that guy never touches anyone again."

"No, no, no. Please, don't tell anyone. Matteo won't do that again."

"You know that guy?"

"Yeah, he is a family friend."

"Friend?" That didn't look the least bit friendly.

"Well, his father is friends with my father, but that doesn't matter. Please, don't tell anyone. My dad would never let me go out again if he found out."

"But you didn't do anything."

"Please, Aspen. You don't understand. Please... here, take this."
She shoves something into my hand. I look down at my fingers and find a thin rose gold bracelet with a sparkly charm wrapped around my fingers.

"I can't take this." I look back up just as Adela slips past me. "Keep it. It's a thank you and a good luck charm."

I've kept that bracelet on me for a long time, and even now, I keep it close to me. Maybe not close enough. Because luck has abandoned me completely as I find myself in the clutches of these assholes.

"You're nothing but a dirty pig. Do you have to force all the girls because you can't find someone who actually wants you?"

"I could, but that wouldn't be as much fun." Matteo chuckles before ordering, "On your knees."

"No..." One of the guys kicks my legs out while the other pushes me down to my knees. Pain radiates up my thighs when I make contact with the unforgiving concrete floor.

"Now, let's see how many times I can shove my dick down your throat before you pass out."

I'm just about to start screaming when the shadow of a figure comes up behind Matteo.

"What the fuck are you doing?" Quinton's voice meets my ears moments before my eyes can focus on his face. He takes in the whole situation, his gaze ping-ponging between Matteo, me, and the other two guys. For a split second, I feel relief. I actually believe he will help me, that he will stop them and let me go.

"We're finally putting her mouth to good use. Wanna join?" Matteo offers.

The space falls into a deafening silence. Yet again, I think Quinton will stop this and protect me from them like I protected his sister that night at the fundraiser.

Quinton's eyes bleed into mine, a million unsaid words lingering in the air between us.

"What do you want to do, Q?" Matteo presses.

Without ever breaking eye contact, Quinton says, "Only if I get her first."

13

QUINTON

She is on her knees, looking up at me in disbelief before fear takes over. Nash and Marcel are kneeling next to her, holding an arm each, immobilizing her completely. Both watch with excitement as I undo my pants.

Matteo moves around Aspen and stops right behind her. He appears less excited and more annoyed. Too bad for him that I don't give a fuck about how he feels. All that matters right now is Aspen on her knees in front of me.

My cock is so painfully hard, I have to swallow a groan when I take it out. Through her lashes, she gives me one more pleading look, begging me not to do this without words, but it's too late. I'm too far gone to stop now.

"Open your mouth, and don't even think about biting me. If I feel even the slightest graze of your teeth on my dick, I will fuck your ass instead, and guess what? I didn't bring any lube, so I can guarantee it would be an unpleasant experience... for you, at least. Got it?"

"Why not do that anyway?" Matteo chuckles, leaning down to grab her ass.

"Don't fucking touch me," she spits at Matteo, trying to break free of his hold. He simply laughs at her feeble attempts and slaps her ass, the sound bouncing off the walls.

Grinding my molars together, I rein in the anger I don't understand. So what, he wants to fuck her? I should let him. I should let them all fuck her. *I should, but I won't.*

"I said, hold her still, not grope her so she'll fight more," I grit out.

Matteo nods, although he is clearly unhappy about my order.

Fisting my cock with one hand, I grab Aspen's chin with my other to tilt her head up to me. "Be a good girl and open your mouth."

Her eyes are still defiant, but she knows this is a battle she can't win, and cooperation is going to save her pain. Her mouth opens slowly, her bottom lip trembling as her gaze turns hazy.

The same calm I felt before washes over me once more. I'm in control. Everything happens because I say so. This is my game, my rules.

Precum leaks out from the tip of my cock as I bring it closer to her mouth.

I hiss in pleasure when the mushroom head makes contact with her soft tongue. The guys hold Aspen completely immobile while I push deeper into her hot mouth. She closes her plump lips around my girth, and I almost come undone.

Never breaking eye contact, I start fucking her mouth with shallow thrusts, noticing how she tries to close her throat so I don't go too deep. I let her have her way for a few minutes before it's time for my way.

"Open your throat," I demand, watching as panic flickers over her features. She didn't actually think I was just going to fuck her mouth with slow, lazy strokes, did she?

Using both of my hands, I cradle her head between them and hold her in place. "Open your mouth and relax your throat."

She does as I instruct. A whimper passes her lips, and she lets her mouth fall open. For the first time since we started, she closes her eyes. A part of me wants her to look at me, to keep that connection, but the other part is glad that I don't have to see that desperate plea in the depths of her baby blues.

Plunging my cock deep inside of her mouth, I watch as she gags when the tip presses into her throat. I hold it there for a moment, watching as she struggles to take me before I pull back out to let her breathe.

I only give her a few seconds, and then I repeat the action, forcing my cock so deep that my balls are pressed against her chin. Still holding her face in my hands, I use my thumbs to wipe the tears from the corners of her eyes as I start to fuck her face in earnest.

Losing the last thread of control I was holding, I thrust my cock into her throat mercilessly. Over and over again, I shove myself into her warm mouth, making her gag at the intrusion. Thick spit coats my cock, dripping down onto my balls and her chin.

"Fuck yes, make her choke on it." Matteo grunts, and I try my best to ignore him. "I can't wait to fuck her next."

"I'm next after," Nash chimes in.

"Fuck you guys," Marcel groans.

Aspen keeps her eyes squeezed shut, probably wishing for this to be over. Little does she know, we have just begun.

Everything around us fades away, and all that's left is her and me. The sound of her gagging mingles with my pleased grunts, and I can feel the orgasm building at the base of my spine. I thrust into her one last time, then hold myself there. I come so hard stars dance across my vision. When my release finally ends, and I pull out of her throat, she sucks in a panicked breath and starts coughing furiously.

I let go of her face, and the guys release her arms. She slumps forward, trying to get her breathing under control. Her whole body is shaking, and my conscience roars to life as I look at her small body huddling on the ground in front of me.

"Hurry up and catch your breath." Matteo laughs, patting her on the back. "I'm next, and I won't be gentle either." He starts unbuckling his belt.

Aspen is still gasping for air when I step aside and tuck my now deflated dick back inside my pants. Matteo steps in front of her, taking my place. Grabbing a fistful of her blond hair, he pulls her head up, forcing her to look at him.

"Suck it good because your spit will be the only lube you'll get," he warns.

Her tearful eyes flare with anger, and then she spits in his face. "Fuck you!"

"You stupid bitch!" Matteo wipes his face with the back of his hand before swinging it back toward her.

Without thinking, I grab his arm, stopping him from hitting her. "That's enough. Let her go."

"Are you fucking serious? We're not done with her," Matteo interjects. As soon as the words leave his mouth, he knows he's made a mistake by talking back to me.

Instead of letting go of his arm, I twist it around until he yelps in pain. Nash and Marcel let go of Aspen and step away with their palms up in surrender. Smart move.

I release Matteo with a shove, and Aspen doesn't waste any time. As soon as she is free, she is on the move, but instead of simply making a run for it, she gets up and throws her fist into Matteo's kidney. He grunts and slumps over in pain while she takes off before he can recover.

"You fucking bitch!" he calls after her. "You're gonna regret that." It takes him a moment to recover. When he straightens back up, he turns to his guys. "I'm gonna make her pay for that. Next time, she'll get more than a dead rat in her bed."

"What the hell are you talking about?" I question.

"We left a dead rat in her bed yesterday," Nash explains proudly. "Pinned it to her mattress with a knife."

"It was great." Matteo chuckles. "But nothing compared to what's coming next."

"How the fuck did you get into her room?"

"Easy." Marcel shrugs. "The janitor made us a copy of her key card. We can get in any time we want."

"Give it to me," I demand, holding out my hand.

Marcel looks a bit stunned but reaches back into his pocket and pulls out his wallet. He finds the card and hands it to me.

"You only have this one?" I look around into all three faces. When everyone nods, I continue, "No one goes into her room besides me. No one touches her besides me. No one torments her besides me. She is mine and mine alone. If I find any of you are doing anything to her, I will cut off your balls and shove them down your throat. Is that clear?"

Nash and Marcel nod their heads furiously. Matteo isn't that smart. He studies my face for a moment, his jaw clenched and his eyes glaring. I know he wants to tell me to fuck off, but he manages to refrain and nod ever so slightly. He'll be the one I have to watch.

"Good." I slide the key card into my pocket. "I'll see you guys around."

I walk away with an unsettling feeling deep in my gut. That only spreads like a wildfire as everything that has happened today replays in my mind. It's like watching a movie for a second time, but now you have more information. You know the ending, details you weren't aware of before.

They went into her room and destroyed her bed right after I gave her a new blanket. All the pieces click into place. She thinks it was me, and I can't blame her for that conclusion. She thought I played her, and that's why she made the scene in the cafeteria.

Still, she made a scene, making me look weak in front of the entire school. I had to do something to retaliate, no matter her reasoning.

I don't feel guilty about what I did to her just now, but I do feel uneasy about Matteo. He's not going to let this go. I don't know when or how, but he will strike back. Too bad for him, I meant what I said. She is mine to torment, mine alone to control, and I will not let anyone take that away from me.

The gravity of my statement only starts to sink in when I reach my dorm door. I unlock it and walk in. The place is dark and quiet, letting me know Ren is already asleep. Checking the time, I realize it's after one a.m. already.

Quietly, I head to my room. I briefly think about taking a shower, but that would mean washing Aspen away from my body. The thought of her dried spit remaining on my cock makes the fucker twitch in my pants. God, I'm fucked up. My mind twisted and depraved, but instead of feeling apologetic about it, I embrace it. Embrace the darkness running through my veins.

I was born into this life, and I have no plans on fighting it. Slipping out of my boots, I undress quickly but forgo the shower.

Falling into my bed, I stare at the ceiling, knowing there is no way I'm going to sleep any time soon. So instead, I let earlier run through my mind on repeat...

The way her tongue felt on my cock, her soft whimpers, the

tears in her eyes. Her helplessness and the power it gave me in return. Fuck. It's like a drug I can't get enough of. My dick is already hard again, and I pull it out of my underwear.

Wrapping my hand around the length, I start stroking myself and imagine going to her room. With the key card, I could slip inside unnoticed, climb into her bed, and pin her beneath me before she even wakes up. Closing my eyes, I picture her lying there, only wearing a flimsy pair of sleeping shorts I can easily pull down before plunging my cock deep inside her tight cunt. I would shove her body into the mattress with each thrust—

My little fantasy comes to an abrupt halt as I wonder if she is even in her room now. Matteo said they fucked with her bed. Surely, she won't sleep in it after they put a dead rodent in there. But where else would she sleep? Did she get a new bed? New room?

Not knowing is slowly driving me insane, and no matter how hard I stroke my cock, I can't get back into it.

"Fuck." Climbing out of bed, I fix my boxers and pull on the clothes I took off earlier. I pat the pocket to make sure her key card is still there as I leave the room and head across the dorm.

It's almost three in the morning now, and the corridors are completely void of students and noise. The only sound disturbing the dorm silence is that of my footfalls.

When I get closer to her room at the end of the hall, I notice her blood-soiled mattress and bedding left in the corner. Frowning, I pull the key card out and swipe it through the slide above the knob. The lock disengages, and I push the door open quietly.

Her room isn't dark, the light in the attached bathroom is on, and the door to it has been left open. My eyes fall on the empty bed. Since the mattress is gone, and the only thing left is the iron rails below. Scanning the rest of the small space, I quickly discover she isn't here. I check the bathroom and find it empty as well.

Only when I exit the bathroom do I notice the small set of feet sticking out of the shadowed corner. I move closer until I'm at the head of the bed, and that's when I see her. She's huddled up behind the bed, her legs drawn up to her chest, with her head resting against the back of the headboard.

Her eyes are closed, but her face still seems pinched, as if she is having a bad dream, or maybe she is just cold since the only thing she has to cover up is a towel.

I shouldn't care about her comfort or where the fuck she sleeps, but something in the back of my mind is telling me I should. Maybe it's the part of me that craves control, or maybe it's something I don't understand yet. Either way, I have to find a way to make it stop. I can't afford to have a conscience.

Not now, not ever, and especially not toward Aspen.

14

ASPEN

My eyes fly open, and I'm dragged out of sleep when I hear the sound of the door closing. Immediately, my heart is racing, and I'm wide awake despite being so exhausted I could fall asleep standing up. Panicking, I search for the knife I must have dropped when I dozed off. Sliding my hand across the floor, I search the space beside me and let out a sigh of relief when my fingers slide over the metal.

Wrapping my fingers around the cold handle, I hold the knife out in front of me. It's only a butter knife I took from the cafeteria, but it's better than nothing.

I refuse to go down without a fight.

Holding my breath, I listen intently for the intruder, but I'm only met with silence. Clutching onto the knife tightly, I carefully stick my head out around the headboard to scan the room.

It's empty. Maybe I imagined the sound. My mind is starting

to play tricks on me, which is either from a lack of sleep, lack of food, or both.

Taking a few deep breaths, I slump back into my corner behind the bed. It's uncomfortable, but it gives me this weird sense of comfort and safety. I already know people can enter my room, but if I sleep like this, they won't see me until I'm ready for them to see me.

I lean my head back against the wood. Pulling the towel tightly around my upper body, I try to find an inkling of comfort, just enough to let me sleep for a little while. I'm so fucking tired. Tired of this school, of this room, the bullying... I'm tired of my life.

Squeezing my eyes shut, I force the darkness to take me, to let me forget everything for a couple of hours. I'm just starting to fall asleep when something startles me awake once more, but this time, it's not a sound I imagined that's waking me up. It's something tugging at my towel.

Panic grips me by the throat, and without thinking, I start thrashing around me, kicking out my legs, hoping one of my limbs will connect with anything that hurts. My eyes are wide open, but the room is pretty dark—only some light from the bathroom is filtering into the space.

"Calm down. It's me." Quinton's voice breaks through the fog of panic, but it doesn't stop me from struggling. He'll hurt me and break me if I let him.

My hands are empty, and I have no clue where the knife went, so I have to use my fists to try to fight him off.

I don't get far, and the next thing I know, Quinton is grabbing onto my ankles. He pulls me toward him, so I'm flat on the ground, the back of my head almost hitting the floor.

Then he climbs on top of me, his mammoth frame blanketing mine, pressing me to the floor and leaving me completely immobilized. I turn my head to the side, and Quinton dips his face into the crook of my neck.

My back is cold from the concrete floor, but my front is warm from Quinton's body heat. It only takes a moment until all I can feel is him, the weight of his body, the press of his thighs against mine.

"Just calm down," Quinton repeats, his voice low, soft, and it's only then that the words he said sink in. When I woke up, he said, *"Calm down. It's me."* As if the fact that it's him visiting me and not someone else would calm me down.

Is he really that delirious?

Unable to move even an inch, I do the only thing I can and concentrate on my breathing. To my surprise, Quinton neither moves nor lets all his weight settle on mine. His arms are on either side of me, caging me in but also supporting some of his weight so as not to risk crushing me.

"I'm calm," I whisper into his shoulder, trying my best not to breathe his manly scent into my lungs. It's spicy and intoxicating, and I don't want to admit for a second the way it makes my head spin.

He stays still for another few moments before pushing off me. I follow his movements and sit up, pressing my back to the wall.

"What do you want?" I finally manage to ask, still trying to figure out why he is here.

Uncertainty flickers in his eyes as he reaches for something beside him. I pull my legs up to my chest protectively. I'm terrified of what he might do next. After what he did in the corridor to me, I don't think I'll ever trust him.

"I just brought you this." He picks up a comforter and hands it to me. I look at it, desperately wanting to take it, but I'm not stupid enough to do that. Not again.

"No, thanks."

"Just take it."

"No! Do you think I'm that stupid? This can only be one of two things. Either you're giving me something to play fucked up mind games with me, or this is some kind of payment. Is this your 'I'm sorry' gift?"

"I'm not sorry." He shrugs. Of course, he's not. Someone like him doesn't feel remorse. "And this isn't some mind game. I told you I would get you a new blanket, and I'm keeping my word. I didn't put that rat in your room."

"Great, so everyone in this school has a key to my room?"

"Not anymore. Only I have a key now."

"Is that supposed to make me feel better?" As I say the words, I already know that it does, and I hate it. I hate that out of all people in that group of guys, Q makes me feel like he is the lesser of two evils.

"I don't really care how you feel. Now, take the fucking blanket and go back to sleep."

"No." I shake my head and wrap my arms around my legs so

I can rest my cheek on my knees. "Just leave me alone." The words come out half-hearted, knowing he won't listen anyway. Still, I close my eyes and hope for the best.

Of course, I was right. He is not going to leave me alone. Instead, he throws the blanket on top of me. Startled, I try to kick it off, but before I can manage, I'm lifted off the floor and pulled onto Q's lap.

"What the hell are you doing?" I object but stop struggling immediately because I involuntarily rub my ass over his crotch with every move I make.

"Just shut up and go to sleep."

Stunned into silence, I stay quiet as he wraps the blanket around me and holds me to his chest tightly, cradling me like a small child. I don't realize how stiff my body is until my muscles start to hurt, shaking with exhaustion, and I'm forced to relax a little.

As soon as I do, I sink deeper into his hold, and I inwardly curse myself for letting this happen. I know it's a trick, a game he is playing, but I can't help but grab on to this small amount of comfort. Even if it's not real. I'm so fucking tired. My body is drained, and all I want to do is sleep.

My eyes flutter shut without my permission, and I let my cheek rest against Q's chest. He is so warm... and he smells good... I still hate him, though. I hate him for who he is and what he did to me today. I hate him.

"I hope I slobber all over your stupid shirt," I murmur against his chest, drawing a low chuckle from him. That's the last thing I remember before falling into a deep, dreamless sleep.

FOR THE FIRST time since I got here, I wake somewhat rested. It takes me a moment to get my bearings and realize where I am. I'm still curled up on the floor, hidden behind my bed, but instead of cold and unbearably uncomfortable, I'm wrapped up in a cocoon of thick blanket, my head resting on a fluffy pillow.

Still slightly disoriented, I look around the room and find it empty. If it wasn't for the pillow and blanket that smells of him, I would say last night was a dream. I still don't know why he showed up and pretended to care, but I already know nothing good will come from it.

He said so himself. He isn't sorry about forcing me to give him a blow job in front of his friends. The memory of that invades my mind, and my stomach churns. He used me to get off before, but no one saw that. It was easier to twist it in my mind and make it into something it wasn't.

Nothing about what he did to me in front of those guys can be sugarcoated. It was nothing but degrading and violating. I have never felt so used and helpless in my life. I've also never experienced so much relief as when he made them stop. Quinton doing what he did to me is bad enough, but Matteo? I don't think I would have survived his cruel touch.

I try not to read anything into it, knowing Q just doesn't want to share his new toy. I already know that's not going to last forever. He might have protected me from Matteo last night, but he won't do that for long. I'll need to find a way to protect myself if I'm going to make it another year, month, or day here.

I pull open the nightstand drawer and slide my hand to the back. When my fingers touch the cold metal, I wrap them around the thin chain and pull the bracelet out.

I put it there as soon as I arrived. Over the years, I have often carried it with me, waiting until the moment I could return it to Adela. Since that opportunity hasn't presented itself yet, I've used it as a beacon of hope. A reminder that I'm strong and don't need to conform. She gave me that bracelet during one of her moments of weakness, and I've used it as strength through some of my own. *Strength.* That thought reminds me that I'm late for PE.

Shit. I shove the bracelet back into its hiding spot. The PE class that is supposed to teach me hand-to-hand combat. *Ugh.* I want to curl back into this blanket and go to sleep, but I can't. I can't skip that class because that's what they want. They want to break me and make me stay locked in my room to lick my wounds.

Fuck them. The thought gives me enough strength to get up from the floor and throw the blanket and pillow on the empty bed rails. Raising my arms above my head, I give my body a good stretch before going into the bathroom and getting ready for class.

The first thing I notice as I take off my bed shirt is the finger-shaped bruises on my upper arms. I press down on the tender flesh, which is already turning purple. It's sore, but I've experienced worse. These bruises will fade, but the memories of last night won't. They will linger in the dark corners of my mind forever.

Checking the time on the clock, I realize I'm actually running late and kick my morning routine into high gear. I pull the clothes I hand washed yesterday off the shower rail where they are hanging to dry. I get dressed and slip into my sneakers, pulling my hair into a ponytail as I rush out of the room.

I'm in such a hurry that I don't even notice the odd stares I get as I pass people. Everyone must have heard about the scene in the cafeteria yesterday because I don't want to think about the alternative.

At least no one bumps into me on purpose, which is a step up from my average day.

I take the elevator up to the upper level and speed walk into the gym, where the instructor's already started teaching.

Most students are standing around Quan in a circle, paying attention to what he is telling them. All except Quinton, who I spot leaning casually against the wall, looking bored.

Without even thinking about it, I walk around the other students and right up to him.

He turns his head toward me, raising an eyebrow as I approach. I force my feet to stop, wondering what the hell I'm doing? Why am I walking toward him, like a moth to a flame? I know better than to approach the beast, but here I am, marching right into his trap.

A grin spreads across his face, and he motions for me to come closer.

Shaking my head, I look around the room just as Quan announces, "Okay, partner up."

Shit.

Scanning the crowd, I hope for a miracle of finding a girl willing to partner up with me. Of course, everyone just shakes their heads at me. It doesn't take long for everyone to find a partner, leaving Q and myself to be forced together again. I trot over to him with my head held high.

"I don't know why you even try. No one's gonna partner up with you."

"You don't know that. Someone might change their mind one day."

"They won't," he says, sounding nothing but sure of himself. "I'm surprised you came."

"I'm not scared of you," I lie. I'm terrified, but I'll do whatever it takes to pretend I'm not. "And you can't control me," I add, that one is less of a lie.

"The second one might be true. I can't control your mind, but I'm going to try anyway." He winks at me like he just made a joke or said something flirty. "Now, come at me."

"Huh?"

"Attack me. You came to class, so are you going to stand around for the next two hours, or are you going to train with me?"

"I was hoping to train with someone more my size. Not with you... *again.*" I fold my arms over my chest.

"You need to be able to fight off anyone who's a threat, not only people your size. You think some guy in a back alley won't attack you because you weigh less than him?"

Damnit, he's got a point.

"Fine, let's do this. Preferably without the choking me out part."

"I can't make any promises. It seems you bring out the worst in me." He smirks, which gives me the push of anger I need. Using that energy, I charge him and throw my shoulder into his stomach. Or at least I try to. He easily grabs me and pushes me away like an annoying bug before I can even make contact.

Wrapping his arms around me, he takes me into a bear hug from behind, and his scent invades my nose. He smells as good as he did last night when I fell asleep in his arms.

"Get out," he says casually like it's an easy thing to do.

I start to wiggle around, but his grip around my arms is iron, pinning my useless limbs to the side of my body. Finally, I give up struggling and take a moment to catch my breath.

"I can't get loose," I say, defeated.

"Yes, you can. You just have to know how. I'm stronger than you, so we both know you are never going to overpower me. The next best thing is to be smarter than me."

"How does that help me get away? I can't use brainpower. I'm not a Jedi."

"You have to use my body's mechanics against me. Besides flailing around, try this. Drop your hips into a squat like you're gonna piss in the woods. At the same time, put your hands on your chest like you're a vampire. Bring up your arms and shoulders simultaneously. Then turn into my body and elbow me as hard as you can in the ribs. Do this all at once, and you'll be free."

I look over my shoulder at him in disbelief. I'm sure this is a trick. Some game he is playing to get me to do what he wants. I'm about to tell him to fuck off, but what then?

Honestly, my best bet is to play along. This is better than him threatening and assaulting me.

"All right, whatever. I'll try it."

I do as he instructs. It takes me two attempts before I'm able to coordinate the whole move, but when I do, it works. I get free and swing my elbow into his ribs, drawing a groan out of him. Shocked beyond belief, I watch with my mouth hanging open as he doubles over, cradling his side.

I knocked the breath out of him.

"Fuck. I didn't know you could actually hit that hard."

"I didn't know either."

He recovers quickly, straightening back up. "All right, again."

We run through this move two more times before he shows me three more. I can't seem to shake away the thought of this being some kind of joke to him, but at this point, I have no idea why he would offer to help me defend myself, even more so when he knows I could use these same moves on him.

By the time Quan lets us out of class, I've built up a good amount of sweat, and my muscles tense, telling me I'm going to be sore tomorrow. Quinton leaves class without a word or good-bye, not that I was expecting him to say anything.

Grabbing a bottle of water on the way out, I down it and fill up another one. I still find myself speed-walking back to my room. I need to grab a quick shower before going to my next class to avoid being stinky.

I'm alone in the elevator and thankful for the moment of solitude. When the doors open, I step out, keeping my head down. That turns out to be a mistake because if I had looked around, I would have seen Anja and Marcel waiting for me.

By the time I do see them, it's already too late. There's no avoiding them, and instead of hanging my head, I lift it high and stare straight ahead at them. Marcel is the first to react, a slimy grin appearing on his lips.

"Oh, look, it's the rat scurrying away, ready to tell another lie about someone."

"Don't you have anything better to do than harass me?" I pipe up, refusing to let myself be walked on.

"Is it harassment if it's true?" Anja adds, and they both break out into laughter. My cheeks heat, and I decide to hit Anja where it hurts.

"You're just jealous because Quinton pays more attention to me than you." It's a stupid comeback and not my best, but I know it hits its mark when Anja's nose wrinkles and her lips turn up in a snarl.

"He doesn't like you. He likes tormenting you. There's a difference."

I mean, she's not lying, but it doesn't change the fact that he shows more interest in me than her.

I shrug. "Whatever makes it easier for you to sleep at night."

Anja looks like she wants to punch me, and Marcel places a

comforting hand on her shoulder, stopping her from following through on the thought.

I turn and continue walking toward my room. I've only made it a few feet when I hear Marcel yell, "That's right, scurry back to your garbage can of a room, you dirty fucking rat."

There aren't many people in the corridor, but enough to draw a few eyes, leading to unwanted attention. I can feel their eyes on me, so I force my feet to go faster.

I'm down the hall and locked inside my room in less than a minute. Stripping out of my sweaty clothes, I hop in the shower, turning the water all the way to hot. At least I can let my muscles relax for a few minutes before I have to head to my next class. When I'm out there, I don't have the luxury of relaxing. Everywhere I turn in this house of demons, I have to watch my back. People want me dead, and since they can't kill me, they'll do much worse things. I have to be prepared for anything.

15

QUINTON

The days pass in a blur, and I sink deeper into my routine. Breakfast, classes, and phone calls home. I do my best not to think about Aspen or the slight bonding time we shared in PE. I don't care about her in any sense, and I don't need her thinking I do. Still, I won't lie. Her presence affects me in a deeper way than I ever thought possible.

I've just fallen back onto my bed when the door to my room opens, and Ren steps inside. He closes it behind him like someone else is in the apartment or something.

"What's up?" I ask, a brow raised.

Ren runs a hand through his hair, almost like he's flustered. "Matteo just showed me a video. It's from the other day..."

My brows pinch together in confusion. "Yeah, what about?"

"What you did with Aspen. The forced blow job. Matteo took a video of it and saved it on his phone."

Fuck. My first thought is to go and find the fucker and beat his ass, but I shove the thought away... for now. There will be a time for that.

"Look, you know I don't give a fuck what you do, and I hardly ever make comments about shit. I mean, our parents are fucking criminals, but don't you think...?" Ren drags his feet, and my frustration toward him mounts.

"You're being weird and vague as fuck. If you have something more to say, then spit it out. When have we ever minced words?"

Ren shakes his head like he's shaking away whatever is bothering him. "Never, which is why I'm telling you I think you took it too far."

All I can do is blink while staring blankly at him.

Did he... did he just say I took it too far?

"What the fuck?" I lash out, unsure why he's suddenly sympathizing with her. He was talking about torturing her when we first got here, and now a blow job is too much?

"I don't want to piss you off, but the video just pushed it over the edge for me."

I'm shocked, almost into complete silence. I don't understand what he's trying to get at.

"You have thirty seconds to explain yourself."

Ren's jaw tightens, and his eyes dart away from mine. Whatever he's going to say, he knows I'm not going to like, and even less than what he said before.

"I saw the video, and then Luna called me a little bit after, and it made me think... if someone ever did that to her. I'd be filled with murderous rage. There would be nothing to stop me from slaughtering those fuckers."

"If you're trying to make me feel like shit, it isn't working. You know what her family did to my family. You know the pain they caused."

Ren frowns. "I do, but as your best friend, it's my job to keep you checked in with reality. I can't let you slip too far off the rails." He pauses, and while he does have a valid point, it's not valid enough to tell me that I have no cause for what I did. I don't feel guilty for putting Aspen on her knees and fucking her throat. The only thing I hate is that there were others there to see it, but that's what was needed to drive home the point that she is still lesser than me. "What if something like that happened to Scarlet? If someone did that to her? How would you feel?"

My sister's angelic face fills my mind. The thought of anyone hurting her or touching her in a way that would make her feel degraded or less than ignites a fire in my veins. Still, all the anger from that statement gets directed at Ren.

"What the hell is wrong with you?" I growl. "Scarlet and Aspen aren't even on the same playing field, and that's my fucking sister. Don't ever talk about something like that happening to her again." Anger rushes toward the surface, and it's the uncontrollable kind. The kind I need to get out at the gym, so I can punch the sandbag instead of Ren's face.

Ren shakes his head, a look of disgust filling his features. "What's wrong with me? Why don't you ask yourself that? You fucked a girl's face in front of all your friends and recorded it.

Then you let the other guys have a turn. If you ask me, it sounds like you're the one with the problem, not me."

"I didn't let anyone do shit."

"That's not what it looks like on the video. You stepped away and let Matteo take your spot."

"I stopped it right after," I defend.

"The video cuts off after you are done with her. The last thing I saw was you walking away, and Matteo stepping in front of her. It didn't look like you were making anyone stop doing anything."

My hand clenches into a fist without thought. It would be so easy to swing at Ren right now, but one punch wouldn't be enough for me. I need something deeper, and fighting with my best friend over what is right and wrong isn't going to sedate the beast pulsing with life in my veins.

"Whatever, I'm going to the gym." I push off the bed and grab my Nikes before brushing past him and out of the room.

I shove my feet into my shoes and walk out of the apartment, slamming the door behind me. Normally, I would walk to the gym, but I jog over, hoping to let some of the tension out.

That doesn't seem to work, and as soon as I walk into the gym, I head for the sandbag and bang my fist against it until my knuckles ache. Then I head for the treadmill. I'll exhaust myself before I get into a full-on fight with Ren, even if he does deserve a right hook to his nose.

I run for the next hour. The sweat pours off me, and my lungs burn, but it's exactly what I need.

With each step I take, I consider what Ren said more and more. About how I would feel if someone did that to Scarlet.

Near the end of my run, I start to think about a way to make things better. I can't take back what I did, not that I would if I could, but I could handle things with Matteo. I could go to him and make him delete the video, but the message that video brings is worth Ren's backlash.

While it might make me feel a smidge guilty, that video will make others fear me. It will tell them if you mess with me, you could be next. Once I'm done running, I do some sit-ups, chin-ups, and light weightlifting.

Even after spending two and a half hours in the gym, I still feel ragey. Though the feeling has dimmed, it's still there, simmering like a stew on the stove waiting to be served.

I leave the gym and head back toward my apartment, but after a few steps, I pause and turn around to start walking toward Aspen's room.

It's so fucking stupid how drawn I am to her. Not in a way that makes her anything special, but I feel this bond forming between us, a connection that is merely physical.

In this place, she is my outlet, and I am her savior, her protector of sorts, even if I'm the bully as well. Rat is still painted on her door, and I consider telling someone to fix that for her. I can use it as a tactic to get her to do something I want. I search my wallet for the key card to her room and slip it into the slot, smiling when it turns green.

I turn the handle and put my wallet back into my shorts as I walk into her room. I still can't believe how tiny and cramped the space is. As soon as I walk inside, her head snaps up from where she is sitting on her small desk, a book with some half-naked guy on the cover in her hands, titled *Pretty Little Savage*.

"What are you reading?" I ask, closing the door behind me.

"I think the more important question is what the hell are you doing here? You do know this isn't your room, right?"

I shrug. "It's whatever I want it to be. Now, what are you reading? And why are you sitting on your desk?

"I'm reading a book, and I'm sitting on top of my desk because I don't like turning my back to the door in case some psycho walks in unannounced."

"I told you, I'm the only one with a key."

"The person I'm referring to as the *psycho* is you."

"You are really mouthy today. Didn't you learn anything from your lesson the other night?"

"The only thing I learned is that you are a monster."

"Would a monster bring you a blanket so you don't freeze to death at night?"

She lets out a humorless laugh. "Do you think because you give me some bedding, you're suddenly a good person? Or that it makes up for you and your friends assaulting me?"

"I never said I'm a good person... hell, maybe you are right. I am a monster. So why not embrace it?" She wants a monster? Fine, I'll give her one.

"What do you want?" she asks, her voice slightly trembling at the end.

"I want you to take off your clothes—"

"No. Not happening." She climbs off the desk and steps away from me.

"I can make you do it." I stalk toward her. She takes two steps backward until she is at the wall with nowhere else to go.

"Then do it," she taunts. "But I will never do it willingly."

Her statement has me grinding my teeth together. She's right. I can control her body, but not her mind, and that pisses me off more than I can say.

"How about a deal? I'll get you a new mattress."

"So you don't have to fuck me on the floor? No, thanks. I'd rather you be uncomfortable too." She crosses her arms in front of her chest defensively, but all I can see is her tits being pushed up.

"You're right. The mattress would be for both of us. What else do you want?"

"I don't give a shit about a new mattress. I'll still sleep behind the bed." She nibbles on her bottom lip, thinking. "What I really want is for you to keep Matteo off my back. If you promise me that, I'll do whatever you want... for one hour."

I hide my amusement. She has no idea I've already told Matteo to leave her alone, but there's no way I'm going to admit that out loud and miss out on her giving me an hour of her time.

"So, you want me to keep Matteo off your back indefinitely? But you'll only give me an hour of your time? That hardly seems fair."

"We both know it would only take you two minutes to tell him to leave me alone, and he would listen to you. Letting you do whatever you want to me not only goes against everything I am, but I'll have to live with that for the rest of my life, just like I have to live with what you've already done to me."

"Well, when you put it that way, I suppose I'm coming out pretty good on this deal." I lift my arm, extending my hand out to her. "I'll keep him off your back, and you'll give me an hour of full control."

For a moment, she examines my hand like it's a foreign object before she hesitantly puts her delicate hand in mine.

"Deal."

"Anything I want? One hour?" I clarify, holding her hand tightly.

She hesitates, and I can see her mind working up all kinds of scenarios. "You won't hurt me... like no weird kinky torture stuff, right?"

My lips tug up into a grin. "No. I'm not into pain or inflicting pain. None of what you are thinking of."

"Okay, one hour," she confirms, and my smile widens. Letting go of her hand, I cross the small space that is her room and take the chair in front of her desk.

The flimsy wooden chair creaks under my weight, and for a moment, I consider sitting on the desk instead, but I already have plans for that flat surface, so I keep my ass planted where it is.

"Strip for me. I want you completely naked... and take your time. We've got an hour, after all. Let's savor it."

She sucks a shaky breath into her lungs and slowly reaches for the hem of her sweatshirt. She pulls it up and over her head, revealing that she's not wearing anything else underneath. I've already seen her tits when she was lying down on her bed, but now that she is standing, they look even better. Perky, just the right size, with small pink nipples demanding attention.

As her fingers dip into the waistband of her leggings, my eyes are drawn to her stomach. She's always been a skinny little thing, but now that her baggy sweater is gone, I can tell she is even skinnier than usual. Her stomach is caved in, her hip bones are more pronounced, and when she leans over to pull her leggings off, I can see her ribs sticking out.

Is she not eating? The image of her yelling at the cafeteria staff pops into my head, and I wonder if they're giving her enough food. Surely, they'll feed her something. Either way, I store that information, knowing I can use that to my advantage in a new deal on another day.

"It's too fucking cold in here to be naked," she mumbles angrily while she pulls off her white cotton panties. They fall to the ground, and she straightens back up, glaring at me like she wants to murder me.

"Maybe I should have included a no complaining clause in our deal," I say as I take in every single inch of her body.

Her hair falls down her shoulders in golden waves, and I can't wait to wrap it around my hand. As I let my gaze roam down her body, I notice the faded bruises around her slender arms, and I'm glad I already decided that Matteo is never to touch her again.

My eyes finally land on the junction between her thighs. To my surprise, her pussy is shaved bare.

"Come here," I rasp, motioning for her to come to me. "I'll warm you up."

Her steps are small, each one more uncertain than the one before. She stops just short of bumping into my knees. Her flowery scent fills my nostrils, and I breathe it deep into my lungs like a drug, letting it cloud my mind.

Now that she is closer, I can see she is shaking. Taking the room temperature into consideration, I figure it must be from the cold.

"Are you just going to gawk at me for an hour?" She folds her arm over her stomach, not covering up her tits, but to keep warm, I'm guessing.

"Oh, don't worry. I'll be doing much more than looking at you, and since you keep mouthing off like a brat, I think I'll treat you like one too."

16

ASPEN

*W*hy can't I just keep my mouth shut for once?

Then again, Quinton wouldn't use a free-for-all hour to have a chat about my book. He came here to hurt me and play out his sick fantasies. No matter what I do or say, we always end up here... with Q eyeing me like I'm a lamb ready for the slaughterhouse.

"Turn around," he orders, his voice more raspy than usual.

Against every fiber in my body, I spin around slowly until my back is turned to him all the way. At least I can momentarily let my mask slip. It's tiring to pretend not to be scared. No matter how much I tell myself that this is the better option, knowing that I'm giving my virginity to someone who loathes me is not what I wanted.

Especially not here, in this shithole of a room that doesn't even have a real bed. Which means that not only will my first time be with Quinton, but it will also be on a dirty floor of a school I hate. Tears prick at my eyes, but I blink them away. I'm not gonna cry about this. At least it's my choice, and it's not Matteo forcing me.

I'm so lost in thought that I flinch when Quinton touches my back.

"Relax," he grunts as if him ordering me to relax would actually work.

He grabs my hips and pulls me even closer to him until my legs are wedged between his. My breath hitches when his hands move to my ass, massaging each cheek before spreading them apart like he is inspecting me. I feel so exposed and humiliated, I could cry, and I'm so fucking glad I'm turned away from him because there is no way I could hide the way I'm feeling right now.

"Sit on my lap," Quinton directs while already pulling me down onto him.

My cold, naked skin meets the welcoming warmth of his fully clothed body, and I lean back on instinct, trying to get closer.

He wraps his arms around me from behind, cupping my breasts in his palms as he buries his face in my hair.

"Move your hips, grind your ass over my dick."

Closing my eyes, I start to shimmy my butt, dragging it over his already hard cock. He groans, letting his hands fall from my breasts, and grabs my hips instead, guiding me to move the way he wants.

"Like this," he says, returning to play with my tits while I keep the rhythm he set.

He rolls both of my nipples between the tips of his fingers, making me gasp with shock. It's almost painful, but not quite. Goose bumps spread across my skin, and for the first time, it's not from being cold. A low heat builds deep in my core, and it's one I've never felt before.

That heat evaporates into thin air when Quinton opens his mouth again, ruining the moment. "I'm gonna fuck you so hard, you won't be able to walk tomorrow."

My body goes stiff, only making him chuckle.

"Don't worry, I'll make sure you're nice and wet. I'll even make you come as long as you do as I say." I know he is patronizing me, but his words set off a swarm of butterflies in my belly. No one has ever made me come, and if he lets me enjoy this too, it won't be so bad. Maybe I can pretend that I didn't sell my virginity, even if it is for safety.

"Spread your legs and hook them over mine."

As instructed, I let my legs fall open and dangle over his spread knees. Cold air washes over my exposed center, sending a shiver down my spine. He repositions me slightly, so his hard cock is nestled between my ass cheeks. Again, I'm glad I'm facing away so he can't see my face redden in shame.

His right hand moves from my boob back down, over my stomach, then lower and lower. His fingers brush over my spread folds, and I freeze, my body going rigid again as his fingertips run over my clit slowly.

"I didn't say to stop moving," he whispers into the shell of my ear while he leisurely draws small circles over the small bundle of nerves.

"Sorry... I..." *I what?* I can't think with him doing that. My brain seems to be fried at the moment. I try to continue rolling my hips like he showed me, but my movements are choppy and uncontrolled now.

His skilled finger dips lower, and he starts circling my entrance. I briefly wonder if I should tell him I'm a virgin, but I'm pretty sure he already knows. It doesn't take a genius to figure it out. Plus, I don't think it would change anything, so I simply keep my lips sealed and hope he won't be too rough.

He enters me slowly, and I still once more, unable to move another inch. My breathing is labored like I've just run a marathon, even though all I did was shimmy my ass a little.

"Relax," he growls, pulling me closer to his chest at the same time as he pushes his finger deeper.

"I'm trying," I say, but it comes out more like a whining sound.

He pulls his finger out slightly just to push it back in a little deeper, drawing a whimper from my lips. Then he suddenly stops.

"Are you a virgin?" he asks like he is shocked by the possibility.

"Yes," I huff out.

For a long moment, he is quiet. His finger remains buried in my pussy, but he doesn't move. I don't know why, but I feel like I have to explain myself.

"Is it really that much of a surprise to you? I'm only eighteen... and my life has been a little crazy for the past year." I whisper the last part, not wanting to remind him of my father's betrayal while his finger is buried inside me.

"So you're gonna let me fuck this virgin cunt?" he asks, starting to move again.

"Y-Yes," I stutter as he continues thrusting his finger into me.

He briefly takes it out, just to reenter using two fingers. I try to remain relaxed, but two fingers are stretching my tight opening now, and it takes a moment to get over the discomfort. To adjust to the intrusion, Quinton starts rubbing his palm over my clit while fingering me.

At the new sensation, I throw my head back, letting it rest on his shoulder. He continues to use his palm and fingers to stimulate me, driving me further to the edge of an orgasm. Suddenly, I'm not cold anymore. I'm hot, my skin feels like it's on fire, and I'm ready to burst at the seams.

I'm almost there, so close to release, I can taste it. He pushes me all the way to the cliff, but right before I'm going to tip over, he stops and pulls his hand away. A disappointed whimper escapes my mouth, and I regret it immediately.

His chest rumbles with a laugh as he pushes me off his lap. "Go get the pillow."

On unsteady feet, I pad across the room and grab the pillow from my sleeping spot. When I turn back around, I find Quinton pulling down his shorts, his very hard cock springs free, and I automatically clutch onto the pillow, holding it in front of me like a barrier.

"Put the pillow here," he points at the ground between his feet, "and get on your knees."

This is the lesser of two evils... I keep reminding myself, but my body protests as I drop the pillow and get on my knees. Memories from the other night rush back, and all the warmth I felt earlier vanishes, leaving behind an icy coldness.

"I'm not gonna make you use your mouth since I went to the gym right before I came here, but I want you to jerk me off." Quinton grabs my upper arms surprisingly gently and positions me just the way he wants to. He closes his legs enough to where they are pressed against my sides, lending my chilled skin some much-needed warmth.

"Oh," I say, kind of surprised. I wonder how much time has passed since we started, which makes me realize I don't even know what time we started. "What time is it? I mean... I didn't check..." I stumble over my words, more nervous than before now that he can see my face.

"Don't worry about the time. I won't keep you longer than an hour."

"Is this all you want me to do?" I glance around the room, trying to look anywhere but him.

"I don't know yet. Depends how well you do."

"I've never done this before." I half expect him to laugh again, or at least make a snarky remark, but he simply grabs my wrist and holds it up.

"Start with spitting in your hand."

"What?" I sneak a peek at his face to make sure he isn't making fun of me. "Are you serious?"

"Yes, spit on your palm." Gathering saliva in my mouth, I hold open my hand and spit in it while he watches me with hungry eyes. "Now wrap your hand around my dick and stroke it up and down."

Even though I feel weird doing it, I follow his directions and use my wet hand to grab his length. The spit starts to make sense when I realize how easily my hand slides up and down, and now I feel stupid for not knowing this before.

My inexperience never bothered me before. I just had so much stuff going on in my life that sex and boyfriends were the last things on my mind.

"That's good," he praises. "A little faster." I pick up speed and watch with heightened curiosity how Quinton's face contorts in pleasure. His eyes are closed, and I take that moment to really take him in. He is as beautiful as he is evil. A perfect disguise for a predator.

As if he hears me thinking about him, his eyes fly open, and I look away, feeling caught even though I didn't do anything wrong.

"Open your mouth," he orders, wrapping his large hand over mine. "Open," he grits out again while starting to jerk himself even faster, tightening his grip around both my hand and his cock.

I let my mouth fall open. Quinton lifts his free hand and grabs the back of my head, holding me in place right in front of him.

"Fuck... keep your mouth open," he growls at me. Threading my hair through his fingers, he tugs on it slightly as ropes of cum start to shoot from the tip of his mushroom head onto my lips, face, and into my mouth. Thick, salty liquid hits my tongue, and Quinton's pleasured groan echoes through the room.

"Swallow it."

Closing my mouth, I swallow the bitter cum, trying not to cringe at the taste.

"Good girl. Now don't move." He scoots the chair back and gets up, leaving me to kneel on top of the pillow with my hands in my lap like some kind of sex slave. My stomach sinks. Is that what I am? A sex slave?

Quinton disappears into the bathroom. I hear him trying to turn the water in the sink, but all that comes out is the screeching sounds the pipes make.

"The sink is broken. You have to use the shower," I call after him, and a moment later, I hear the shower turn on.

I can't figure out what he is doing until he returns, holding a wet washcloth in his hand. Instead of handing it to me, he leans down, cradles the back of my head with one hand, and uses the other to wipe my face of his cum.

When I'm all cleaned up, he throws the dirty washcloth on the ground close to the bathroom door. Next, he grabs me under my arms and lifts me off the ground like I weigh nothing. Panic bubbles back to the surface when he places my naked ass on the desk and pushes my body down.

"Lie back and spread your legs."

I do as I'm told and spread my legs wide, giving him an up-close and personal view of my pussy. My fingers grasp onto the wood, and I know where this is going before it even gets there. Quinton peers down at my most private parts, and it feels like he's inspecting me.

I shouldn't care what he thinks about me, but a part of me does, and in the back of my mind, I wonder what he's thinking.

"Just because I do this doesn't mean I like you. It doesn't mean you're anything to me. Do you understand?"

"Y-Yes." My voice cracks as I speak, and a tiny shiver zings down my spine at the way his dark gaze trails down my body.

His fingers sink into my thighs, and he parts my legs wider to accommodate his size. "Let me guess, you've never let a guy eat you out before either?"

I can feel the heat of embarrassment in my cheeks. "Like I said, I've been busy with life and..." Whatever I was about to say, I can't recall because, like a starved beast, Quinton leans forward and latches onto my clit, his tongue lapping against the little bundle of nerves.

The pleasure starts to build at my spine almost immediately. He works my clit with his tongue in a way I never could with my own fingers, alternating between flicking it and sucking on it. Fire ignites deep in my belly, stoking the flames of my desire, and I can feel myself getting wetter. For a fleeting moment, I am brave and spear my fingers through Quinton's dark hair. The strands are silky smooth, and I tug on his hair lightly, enjoying the brief groan he makes against my folds. He pulls away a second later, and I let out a low whine of disapproval.

Letting out a chuckle, he looks up at me from between my

thighs. "I can't wait to claim this pussy, to fill it with my cum, and see its virgin blood on my cock."

Nothing about what he's said should turn me on, but it does. It turns me on so much, it terrifies me.

"Quinton..." I whimper, wanting to come, my pleasure clinging to every pore on my body. A dark shadow creeps onto his face, and a gasp slips past my lips as he plunges his middle finger inside me in one swift movement. I'm so wet that there's no discomfort, but I'm shocked by the sudden movement and change in his demeanor.

"Beg me for it. You want to come, then beg for it."

"You can't be serious?" I'm not sure how I manage to get the words out, not with his finger moving in and out of me at a delicious pace.

Q smirks, and I swear it's like looking the devil in the eyes and begging him not to strike you dead. "Oh, I'm dead fucking serious, so serious I'll leave you tied to the bed frame until tomorrow with no way to relieve yourself. Now beg, and make it believable..."

Fuck... I can feel myself climbing higher and higher, my walls tightening, and it won't be long till I crumble to the ground. Like a high, I chase the orgasm, but it's just out of reach.

"Please..." I beg, my tongue darting out over my bottom lip.

"Please, what?" He seems unaffected by my begging, but I can see his cock growing in his pants, and the power of arousal makes me feel like I'm a queen. Even if he doesn't want to believe it, some part of me has a tiny bit of control over him.

"Please, let me come." I gasp once more as he adds a second finger—a tinge of pain mixes with the pleasure at the intrusion, but the ache in my core intensifies.

I'm rushing toward the finish line, and he knows it, his own movements get faster, and when his thumb brushes against my clit, sparks fly.

Gritting his teeth, he looks up at me, the blue of his eyes intense. "Your pussy is so sloppy. It's making a mess of my hand."

"Oh, god." I tip my head back, the pleasure rising. My nipples pucker, and my entire body trembles like I'm walking a tightrope.

"I want you to remember who owns you here. I want you to remember that I can do whatever I want to you, whenever I want to. Say it. Tell me it's true."

Unable to stop myself, caught between the pleasure and the need for him to continue, I let out a strangled, yes, and like the asshole he is, his eyes gleam, and he pumps into me faster until I'm cresting the wave of pleasure.

Light blinds my eyes, and my entire body is suspended in time. My muscles twitch, my core tightens, and my channel clenches around his fingers. My entire body trembles as I float down slowly from heaven, and back down to hell, my current reality.

By the time I've come down from the high of coming, I'm a goopy mess, and Quinton makes quick work of wrapping me in a blanket, swaddling me like a baby, before placing me on the floor next to the bed. My head hits the pillow, and I'm out almost immediately.

I WAKE UP DISORIENTED. So much so that it takes me a moment to realize where the loud banging sound is coming from. I fight my way out of the blanket that is tightly wrapped around my naked body and look around the room. The loud banging increases, and I know it's coming from my door.

My first thought is that this can only be Quinton, but he has a key card, so he wouldn't knock.

"Hold on," I croak, getting up, forcing my stiff limbs to move.

As soon as I'm standing, the room starts spinning, and I have to put my hand against the wall to steady myself.

There is another knock on the door, and it's like the sound has a direct line to my brain, making a rattle inside my skull.

"Jesus, hold on. I'm coming!" Dropping the blanket around me completely, I make quick work of finding my clothes and getting dressed. I pull the door open ready to cuss out whoever's interrupting my sleep, just to come to a screeching halt when I see the janitor on the other side, a brand new mattress propped up next to him.

"I'm supposed to drop this off," he says before sliding the mattress into my room. It's only halfway in when he turns around and walks off, leaving me standing there dumbfounded.

Coming back to my senses, I pull the heavy thing inside and

close the door with my foot. It takes all my strength to push it up on the bed and let it settle on the bed rails. I'm out of breath, and another wave of dizziness comes over me. I don't know why I'm so freaking weak until my stomach growls, reminding me of the lack of nutrition in my life. I guess the food deficiency is finally catching up with me.

Checking the time, I play with the idea of walking to the cafeteria and seeing if they have anything I can eat, but even that seems like such a waste of energy. All I wanna do is lie down and go back to sleep. Maybe I still have some leftovers that will tide me over.

Still half asleep, I start scouring my room for anything, for any snack that I possibly could have forgotten about. Inwardly, I scream eureka when I find a half-eaten wrapped-up cheese sandwich. I try to remember when I picked it up and how old it is. But the thought evaporates when I unwrap it, and the scent of rotten food greets me.

Immediately, my stomach turns from hungry to sick. Gagging, I slap my hand in front of my mouth and run into the bathroom. I make it to the toilet just in time to start hurling and throw up every tiny thing I got to eat yesterday, which isn't much. Still, I keep heaving until my throat hurts and my back muscles are sore. It feels like I'm throwing up for a good ten minutes, and all that's coming out now is stomach acid.

Slumping next to the toilet, I catch my breath. When I feel like I can finally get up, I push to my feet but have to hold the sink a while just to be able to make it into my room. I down a bottle of water I had sitting next to my bed, then grab the blanket and pillow from the ground and climb onto my new mattress, curling up in the fetal position. I hope that this will pass quickly, and I can get something real to eat today.

Maybe I should have bargained for food instead of for safety from Matteo. Food... that will definitely be the next thing I ask for. If there even is a next time?

Then Quinton's words from last night ring in my ear... *"I can't wait to claim this pussy, to mark it with my cum, and see its virgin blood on my cock."* He is already planning on doing this again, making deals with me for whatever fantasy he wants to play out. Next time, I'll be better prepared. I'll use his needs to my advantage, to fill my own.

Closing my eyes, I try my best to calm my stomach and go to sleep, at least for a little bit longer. But the constant nausea mixed with the aching pain of hunger makes it hard to find any rest.

For the next few hours, I fight a losing battle between sleep, hunger, and pain. A part of me knows I would feel better if I got something to eat and drink, but I can't muster up the strength to get up and go to the cafeteria.

Suddenly, I start feeling really cold, even with a thick blanket wrapped around me, and I start shivering so hard my teeth clink together. The next thing I know, the cold is gone, replaced with a heat so strong flames are dancing over my skin. I kick the blanket off, and even with only wearing a thin shirt and leggings, I feel so hot. When I run my hands down my clothes, I notice they are soaked in sweat.

Fuck, I must have a fever. I try to get up, but my legs give out as soon as my feet touch the floor, and I crumple to the ground like I'm boneless. As I lie in a heap on the floor, the only solace I can find is that the cold concrete actually feels nice on my burning skin.

Not in a million years would I have thought I would ever wish for Quinton to waltz into my room unannounced, but I do now. I think he would take me to the doctor. After all, he can't torment me if I'm dead, and right now, I sure as hell feel like I'm dying.

17

QUINTON

It's been almost forty-eight hours since I left Aspen's cocooned body in her room. Even though I've showered twice since then, I swear I can still smell her on me. Her sweet floral scent makes my cock hard.

I should have known she was a virgin. I shouldn't have been as shocked as I was. The knowledge of knowing that I'm going to be her first is enticing. I really wanted to go and fuck her last night, but I also want to savor the control I have over her. I want to draw it out and build up to the main event.

Plus, I love having her on her knees, looking up at me with those innocent doe eyes of hers. An innocence I'm going to snuff out. My cock is getting hard thinking about it, and a plan forms in my mind. I'm going to visit her in her room tonight and make her another offer. She is desperate, and I'm going to use that to my full advantage.

"Do you ever sleep?" Ren asks, his voice raspy. He is sprawled out on the other couch with his eyes half-closed.

"Sometimes." I shrug.

"Well, some of us do it every night. So, that's what I'm doing now," he groans, pushing himself up on his feet.

"Before you go to bed, did Matteo say anything else about Aspen?"

"What do you mean?"

"I told him to stay away from her. I just want to make sure he's listening and not going behind my back to talk a bunch of shit."

Ren's eyebrows shoot up. "Is that so? Why the sudden change of heart?"

"There hasn't been a change. One, Aspen is mine to torment. Two, Matteo needs to learn his place."

"The only thing I heard him say is that she didn't show up to class today and that she's probably hiding in her room or something." He shrugs.

"All right."

Ren nods and disappears into his room.

I wait a few more minutes before I get up and slip on my shoes. I smile deviously to myself. It's time to pay my little toy a visit.

With her key card in hand, I make my way across the dorm to her room. While I'm walking, I think about how I didn't see her today or hear anyone talking about her either. Normally, there is at least a little bit of chatter about the *rat*, but there was nothing today or yesterday.

Could she really be hiding out? Maybe she is ashamed about how I made her come, ashamed of how much she liked it. The thought makes me smile with glee.

When I get to her door, I slide the card quickly and push into her room. Before I'm even all the way in the room, I know something is wrong. Instead of the normal flowery scent that is Aspen, the space reeks of puke and sweat.

Wrinkling my nose, I step into the room and pause. My eyes land on the small body sprawled out in the center of the room. For a single moment, my heart stops, and I'm frozen in time. In my mind, I'm rushing toward the unconscious girl, but my limbs won't work. All I can do is stand there and look at her.

She's on her stomach with her cheek pressed against the concrete floor, facing my way. Strands of her blond hair sticking to her forehead as if she is sweating, her eyes are closed, and her lips are parted slightly. Her skin is so pale; it's basically white. The only coloration is the purple around her eyes.

The room is completely quiet; the only thing I can hear is the rapid beating of my heart and my shallow breathing. Only when I hear the raspy sound of a labored breath does my body seem to work again.

I shove into the room and kneel next to her. Using the back of my hand, I touch her cheek, hoping that will wake her up. I pull my hand away quickly as if burned by a hot iron because that's what it feels like. She's so fucking hot. She's burning up.

Sliding my arms under her, I lift her body off the floor, noticing how light she feels. Way too light.

It's after midnight, and there's no one out in the hall, so I jog almost the whole way to medical. I hold her to my chest tightly, making sure her head doesn't bounce around like crazy, but even the continual jogging doesn't wake her. With each rushed step I take, I get more worried.

How long has she been lying there like this?

The school medical building is basically a small state-of-the-art hospital, so I'm not worried about them not being able to help her. I just hope someone's there. As I get closer, I see the light inside is on, and I let out a sigh of relief.

Using my shoulders, I push open the large double doors. Like a small emergency room, there is a nurses' station up front, and right past it, the open space of sections for patients. The sound of the doors opening has one of the nurses rushing to the front to greet me. As soon as she sees me, her face goes pale, and her eyes widen.

She waves me over to a bed. "Here, put her down right here."

I carefully place her on the bed, and the nurse starts working on her immediately, taking her vitals and firing off questions at me.

"Do you know what happened to her? How long has she been unconscious? Is she allergic to anything? Any family history of diseases? How long has she had a fever?"

"Lady, I don't fucking know. I don't know any of this."

"Okay." She continues working on her, and then a machine starts beeping. "Fuck!"

"What?"

"Her temperature. It's 107.1. We need to get her fever down

before we do anything else. If she's been like this for a while, she is in serious trouble. You need to get some wet towels. Over there, in the cabinet. Get all the towels, get them wet and bring it here," she orders while prepping Aspen's arm for an IV.

I spring into action and walk over to the cabinet. Opening it, I grab as much as I can, and dump them in the sink to get them back, before bringing them to the bed Aspen is in.

"Just drape them over her."

When I return with the wet towels, I start spreading them over Aspen's body while the nurse draws blood from her other arm.

"She's dehydrated. I can barely find a vein."

"No offense, but shouldn't we call a doctor?"

"I am the doctor," she states without so much as glancing at me. I stare at her a little bit longer. She looks way too young to be a doctor. As a matter of fact, she looks too young to be a nurse.

"Is there anything else I can do?"

"No, not right now. Just stand back a little bit and let me work."

I take one tiny step back, but I can't bring myself to put more distance between Aspen and me. Silently, I watch the doctor work, hooking Aspen up to machines, taking samples, and running back and forth to her desk.

I hate hospitals. The smell, the bright lights, the machines. I hate it all because it reminds me of Adela. Of her time at the hospital, a time when we still had hope that she would recover, that she was gonna be okay. The doctors gave us hope, but we lost her anyway.

"Her oxygen is normal, but her iron is extremely low. High fever, dehydration..." The doc keeps mumbling to herself, some stuff I can barely make sense of. "All right, her fever is starting to come down a bit. Let me make some calls."

She walks back over to her desk and picks up the phone. I'm not paying much attention until I hear her voice booming through the room. "I need you to come to the medical bay right now... No, I'm not joking... I said right now, and no, it cannot wait until morning. I said right now!" she yells into the phone before slamming it down on the receiver, and I wonder who the hell she just called.

For the next thirty minutes, I just stand back and watch as the doctor keeps running all kinds of tests. Aspen never even moves, remaining immobile and in complete silence. The only sounds around us are the low beeping of the heart monitor and other machines.

Suddenly, the front door opens, and a very angry, still sleepy-looking Lucas Diavolo walks in.

"This better be good," he grumbles, and then his eyes fall on Aspen lying in the bed, dead to the world. "What's wrong with her?"

"He found her like this earlier and brought her here. She's extremely dehydrated, has a high fever, and is malnourished," the doctor explains.

Lucas looks at me, raising his eyebrow in question, but luckily, he doesn't ask where I found her and why I brought her here. Instead, he directs his attention back to the doctor. "So give her some medicine."

"I have, but her fever was over 107 when she got here, and I don't know how long she was like that. You need to call her parents and get them here."

At the mention of her parents, a bad taste forms in my mouth. I know her father is in prison, so he won't be coming, but I know her mother played a role in the betrayal as well, and if she comes here, I don't know that I'll be able to maintain my cool.

"We don't have parents come because their kids are sick. What kind of place do you think this is?"

"I don't think you understand how serious the situation is."

"I get it. She's sick. So give her some meds and send her back to the dorm. I'll excuse her from class for a few days." Lucas waves her off, trying to step past her and back to where he came from, but the doctor stops him with a hand to his chest.

"Lucas," the doctor scolds him, and I'm surprised that she calls him by his first name, "let me make this really clear, so you understand... I don't know if she's going to make it through the night."

Lucas stiffens, standing up a little straighter, and so do I. His eyes go wide, all the sleep in them gone.

"What do you mean she's not gonna make it through the night?"

She drops her hand from Lucas's chest and walks over to Aspen's bed again. "I said I'm not sure if she's gonna make it, not that she won't. She is really sick, Lucas. Her body is weak, but you know me. I'll do everything I can. I got the fever to come down, so that's good. I'm running tests on her liver and kidney function, but from what I can tell just by examining her, it looks like her organs are failing."

"Fuck! Okay, I'll call her parents." Lucas nods, his face suddenly pale. "Keep me updated."

He leaves, and the doc sits down by Aspen's bed, taking her hand into hers and simply holding it.

"Come on," she whispers. "You need to fight. You are too young to die."

The words slowly sink in. Aspen could... she could actually die...

I'm no stranger to death by any means, but this feels different. Most people think, me being who I am, I must have killed people before. But the truth is, I haven't. I've seen people die. I've beaten people up, tortured them for information, but I've never actually killed someone.

If Aspen dies, it will be partly my fault. I knew she hadn't been eating or at least not well. I watched her leave the cafeteria empty-handed. I saw how skinny she was, but instead of offering her food, I held on to that information as a bargaining chip.

If she dies today, her blood will be on my hands.

18

ASPEN

I blink my eyes open and wish I hadn't the instant I do. Bright yellow lights shine from above. The world around me spins, making my stomach churn. Dear Lord, do not let me throw up again. A groan slips past my dry lips as I roll to my side only to realize that I'm on a bed, well, a cot, and no longer in my dorm room.

Disoriented, I force myself to sit up a little faster than necessary and almost tip over.

"Slow down. You're going to make yourself sick." A voice carries into my ears, and I swing my head in the direction of the voice, only to discover a young woman and Quinton in the small room that is definitely not my dorm.

"Where am I?" The last thing I remember is being so hot it felt like my skin was on fire. Now I don't feel nearly as hot, but my thoughts are sluggish, making it hard for me to piece the puzzle together.

"How do you feel?" The young woman steps closer, her eyes examining my face.

"Dead," I joke. Then I add, "Like I got hit by a truck."

The woman nods but doesn't reply. I peer over at Quinton as I can feel his eyes on me. The way he's looking at me—like I died and came back to life—makes my skin crawl. I do not want to be the center of his attention, not now or ever.

The nurse busies herself checking my heartbeat and temperature, then asking me to follow her pen with my eyes. I do as she asks, and when she hands me a paper cup with water in it, I swallow it down, letting the cool liquid coat my throat.

"Now can you tell me what happened, and where I am?" I ask once she takes a step back and seems to be happy with her findings.

"You're in the school emergency room, and I'm sure I don't have to tell you this, but you have a lot of explaining to do."

My brows furrow in confusion, and I look at Quinton, whose face is still and void of all emotions, giving nothing away.

"I don't understand. I don't know how I got here or what you're talking about." My head is pounding. I'm confused, and all I want to do is fall back asleep.

"He brought you here." The nurse or doctor, whoever she is, hooks her thumb in the direction of Quinton. He must've taken a trip to my room only to find me half-dead on the ground, ruining whatever plan of damnation he had for me.

"Now explain to me why you haven't been eating?"

"Eating?" I almost mock.

"Yes, eating. Your blood tests revealed that you're malnourished, have very low iron and multiple vitamin deficiencies, and most likely a bad case of food poisoning. You should be grateful that you didn't shrivel up and die."

Well, that explains a lot of things. I lift my hand and notice the IV in my arm, clear liquids pump into my body, and the significance of the situation starts to weigh heavily on my shoulders. *Why you haven't been eating?* Her question repeats back in my mind, and I can feel her gaze narrowing further, burning into my skin.

She's waiting for an answer, and I'm almost ashamed to tell her... *almost.*

"None of this is my fault. The cafeteria staff won't give me any food, and—" Quinton interjects before I can continue.

"She has an eating disorder. She's just lying to cover it up. She's super ashamed of it and doesn't want to admit she has a problem."

In an instant, I'm red hot with anger. I don't have a fucking eating disorder, and I tell him this with a glare. He returns the glare, his jaw clenched, his icy gaze burning into my eyes.

The woman's gaze ping-pongs between us, and I have to wonder if she will really believe him. I swear to God if she agrees with him...

She nods, and her gaze softens a smidge. "That's not all that unusual for a girl of your age." Looking from Quinton and back to me, she says, "We'll get you nursed back to health, and then you really need to consider some form of therapy. You could've died... I really hope you understand that." I want to tell her she is wrong, but there's no way I'm going to, not with Quinton in the room.

"I've got some paperwork to do, so I'll be back in a few minutes with another bag of fluids. You lie back and rest." She pats my leg, and I bite the inside of my cheek until I taste blood. I'm very close to exploding on Quinton.

As soon as she walks out of the room and the door closes behind her, I'm ready to lurch across the room. "What the hell? I don't have an eating disorder, and we both know it."

His jaw clenches tighter, and he speaks through his teeth. "Will you ever learn to keep your mouth shut?"

"I have no reason to keep my mouth shut," I growl. "In fact, keeping my mouth shut is the reason I'm here in the first place. Had I spoken up sooner about not getting adequate meals, maybe I wouldn't be here, half-dead to the world."

Arguing is making my head hurt, and I lie back on the cot and close my eyes, cutting off whatever connection we held looking at each other.

"A thank you is sufficient enough. There is no need for you to throw a hissy fit. You're already a snitch in the eyes of every single student and staff member here. Now you snitch on the cafeteria staff by telling the doctor you aren't being given food?"

"It's not a lie."

"It's a snitch move. Keep your mouth shut. It's your biggest downfall." The sound of the chair scraping against the tile floor forces me to drag my eyes open again, and I see Quinton pushing out of the chair.

"Where are you going?" I ask, trying not to sound like I care.

He's obviously been here a while, and I'm fine now, so what does it matter if he leaves?

"If you must know, I'm going back to my room to sleep for a few hours. I've been here for hours making sure your ass didn't die on me before I can get my full use out of you. I have class in a few hours, and I haven't slept a wink."

All I can do is roll my eyes.

"Of course, all you care about is my usefulness to you."

"Shut up and go to sleep before I put you to sleep."

"You don't have to be so aggressive."

"Go to sleep, Aspen," he orders, shoving his hands into the pockets of his jeans.

I watch him walk to the door and then snap my eyes closed, pretending like I don't give a shit what he does. Really, I don't. I just don't like how dismissive he is of me or the fact that the cafeteria is the reason I'm currently hospitalized. I'm not a snitch for speaking the truth, and I didn't do this to myself, which is what he wants the doctor to believe.

Silence settles around me, and I stay in a temporary state between half asleep and half awake, every little sound startling me. I'm feeling a lot better, which is all that matters to me at this point. I'm not sure how much time has passed or when I finally fall asleep, but the next time I open my eyes, I find Brittney sitting in the spot where Quinton was the first time I woke up.

"Hey, you!" she greets, concern etched into her features.

"Hey," I croak.

"What happened? You look like someone put you through the food processor."

A smile tugs onto my lips. "That's because they did. Apparently, I have food poisoning, and I'm dehydrated and lacking minerals."

Brittney gives me a stern look. "If you want to tell me what's going on, you can. I won't say anything. I just don't want you to hurt yourself or be harmed by someone else." I get the feeling she is referring to that night in the hall, which I never fully explained to her.

"If you're wondering if I did this to myself, the answer is no. It's also a very complicated situation, so I'll leave it at the cafeteria hasn't been offering me good food, and when I say good, I don't mean delicious." Brittney's nose wrinkles. "Whenever I go to get food, it's expired or near expiration. Sometimes, there isn't anything at all, and on those days, I don't eat. Quinton told me to shut up when I went to tell the doctor..."

I realize all too late that I've said too much and press my lips together to stop the rest of the word vomit from escaping.

Adjusting her glasses, she asks, "Quinton, as in the guy who I saw you with in the corridor the night we first met?"

I nod, and part of me wants to tell her he's not really that bad of a guy, a lot unstable and a control freak at best, but I stop myself from doing that because it seems wrong. It seems like I'm enabling his behavior, and I don't want to do that. No matter how fucked up someone is, it doesn't mean they can treat people however they want.

"It's a really long story, and I'm way too exhausted to get into it, but yeah, that's how I ended up here."

"I don't like it. I don't like that they aren't giving you proper food." Anger rises in her features, her cheeks become red, and her brows pinch together. I understand her anger all too well, but I didn't tell her any of this because I want her sympathy or help.

"I don't like it either, but there isn't much I can do about it." I shake my head, feeling like shit for what I'm about to say. "I don't want you to feel bad for me either or to try to help. I've got enough attention on me for things that are out of my control."

"Don't you think your health is important enough to speak up over?" she asks me calmly.

"Yes, but I'm confiding in you as a friend, not a teacher, so please don't make this into a bigger issue than it is. I'll talk to the cafeteria. I'll get it fixed."

And I will, or at least, I'll try.

"Now I'm going to worry about you even more." The words out of her mouth make me still. It's been so long since I've heard someone say they're worried about me or that they even care about my existence.

"Don't worry. I'm okay. As soon as I'm out of here, I'll be back in the library bothering you."

She nods, looking down at her hands resting in her lap before looking back up at me. The way she's looking at me with such a somber, open expression is more than I can take, and I dart my eyes away to look at the blanket covering me.

"If you need anything, Aspen, don't hesitate to ask. I'm here for you, as a friend and teacher. I'll help however I can, whenever I can."

I don't want to admit how much her words soothe me, how much better they make me feel because I'm afraid I might wake up and find out this has all been a dream. I mean, the vomiting and fever could all be a dream.

"Thank you, and thanks for checking on me. By the way, how did you know I was here?" I'm almost hesitant to know the answer to that question, but if the whole school knows already, then I need to prepare for when I'm released back to the dorms.

"Rumors. I heard a couple of teachers talking this morning and had to check for myself. I called down here, and the nurse told me that you were admitted but sleeping. I put off coming down so that you could sleep. I didn't want to disturb you."

Wow, how long have I been in and out of sleep? Obviously longer than I thought.

"Well, at least it's only the teachers that know."

Brittney frowns. "I don't think it'll be that way for long, but don't focus on that. Focus on feeling better."

I nod. That's the only thing I can do right now.

I'll deal with the fallout later. At least I'm not going to die of dehydration or anything else insane, not yet.

19

QUINTON

*E*ven though I don't visit her again, I keep tabs on Aspen through the doctor who helped bring her back to life. I've called down to medical every day, and she's given me a brief overview of how she's doing. It makes me feel less like an asshole for not visiting her, but I don't have anything to prove to her. She's nothing to me, not a girlfriend or even a friend. Just a toy that I don't want broken yet.

The cafeteria is crowded as hell today, and by the time we make it to a table, I'm ready to toss my lunch in the trash and walk out. All the people and commotion make me feel edgy. Ren strikes up a conversation with some kid sitting across from us. His name is Sillas, and he looks like the all-American type, right down to the polo T-shirt he's wearing.

His blond hair is cut military style, and he's wearing khakis. Who the fuck wears khakis? I guess if his overall appearance isn't shocking enough, his next sentence has me spitting my soda out across the table.

"I'm pretty sure my dad sent me here to become friends with other criminals. I'm a hacker, but I haven't really done anything huge. He wants me to break outside my comfort zone and get into the dark stuff."

"Hacker?" I choke on the remaining liquid in my throat.

"Yeah, it's kind of a family thing." He shrugs like it's no big deal, and really it isn't. Hackers aren't a new thing, but it's a big deal to me. An idea takes root in my mind, growing to life right before my eyes, and I can't stop it.

Ren slaps a hand on my back while laughing. "You going to make it?"

"Yeah, I'm fine." I lean across the table and look Sillas in the eyes. He seems like a straight shooter, but you can't judge someone by their appearance and know they're worth trusting. Still, I'm not afraid. My father knows that I want answers. I'm not hiding anything or doing wrong by asking someone to find information for me.

"I need you to do something for me, and while you probably don't need it, I'll sweeten the pot by throwing some money in too."

Sillas's face becomes serious in an instant, and he sheds the all-American boy image right before my eyes. "What do you need done?"

I keep my voice low as I say, "I need you to help me find someone... my mother."

Sillas visibly gulps, and he looks like he might be sick.

"Your mother is missing? Wouldn't your dad—"

"Ella Rossi is not my biological mother. I want you to find my birth mother," I explain and watch as pure shock forms on his features.

"I can try. I'll need as many details as you can give me, and then I'll reach out to my dad."

I shake my head. "No. I want you to do it. Don't involve anyone else. This is between you and me. Prove yourself to me, and you won't have a thing to worry about in this place." I add the last little bit for effect, even if it is true. No one will mess with him here, not if he's walking alongside me.

We finish up our lunch, and I let Sillas know that I'll text him the details about my mother that I know. Which isn't much of anything. On the way out of the lunchroom, Ren nudges my shoulder.

"Are you sure about this? Going behind your dad's back?"

I stop in my tracks and pin him with a stare. "Nothing I do here is a secret, and it's not like he doesn't know I want answers. He refuses to give them to me, so I'll find another way, my way." The venom in my words must stop Ren from pushing forward with any other questions because instead of continuing the conversation, we move on to discussing Luna and how excited she is to visit Ren.

"I miss her like crazy but really wish I could spend time with her somewhere else."

"She's coming here when she graduates, right? Why not let her come and get a feel for the school? That way, she's not just dropped on her ass out in the middle of nowhere like us."

Ren shrugs. "If I'm being honest, I don't want her to come here. I don't want her to have anything to do with this life. I want her to go to school, get a good job, live her best life, and get married and have kids if that's what she wants."

I almost laugh. "You're going to let your sister date?" I can see it now, Ren murdering so many guys our family can no longer cover it up.

"No. It will have to be an arranged marriage kind of thing. I've got to make sure he is perfect for her and that he's not going to hurt her or make her cry. I mean, you'll probably be the same with Scarlet."

The mention of her name reminds me of how soon she will be an adult, and before long, here alongside me.

"I don't mind Scarlet coming here because it will be safer than any other place. Plus, I can keep an eye on her here. At least until we graduate."

Boys will be interested, and she'll be able to make her own decisions. Decisions that could get her hurt or even killed.

The lack of control I have over the people I love terrifies me. I block out the rest of the conversation, and when we reach our dorm, it's right as one of the maids is walking out. She moves out of the way and starts pushing her cart toward the next room.

I'm reminded of the condition that I found Aspen in and the way her bedroom looked. I know she'll be released soon, and by making sure her room is clean, she'll owe me an hour of her time. Stopping in front of the cart, I force the maid to stop or hit me. Thankfully, at the last moment, she looks up at me through her lashes and stops moving.

"I need you to clean Aspen Mather's room."

She shakes her head, her dark brown ponytail swaying. "I cannot do that. Mr. Diavolo gave us instructions that we're not to clean her room. I am sorry."

Something in me snaps, and I grip the edge of the cart with two hands, ready to toss it over my shoulder.

"I don't care what he told you. I'm telling you to go clean her room. Now go do it, or I'll be sure to let my father know that you tried to steal something from our room and that I caught you red-handed doing it. I imagine the wrath of my father will rival that of Mr. Diavolo."

The young woman's cheeks become as red as a tomato, and her gaze turns submissive. "Of course, Mr. Rossi. I will be sure to clean her room for you."

I nod and move out of her way, allowing her to pass by without incident. I can feel Ren staring a hole through me.

"What the hell are you looking at?"

"Just trying to figure out why having Aspen's room cleaned means so much to you?"

I don't have to dive into the deal that Aspen and I made with each other. That's none of his business, so I do what I do best. I put up another wall.

"Don't worry about it."

"I hate to say it, but you're acting weird."

I roll my eyes. "No, I'm not."

"Yes, you are, and I don't like it."

Ren and I have always been close, and while we still are, and I can trust him with anything, I don't need to divulge all the things I do with other people, least of all, Aspen.

"Sorry, but you're wrong, and I really don't care what you like," I say as we walk through the door and into the apartment. The smell of antiseptic hangs in the air. The living room is clean, and the kitchen counters are wiped down.

Ren changes the subject. "Want to have a couple of beers and maybe invite the guys over for a little bit?"

The idea of sitting through an entire evening with Matteo makes my blood boil. I don't like the way he looks at Aspen— like she's a piece of meat or that she belongs to him.

"Nah, I've got homework."

Disappointment fills Ren's features, making him appear more like my father than my best friend. "Whatever is in those books isn't anything we haven't learned. You said so yourself." And I did, but that was before I realized Matteo was a douchebag. If he showed up here tonight, blood would be drawn, and it wouldn't be mine.

"Yeah, well, I don't care. I'm spending the rest of the afternoon in my room."

Ren shakes his head and walks away, and I walk into my room and close the door behind me, clicking the lock into place. I feel a little bad about turning Ren down, but I'm not going to hang out with Matteo, no way in hell.

I flip open my laptop and log in, wanting to check my email and social media a bit. As soon as I open my account, I spot an email from Scarlet. My fingers linger on the keys as I stare at the screen, reading the message.

HEY! I got the official invitation to the founders' ball. I'm so excited to see you! You better be ready for me to hug you. Mom and Dad are excited to see you too. Only a short while before we can visit. I miss you so much. Oh, and I can't wait to meet your date.

MY DATE? What the hell is she talking about? I can't get my fingers to type out a response, so I stare at the screen in bemusement. *Date?* I don't have a date.

Hell, I didn't even want to go to the founders' ball, but it doesn't appear I have much of a choice, and it looks like my father is up to no good, as I am certain he is the one who hand-selected my date. The idea of seeing my father again makes me want to stab someone. I can only hope the night doesn't end in bloodshed.

20

ASPEN

he days blend. Quinton never returns to medical to check on me, and I'm not sure how I feel about that. On the one hand, I'm happy, but on the other, I'm confused. Why would he make the effort to bring me here and ensure I'm okay, only to never return to check on me later?

I don't bother trying to make sense of it. What Quinton and I share behind closed doors doesn't matter, and him bringing me here has nothing to do with him actually caring. It has everything to do with him ensuring his little toy doesn't get broken to the point where she is no longer useful.

That's what I feel like, too, a toy that's been placed on the shelf and only pulled out when the occasion arises. Not that I want to be anything to him. I'd rather he ignore my existence altogether, but I would never get so lucky.

"Make sure you're eating and getting lots of vitamins and minerals. If you end up back in here with the same issue, I'm calling for a psych evaluation. You won't have a choice on seeking therapy or not because I'll make you."

I try not to roll my eyes at the doctor, who has been a lot kinder to me than most of the other staff here. Still, she believes I'm starving myself, which pisses me off.

"Got it," I say.

It's been a long time since I've felt this good, probably since I arrived. I don't look back when I leave the medical center and walk back to the dorms slowly. A few students linger in the corridors, but none of them pay me any attention. As soon as I'm inside my room, I sigh, almost happy to be in my own space again.

I'm surprised to see that the floor has been cleaned, the smell of bleach tickling my nostrils. I notice the mattress on the bed and remember it being delivered, but everything after that is a little fuzzy. On the mattress is a brand new sheet, and a bag is sitting there. I briefly wonder if Quinton had something to do with the room being cleaned. I don't want to owe him anything else.

Curious, I walk over to the bed and peer inside the bag. Its contents include a couple of granola bars, small bags of trail mix, and two candy bars. There's a small note at the bottom, and I really hate that this bag makes me smile.

A person should not be this excited over something so mundane, but I am. Opening the note, I read it back to myself.

YOU OWE ME ANOTHER HOUR.

I'll collect at my leisure.

-Q

I ROLL MY EYES. Of course, he would expect something in return for cleaning the room and getting me a small bag of food. Almost apprehensively, I open one of the granola bars and sniff it. After eating bad and expired food, I've developed a bit of PTSD toward eating. Nothing odd catches in my nostrils, so I take a bite of the bar, chewing it slowly before swallowing.

I wait for something bad to happen, for my stomach to revolt in some way, but nothing does, so I continue eating it, devouring every morsel like it's the last thing I'll get to eat.

A granola bar won't sustain me, so I'll have to make a trip to the cafeteria this morning. The idea of fighting with one of the staff is exhausting, but I'm not going to let myself end up in the hospital again.

Dusting the crumbs from my lap, I stand and gather my wits. I have to get back into a routine. As I walk to the cafeteria for breakfast, I wonder if the school had called my mother when I was sick. She never tried to call me, but I suspect if she knew, she would've called. The cafeteria is mostly empty when I arrive, and I walk up to the buffet, my mouth watering and my stomach rumbling.

"I don't know who is in charge back there, but..."

"We have your breakfast ready." The guy ignores what I was about to say and disappears into the back for a moment. When he returns, there's a foam cup in his hand, and I look at him, puzzled how my entire breakfast could be in that single cup.

"What is this?" I ask, taking the cup.

"Breakfast. It's got a bunch of different vegetables and fruit, as well as some vitamins and minerals. Not sure how it's going to taste, but it's super healthy and will give you all the nutrients you need."

Based upon everything he's just said, someone must've already talked to the cafeteria, which I didn't want or need. I doubt it was Brittney; if she had talked to them, I'm sure I would have an actual meal in my hands right now, not a liquid version. All fingers point to Quinton or maybe even the doctor.

"This is all I get to eat?"

"You don't need anything else. The items in that should get you through to lunch."

I clench my teeth together to stop myself from lashing out. I'm so tired of people telling me what I do and don't need here.

"Fine," I grumble, instead of arguing with the man, and take my foam cup. It's easy to find an empty table this early in the morning. Pulling the cap off the foam cup, I peer inside of it. A bright green liquid peers back at me, and I gag.

They can't really expect me to eat this, can they? I look away from the contents of the cup, cringing at the thought of drinking it. What other option do I have? None. I have to eat, or I'll end up back in medical, and who knows what will happen next time.

Swallowing back my gag reflex, I lift the cup to my lips and tip it back. The green liquid splashes forward and into my mouth. I try my best not to focus on its taste but instead forcing it down my throat, but that doesn't work all that well.

The bitter taste of the greens is the first thing I notice as well as the thickness of the smoothie, if you could even call it that. Personally, I would love to toss it in the nearest trash can, but I don't, nor will I. I need every drop of nutrients in this cup.

I have a new goal to add to my list, and that includes not returning to medical again. If eating this horrible, not delicious at all, smoothie makes it so I don't, then I'll drink it.

Somehow, I stomach the entire cup without throwing up. I remind myself that it has to be this way and toss my cup into the trash and give the man who handed me the cup a smile before I walk out. I guess I'll kill them with kindness, though they did try to technically kill me.

I return to my room, and as soon as I close the door, my phone starts to go off. Sitting on the edge of the brand new mattress, I pull my phone from my pocket and find my mother's number lighting up the screen. She's calling on Skype, so I hit the answer key and wait for her face to fill the screen.

"Aspen?" she says, like she can't believe she got ahold of me when I've been waiting for her to call every day since I was hospitalized.

"Yes, Mom?"

"Oh, thank god, you're okay. I just heard from Lucas about your hospitalization. I'm so sorry, honey. I had no idea that you had an eating disorder."

I have to stop myself from lashing out and expelling all my

anger at her. Especially since, for the first time in forever, she seems genuinely concerned about me.

"I don't have an eating disorder. I tried telling them that, but no one would listen to me. I got sick because of the food the cafeteria was giving me. It was expired most days, and on others, they gave me nothing to eat, so I'm not that shocked that I got sick."

My mother's facial expression doesn't change. Does she really think I'm trying to hide having an eating disorder from her?

"No matter what the problem is, your father and I talked and decided that it's still best if you stay there. You're safer, regardless of the circumstances you're going through." Her words are a kick to the gut. I hate this place, but I hate it more that I don't even have a choice. "Lucas has assured us that you will be provided with plenty of healthy, fresh food now."

My thoughts shift to the foam cup with the thick green liquid in it. It tasted like mulched-up leaves and where dreams go to die.

"I'm sure they will," I mutter under my breath.

It sounds cliché, but she really doesn't understand what it's like here. The danger, the hate, and the fear creeping up my spine. It's like everyone is out to get me for something I had nothing to do with—for a choice that my father made.

"Don't be so ungrateful. Things will get better. I promise you're much safer there than out here." I don't believe that for a second, but it's not like I have a way to leave.

"Well, I'm alive, so you don't have to worry anymore."

"Please, Aspen, don't be like that. Your father has a lot on his plate right now, and I'm stuck in hiding. The rest of us aren't living some grand life."

I want to tell her that maybe she isn't living some grand life, waking up to breakfast served and a maid at her beck and call, but at least she didn't have to wake up every day afraid of what may happen next. There wasn't a permanent fear choking her, making it hard for her to sleep at night. There was no point in arguing with her because no matter what, she would make it seem like her situation was so much worse than mine.

"Look, Mom. I've got to go. Homework and stuff."

Her brows pinch together, and her mouth pops open like she is going to say something else, but I hit the end key before she gets the chance. I can't handle another argument. As I shut off the phone, a tinge of guilt zings through me. I hate shutting her out like that, but for my own mental health, I have to.

Eyeing my desk, I look at the stack of books. Being sick really set me back with homework. I guess I'll spend the rest of the day finishing it and hope that Quinton doesn't pop in uninvited. That would just be my luck.

It's been a week since Aspen was released from medical, and I still haven't gone to see her. I keep telling myself it's because I need her to be healthy for what I have planned for her. I can't fuck her if she's passed out, but deep down, I know that's not the reason. I don't care if she is half-dead; I'd still enjoy fucking her... maybe even more so.

No, the real reason I've stayed away is that Ren is right. I'm getting too close. I shouldn't care if her room is clean or if she is hungry or cold. I shouldn't care about anything, and the fact that I do has a deep sense of guilt settling in my bones. She is supposed to be the enemy, and caring for her in any form is like betraying my family.

I should cut all ties, forget our deal, and let her fend for herself, but my body is winning over my mind. Because my body craves her, craves the control and the sense of peace it gives me.

"What group are you in?" Ren's voice drags me from my thoughts.

"Huh?" What group?

"The range. I'm in group six, going to the range this week."

"Oh, yeah. Me too. That's this week?"

"Jesus, dude. Where is your mind? Yes, weapons training starts today. Not like we need it. Want to skip?"

"Nah, I wouldn't mind firing off some rounds. Plus, depending on what kind of training they'll do, it will be kind of fun. It's not like we have anything better to do."

"True. Well, let's go then." Ren gets to his feet.

"It starts now?"

Ren gives me a look like he is questioning my sanity. "If I hadn't said something, would you just have gone to class in an hour?"

"Pretty much, yes." I'm a little surprised myself. I normally like to have a plan and be prepared, but weapons training simply slipped my mind, which only solidifies my thoughts on staying away from Aspen.

We leave the room and take the elevator up to D level. I've only been on this level once to get familiar with my surroundings. To my surprise, it looks like Ren has been here as well. We walk down the white corridor to the gun range. When we walk inside, three people are already there; the instructor, Matteo, and one student I don't know.

Matteo nods at us, and acid churns in my stomach. Every time I see him, I dislike him a little bit more. Instead of nodding back, I ignore him, pretending he isn't there at all.

Shoving my hands in my pockets, I imagine them wrapping around his throat while we watch students slowly pile into the room. Matteo is talking to the guy I don't know. But his eyes glance over at me sporadically, as if to make sure I won't attack him.

The instructor is someone I also don't know yet. He is tall and bulky with short dirty blond hair and an unkempt beard that looks like he just spent six months being homeless.

Ren is leaning against the wall casually, but I know he can tell I'm irritated. Forcing my eyes away from Matteo, I do a quick count of the people in the room. We're at fourteen now, which means we're missing one student. Each group should be fifteen. The thought has barely left my mind when the door opens, and the last person walks in.

Aspen.

"I'm sorry," she apologizes quietly for being late, her eyes trained on the ground. She hasn't seen me yet, and when she does look up, her gaze is trained on Matteo, who gawks at her like a hungry dog looks at a bone.

"Now that we're all here, let's begin." The instructor raises his voice, silencing all the chatter in the room. "I'm Michael Brooks. You can call me Mike. Just kidding, if you call me Mike, I will shoot you in the leg. You will call me Brooks. If you call me Mr. Brooks, I will also shoot you in the leg..."

Brooks continues talking, but my attention is focused on the blond girl with her back pressed against the door she just came through. When I left medical, she was so pale. Color has returned to her face, but she is still too skinny to look healthy.

Her sweater hangs off one of her shoulders, showing off her pronounced collarbone and thin neck. Her jeans are baggy, looking like they are about to fall off her hips.

"You are about to walk into the only room in this school where weapons are allowed." Brooks's voice breaks through again. "You each will find a stand with three weapons. They are not loaded yet, but the ammunition for each is on the bottom shelf on your stand. Only load one gun at a time, stay in your booth, and don't shoot at each other. Got it?"

A low murmur fills the room, and everyone nods their heads in agreement, except Matteo, who is staring at Aspen like he's taking off her clothes in his mind. Brooks opens the door to the range, and everyone starts heading toward the door, Aspen included. Matteo follows her, and I follow him.

Aspen takes the booth all the way to the left, farthest away from everyone to the left. Matteo tries to take the booth next to hers, and all my conviction about staying away from her goes up in thin air.

"Where are you going?" Ren asks, placing his hand on my shoulder.

Fuck, I forgot he was here for a moment.

"I can't make Aspen's life miserable from over there." Shrugging his hand off my shoulder, I walk over to Matteo. "Move, this is my booth."

Matteo turns quickly, looking me straight in the eyes. "Of course." He nods, forcing a smile. "Catch you later, rat." He winks at Aspen and slithers away like the snake he is.

Ren takes the booth three down from me, and the blond

Russian girl from PE takes the one to my right side. I'm pretty sure her name is Hannah, or Anna, or something like that.

I glance to my left and catch Aspen looking away quickly, like she doesn't want me to notice her staring at me. A smirk tugs at my lips as I take in the gun selection before me.

"We'll start with the two handguns. Put your ear protection on, pick a gun, load it, fire, repeat," Brooks instructs, and the room fills with the sound of guns being loaded and racked.

One by one, I push the soundproof earplugs into my ear canal and load my gun on autopilot. The motion is already integrated into my brain enough to where I don't have to think about what I'm doing.

Raising my gun, I aim at the target and fire off all ten rounds. Every single one hits within the smallest ring of the target, and two are dead center. I release the clip and reload before racking the gun and taking aim once more.

I'm about to take my first shot when I hear an almost inaudible curse beside me. I tilt my head and look down through the glass separating me from Aspen. She is fumbling with the gun, trying to load it with the wrong magazine.

Shaking my head, I put my own gun down. Pulling out one of the earplugs, I walk around the small separation between booths. "What the fuck are you doing?"

"I'm loading the gun. What does it look like?"

"It looks like you are trying to shove a 1911 magazine into a Glock 19."

"Oh, so this is not the right one?" She looks down at the gun like it's a foreign object.

"Are you shitting me right now?"

"I don't know these things. I've never even held a gun before."

My face slackens in shock. She can't be serious.

"Your father is an arms dealer," I point out. How in the fucking world has she never held a gun before?

"I wanted to study medicine." She places the gun on the table in front of her and sags against the wall across from me. Her head is down, her shoulders are slumped, and she looks at the gun like she is about to cry.

Now I'm even more confused. The entire time she has been here, I haven't seen her cry once. Even with all the shit people have put her through, including me, she hasn't shed a single tear in front of anyone. She's always held her head high, yet right now, she looks like she is about to run out crying, and I can't figure out why. Why now out of all days? More importantly, why do I care?

"I don't know how to do any of this."

Shots ring out all around us, but I ignore them as I pick up her gun and load it with the right magazine. "Come here. Stand like this, right foot slightly back, shoulders squared, arms bent. Hold the gun with your right hand, then wrap your left around the bottom like this."

I show her how to stand before stepping off to the side, handing her the loaded gun. She doesn't move, simply stares at the gun in my hand for a few more seconds. When she does reach for it, my instinct is to pull away. I'm handing my enemy a loaded gun, after all. Maybe this is a fucking trick? If it is, she deserves a fucking Oscar.

Hesitantly, she grabs the gun and holds it in her hand awkwardly. She takes a stand like I showed her moments ago. Her aim is off, but I let her fire off a few rounds before I correct her. She pulls the trigger, and her whole body jerks from the kickback that she clearly wasn't ready for.

She steadies herself and shoots the rest of the rounds in the direction of the target. Only five out of the ten rounds actually hit the paper.

"That's terrible." Brooks walks up beside us. "Who the fuck taught you how to shoot?"

"Ahh, no one. This is my first time," Aspen admits, shocking Brooks just as much.

"All right then, you go back to your booth, and I'll go over everything with her." He shoos me away, grabs the gun from Aspen's hands, and starts explaining to her the mechanisms of the gun and the different features.

I move back to my spot, making a mental note to check Brooks out later. He clearly doesn't know who Aspen is since he's the only instructor so far who hasn't treated her like a traitor.

"You going to show me how to shoot now? I could use some help." Blond Russian girl winks.

"You look like you're doing just fine," I say, peeking at her target, which looks a lot like my own. Actually, I'm a little impressed with her marksmanship, but of course, I don't comment on that.

"Maybe you can give me lessons in something else then?" she asks seductively. This is the second time she's blatantly hit on me, and just like last time, I ignore it.

I get back to my own guns, firing off the rounds I have, reload, and repeat until I've gone through all the weapons and four different targets. Brooks spends most of the class with Aspen, showing her how to handle the array of guns. With each passing minute, I get more irritated, and I don't really know why.

All I do know is that by the end of the class, I'm ready to punch a hole into Brooks's face. He walks away and talks about cleaning weapons after lunch. Aspen walks past me, obviously trying to avoid me, but I easily catch up to her.

Grabbing her arm, I pull her into my side and lean down so I can whisper in her ear. "You still owe me an hour."

She pulls out of my grasp with a huff and storms off as if she can get away from me. Doesn't she know that will never happen?

22

ASPEN

*P*aranoia skates down my spine, and every time I walk into my bedroom and close the door, I'm waiting for the second that *he* comes walking in. Not knowing when Quinton plans to collect on his hour with me has me on edge. That's a lie, not just on edge, but hanging off a cliff by my fingernails.

I hate having a favor loom over my head, even more, that it's owed to Q, and I have no say on when he's going to collect it. Scanning my key card, I enter the bedroom and close the door behind me. I press my back against the wood and let out a long sigh.

I don't feel one-hundred-percent safe here, not while Quinton has a key card to my room, but I still feel more protected by these four walls than I do in all the time I spend walking the corridors between classes.

I add books to the stack that already exists on my desk and

toss myself onto the bed, thankful that I have a mattress now. Damn Q and his bartering. If I wasn't so weak, I might say no, but a lot of the things he offers help me, and I can't pass up on a decent bed, food, and most of all, protection.

My computer is sitting on the desk beside the stack of books, and I move to grab it, opening it to check my emails. I don't know why I bother. It's not like anyone wants to talk to me. I almost laugh at how pathetic my life is. No friends, no one who truly cares if I'm alive. My parents act like they care, but do they really?

I'm about to close my computer and take a shower when a Skype call from an unknown number comes in. Moving the mouse to the answer button, I pause. Should I answer this call? It could be anyone. Indecision weighs heavily on my shoulders, and as if fate already knows the answer, my finger slips off the key, and I hit answer by accident.

The air in my lungs stills, and my fingers itch to grab the screen of my laptop and close it, but I choose not to at the last second, which also happens to be the same moment my father's face appears on the screen.

I'm so shocked. All I can do is stare at the screen, wondering how the hell he managed to negotiate a Skype call from prison. On second thought, I don't even want to know.

"Aspen, it's nice to see you." He smiles, and while he still looks like my father—balding head and soft green eyes—the bright orange jumpsuit and weathered look on his face reminds me of all the stress this must be putting on him.

"Hi." My voice cracks. "How did you...?" I shake my head,

"Never mind, I don't want to know how you managed to call me from inside." Right away, my defenses are up. If he is calling, it doesn't mean anything good.

"That doesn't matter, sweetheart."

"Is something going on?"

"No, not here. Your mother informed me that you're having a tough time at Corium. That people are after you."

"After me would be a very loose statement. They want me dead but can't find a way to do it without it causing problems."

"You're stronger than you think, Aspen, and even if it feels like the walls are crumbling around you, they're not. There is no safer place for you than inside Corium."

"It's literal hell here."

"Well, in case you need some leverage, I can tell you this..." He looks away from the camera and then back again like he's trying to determine if someone is listening or watching him. "The answer to his question is Xander."

Xander? And who's question? "What are you talking about?" I ask, confused by the riddle.

"You're smarter than you think, Aspen."

"Smart has nothing to do with it, Dad. I don't understand what you're telling me—"

"I can't say more than I already have since calls from inside are monitored," he interrupts.

My lips part, and I'm about to say something else, but then the screen goes dark, and the call ends. Did he really just hang up on me?

I sit there baffled by the conversation, staring at the screen for five minutes before I decide to close it. What could that mean... the answer to his question is Xander. I already know it's referring to Quinton, but I'm not sure in what sense.

Obviously, my father knows things I don't, and instead of telling me, he's speaking in a foreign language, leaving me to figure it out on my own. My frustration toward my mother and father has reached a new height. They both think I'm safe here, but I don't see it, and I certainly don't feel it. How can they think being hospitalized is safe? I was almost killed for crying out loud. Every day here feels like I'm one second away from being tossed into the pits of hell.

How can I continue forward? How can I make myself as feared as Quinton is? I don't want to hurt anyone, but I have to find a way to make myself stronger. When Q was teaching me those moves in class, I had never felt so powerful, so in control.

In a lot of ways, it gave me strength that I never had before. Suddenly, I feel cooped up inside this room. Normally, I want to keep myself hidden, protected by these four walls, but I'm being driven to seek out something else.

I grab my key card off the desk, and my eyes catch on the edge of the map. There's a book covering the majority of it, but in the bottom corner is the map key, and I notice a single word: *sunroom.*

Shoving the book off the map, I scan a route to the sunroom. I'll push through a crowd of my enemies for a few moments of sunlight. I'm giddy with excitement when I leave the room. After the conversation I had with my father, this is exactly what I need.

The corridors are congested with students making their way back to the dorms. With my head down, I push through the horde to the elevators. An elevator is already going up with a couple of students in it, so I slide inside and press my back to the wall. The two girls inside exchange glances while the remaining occupant, a guy, pays me no attention. I pretend they don't exist and ignore their glares.

At least they aren't saying anything.

The elevator chimes, and I remember then that I forgot to push the button for the sunroom, so when they all step out, and I'm left alone again, I push the "s" button and take a step back, happy once more.

When the elevator chimes again and the doors open, I step out and have to shield my eyes almost immediately. Even though it's afternoon, the sun is still beating down on the covered sunroom. It's been a while since I saw the sun this fully.

I notice chairs and tables with little plants are scattered around the room. It's a cozy vacant space and one that might be my hideaway for when the library isn't an option. Slowly, I walk deeper into the room and take a seat at one of the tables.

The sun beats down on my skin, and I bask in the vitamin D it's providing me. Even through the thick glass surrounding me, I can still feel the hot rays. Maybe I'll be less depressed after this? They say the sun can make you feel rejuvenated. Too bad it can't get rid of all the assholes at Corium.

No. I tell myself and try not to think about anything else bad while I sit with my eyes closed, soaking up the sun. I've already made it this far, and I'm no quitter. After a while, beads of sweat start to form on my forehead, and I know it's time to return to my dorm as the sun starts to set on the horizon.

I can do this. Things are hard here, but they could be worse. My father—though he didn't really explain what he meant by it —provided me with leverage. I have no idea what it means, but if I have to use it, I will. The only thing that matters to me is my own sanity. I need to keep myself above water because as soon as I show even the slightest bit of weakness, I'll draw the students of Corium like sharks to blood in the water.

23

QUINTON

"*L*ook, I did as much digging as I could, but I have to be honest with you," Sillas says, and I can already tell where this is going.

"If you have nothing for me, then just tell me." I look him dead in the eyes. His face is emotionless, his eyes bleeding into mine.

"I tried, but whoever covered this up went all out. I can't find any information on her. It's almost like the person you're asking me to find doesn't exist." When he says whoever covered this up, he means my father.

My hand involuntarily forms a fist. Again, the answers I seek are just out of my grasp. I wish my father wasn't such an asshole and would tell me the truth about what happened to her, but I get the feeling even if he did, I wouldn't like the answer. Knowing the man he is today, I can't imagine he was any kinder before I came along.

"So that's it, there's nothing more you can do?"

Sillas glances down the corridor, which is mostly empty, before looking back at me. "Just because I couldn't find anything doesn't mean it can't be found. It just means my reach isn't as far. There's someone else, someone better who can help you, though."

Great, now we're bringing other people into it.

"I don't want to involve anyone else," I growl. I'm tempted to walk away and find another way. I mean, what good is he if he can't help me?

"Look, she's the best of the best, and you don't have to go far at all because she's a teacher here."

I lift a brow. "You've got my attention. Tell me more."

"The librarian. If you want answers, she is the person to go to."

Shit. That's kind of the last person I want to go to, but if it gets me the answers I want, then I'll do it. I run a hand through my hair, contemplating how I'm going to do this. Her impression of me is already skewed because of that one night in the corridor.

I wonder if Aspen told her anything. She probably didn't. Aspen is many things, but she isn't stupid, and she wouldn't dare bring more attention to herself. But even if she didn't tell her, that doesn't mean she hasn't already made her own assumptions about me.

"I'm going to go talk to her now," I announce, shoving off the wall.

"All right, but just so you know, I don't know what her price will be, or if she'll even do anything. I just know if you want to find something that doesn't seem to exist, she can find it for you."

I nod, not bothering to tell him that I'll pay whatever her price is. Even if she says she doesn't want to help me, I'll find a way to get her to fall in line.

Everyone has a weakness, even if they don't act like it.

"Tell Ren I went to work out. I don't want him following me."

"Sure," Sillas says, and I give him a head nod as I walk away and down the corridor.

Ren's been acting strange, and part of me wonders if he's reporting back to my father about my activities here. I don't think he would. Ren's not like that, and he doesn't have anything to do with my father. I think about all of this as I walk to the library, and as soon as I reach the spot where Brittney found Aspen and me that night, my thoughts change.

My cock grows hard at the reminder of how afraid and weak Aspen looked. I need to see her like that again. I need to have her at my mercy, willing to do anything I tell her to do. I crave her complete submission and thrive off the pleasure it gives me. I'm like an addict when it comes to controlling Aspen, and I never want to stop.

Passing the spot where I had her trapped against the wall, I continue walking until I reach the entrance to the library. I stop in my tracks, surprised by how open and airy the space feels. I won't lie, I expected something dark—a dungeon with books that smell like dust and mildew. Not this bright room with huge windows and rows upon rows of books.

Laughter fills the room, and I continue walking, following it around a corner until I spot Aspen and Brittney standing between bookshelves, each of them with a book in their hand. As soon as Aspen sees me, she places the book on the shelf and stalks toward me.

She's scowling at me, and she tosses her blond hair over her shoulder, revealing the soft slope of her throat. A throat I want to grab ahold of and wrap my fingers around.

"You can't be here," she whisper-yells, tossing a glance over her shoulder at Brittney. I give her a dazzling smile and wave at her. Aspen shoves at my shoulder, and a bolt of lightning zaps through me at her touch. "What the hell are you doing?"

I play stupid and look around the massive room. "What do you mean? This is a library. All students are welcome here."

Aspen shakes her head. "Nope, not you."

The smile slips off my face. I don't like how pushy she is about getting me to leave. It hits me then that it might be easier to go through Aspen to get to Brittney, which means I need to suck it up and strike some type of deal with her because I'm not going to stay out of the library when it's free to any student who wants to use it.

"It sounds like you might want to negotiate some type of deal."

Aspen peers up at me, blinking slowly. "I don't want to do any type of negotiating with you. Any deal I make with you is a loss for me."

I shrug. "It's not my fault your negotiating skills are shitty."

She rolls her eyes and takes a step closer to me. I can feel the heat of her body rolling off her and slamming into me. A light floral scent invades my senses, and the nearness of her body makes my cock rock hard. It reminds me that she still owes me an hour. I won't lie. I love having her in my debt.

"Please, Quinton. This is the only place in the entire university where I feel safe. Where I can be myself. Don't ruin that for me, please." Her voice takes on a slight edge, and I don't like the way the sound slices through me, making me feel a sliver of remorse.

I can't feel bad for her, even if none of this is her fault.

"That sounds like a *you* problem."

"Quinton," she whispers my name and then looks over her shoulder at Brittney, who is putting books away but still watching us out of the corner of her eye.

I lean into her face, and fire ignites deep in my belly as her pulse jumps, her pink tongue darting out over her bottom lip. "Say my name like that one more time, and I will have you on your knees with my cock in your mouth."

"Q, I'm serious."

"So am I." I grin devilishly.

"There has to be something you want more than tormenting me."

I almost laugh. "You don't want to know the things I want from you, Aspen. It would make your nightmares look like fairy tales."

Fear flashes over her eyes, but she quickly covers it up with an offer. "Fine, you can have another hour on top of the one I already *owe* you." She makes air quotation marks around the word owe. "Technically, I didn't agree to that deal in the first place. You just brought me stuff and demanded an hour."

"So you didn't eat the food then? I guess I can take it back and wipe your debt."

Her eyes widen a tiny bit in surprise. "Well, I ate it because I was starving. So are you taking the deal or not?"

"Not... seems like a shit deal. You want me to stay out of the library for the whole school year, but I only get one hour of your time? I want more than that... much more."

She visibly shivers. "I know I'm going to regret this later, but one hour, once a week, inside my room."

I rub at my jaw while considering her deal. "One hour, once a week. That still sounds like you're winning, and I'm losing."

Her little jaw tightens, and flames of fire flicker in her eyes. My cock grows harder. Even her anger turns me on.

"I'm not giving you more than that."

"Hmm... one hour, once a week, but I'm in charge the entire time. You have to do whatever I want without complaining."

"Fine, but you agree to stay out of here. You won't show up whenever you want and harass me. This will be my safe place. You promise?" Her face hardens as she looks up at me.

"I don't make promises, but I also don't go back on my word. You follow through on your end, and I'll follow through on mine."

"Deal, now get out." She pushes me backward, and while she barely moves me, I pretend I'm going to tip over.

"If you wanted to get physical, all you had to do was say so."

"Quinton," she growls.

I back away slowly. "It's okay. I'll save it for another day." I wink at her, and she glares.

It's funny how much she acts like she hates me, but when we're alone in her room, and it's just the two of us, she melts like butter in my hands. In a way, I'm giving us both a reprieve. I get one hour of control, and she gets one hour to let go and pretend we aren't enemies.

"Nice seeing you, Brittney," I call over to the librarian, looking past Aspen and straight at Brittney. Her eyes are narrowed like she's trying to figure me out. She never will, no one can. Not even I know what the hell I'm going to do next. I give her a little wave, which she doesn't return. Out of the corner of my eye, I can see Aspen begging me with her eyes to leave.

It might take some finessing, but I'm determined. I'll get the answer I need, regardless of whether or not my father wants me to have them.

24

ASPEN

By the time I reach my dorm room, I'm exhausted. I toss my books on the desk and strip out of my clothes and hop into the shower. The water takes forever to get warm, but once it does, I stand beneath the spray for ten minutes, unwinding. I barely made it through PE today, and history had me wanting to gouge my eyes out. Quinton never showed up for PE, and I didn't want to think about how that made me feel.

Matteo was there, though, and his watchful eyes were on me the entire time. He didn't say anything, but I know he wanted to. If I could get away with driving a knife straight into his chest, and if I was violent enough to do it, I would.

Giving myself time to relax, I slowly wash my hair and body and shave my legs. By the time I'm finished, the water is cold, and I step out, wrapping a scratchy towel around my body and a second towel around my hair.

I've just taken a step into my bedroom when the door flies open, and Quinton stumbles inside, his head bowed and his face hidden. His sudden appearance shocks me, and I stand there staring at his wobbling frame for a full second before I say anything.

"A knock would be appreciated every once in a while," I say, realizing a moment too late that I'm in nothing more than a towel and that I owe him one hour a week, which I haven't given him yet. I take a step back, and a shiver that acts more as a warning slithers down my spine.

"I'm pretty sure I've told you more than once your mouth will be your biggest downfall," Quinton sneers, his voice smoky, and when he looks up, I gasp at the sight of his face.

His lip is busted and bleeding, and his normal icy blue eyes are hazy like he's under the influence of something, which would explain the stumbling.

"What happened?"

He shakes his head. "Don't ask questions you don't want answers to, and believe me, you don't want me to answer this." Moving with lightning speed, he invades my space. His usual intense woodsy scent filling my lungs, followed by the smell of beer.

"You've been drinking," I squeak out just as his fingers skim the edge of my towel.

"Thank you, captain obvious, now lose the towel so I can fuck you. We've only got an hour."

I blink, trying to figure out when I ever agreed to fuck him. I did say one hour, whatever he wants, but I didn't think he would jump so fast into wanting sex.

"Look, Quinton," I start, but he's got the towel ripped away, his hand over my mouth, and my body pressed into the mattress beneath his before I can get another word out.

I'm held captive by his penetrating gaze.

He smiles down at me, his body pressing into mine roughly. His eyes are blazing; anger and defeat swim deep in the depths. With his hand still firmly over my mouth, all I can do is look at him and feel his rage threatening to spill out onto me.

"I don't care that you're a virgin. I don't care about anything, actually. I'm going to fuck you hard and fast. I don't want you to say a fucking word when I remove my hand. Do you understand me?"

The muscles in my stomach tighten, and anxious energy works its way through my body. I shake my head and plead with nothing more than my eyes. Quinton's brows pinch together, his anger mounting.

"What do you mean, no?" He pulls his hand away, though it's still in the air.

He's never hit me, and while I don't think he would, it's hard to trust him when he's sober, let alone drunk.

"You're drunk, and I'm... I'm not ready." I look away shyly, refusing to acknowledge that I'm stark-ass naked, and his rock-hard cock is digging into my thigh.

Laughter fills the room, but it's a mocking kind. "Did you not hear what I just said?" He growls. The palm of his hand comes down on my breast, the slap vibrates through my body, the sting registering somewhere in my mind. It doesn't really hurt and is more shocking than anything.

When he grabs my nipple between two fingers and twists it hard, pain follows.

"Stop," I hiss, and even though there is pain, there is also a small smoldering fire in my belly from the action.

"We both know you don't want me to stop." His eyes move down over my body, and he slaps a hand against my thigh. "Open your legs and keep them open while I undo my pants. If you close them, you won't like what happens."

The warning is clear: disobey, and you'll pay the consequences.

I swallow past a knot of fear in my throat. Maybe I can get him to come, and he'll leave me alone? I spread my legs apprehensively, watching him as he undoes his jeans and shoves them down his muscular thighs.

My heart beats out of my chest, and when his cock comes into view, my throat tightens. The thick mushroom head is an angry purple, and he's so hard he's standing at attention between my thighs. I'm not ready for him to take my virginity, even if he says it belongs to him.

"Quinton." I whimper when he grabs my thighs, his fingers digging into the flesh, and I know there will be bruises there tomorrow.

His hot stare is centered on my pussy, and he lifts his gaze, trailing it all the way up the length of my body. It's obvious what he is thinking and what he wants.

"Do you need me to gag you, or are you going to shut your

mouth?" His mood seems to be getting fouler, and I don't know how to handle him when he's like this. This isn't about control. There is something deeper here, something heartbreaking. Today isn't about controlling me and getting me to comply. Today is about hurting me and taking whatever he can get.

"Quinton, you said you wouldn't hurt me." I try to reason with him, but he shakes his head almost angrily. Pressing me against the bed with his still mostly clothed body, the head of his cock brushes against my entrance. I'm not wet enough for him, and I'm afraid he's just going to enter me without thinking, so I place my hands on his shoulders and give him a push.

The rageful expression he gives me turns me to ash, and he moves forward, his cock pressing into my entrance. Panic grips me by the throat, and pain spears my lower abdomen. I can't anticipate what will happen next.

Of all the times Quinton has taken from me, it's never felt like this. Even in those instances when he was in control, I still felt some form of power. I still felt that I was on the same level as him.

"You promised me one hour and said I could have whatever I wanted and do whatever I wanted. Are you going back on that promise? Because if you do, I'll take mine back too. I'll be in the library every day, and I won't stand in Matteo's way. Maybe I'll give him back the key card, and he can come to your room instead of me. Is that what you want?" The anger in his voice makes me pause. He's piss and vinegar, and I don't have it in me to fight back against him today.

I twist my head to the side to hide the tears building in my eyes, and I whisper, "No." The word comes out so soft I'm afraid he can't even hear me. "I just... I can't do this tonight. Please, Quinton, please."

As soon as I turn to face him, the tears fall, the wet drops slide down my cheeks in unison. I hate allowing him to see me this broken, but maybe that's what he needs. Maybe knowing his toy is broken will stop him from continuing forward tonight.

His beautiful lips curl with disgust, and he pulls away, running a hand through his silky black hair. I can see the rapid rise and fall of his chest. Feel his pain, and I wonder what happened today to make him this way?

He turns away from me and slams his fist into the brick wall beside the bed. The wall doesn't give, and Quinton pulls his hand away with a grimace. I sit up, ready to come to his aid, but choose not to when he turns on me.

With a snarl, he grabs me by the arm and pushes me down to my knees on the floor. The sudden movement makes me dizzy.

"This will be the one and only time I let you tap out. Don't ever ask me to stop again because I won't. Now suck my cock like you mean it. Prove to me that your mouth is better than your virgin pussy, or I'll change my mind and fuck you anyway."

All I can do is gulp.

I wet my lips, and Quinton spears his fingers through my hair. Pain lances across my scalp as he pulls me forward, holding me in place while he brings his cock to my lips.

He gives me no time to prepare and slips between my lips, a

ragged sigh filling the air as his cock hits the back of my throat, and I gag. I breathe through my nose and try to prepare myself for his next thrust. He pulls out and pushes back in again.

"Look at me while I fuck your throat. I want to see the tears as they slip down your cheeks." His grip on my hair tightens, and I do as he instructs, looking up at him through my lashes. I hate that I grow wet at the look of possession in his eyes.

He doesn't own me, not even a little bit, but this side of me wants him to. Holding me in place, he thrusts his hips forward, fucking my mouth and throat. Saliva dribbles out the side of my mouth with his quick movements, and my eyes water, the salty tears sliding down my cheeks without permission.

With pleasure in his eyes, he watches them, smiling like the devil while he continues using me as a source for his own demented satisfaction.

Just like in the hallway when he first forced me to do this, his focus is on me, and I can't look away, not even while knowing he is using me and that I mean nothing to him.

"Fuck, you look so gorgeous with my cock stuffed in your mouth. Maybe I'll do this more often since it seems your mouth is what gets you into the most trouble."

Anything I might say would be muffled, so I don't bother responding. Quinton smirks and pinches one of my nipples between his fingers. There is a tinge of pain, followed by pleasure that zings straight to my core. I'm ashamed to admit that I want him, even in those instances when I say I don't. Deep down, there is a twisted part of me that only he brings out, that wants him.

"Just like that. Take me deep..." He presses all the way into the back of my throat and holds himself there, and for a second, I can't breathe. Panic starts to bubble to the surface of my mind right as he pulls back, and I inhale oxygen deep into my lungs as he pulls out.

He does this over and over again, his own pleasure rising up until he's close to coming. Without warning, he pulls himself from my mouth and fists his cock in his hand. All I can do is watch, saliva dribbling down my chin and my heart racing. I don't care how I look right now. My only focus is watching Quinton reach the finish line.

"Watch me..." He grits the words through his teeth. I don't dare look away, and with a roar, he explodes. Hot ropes of cum land on my breasts, and a soft gasp escapes my lips at the contact. Quinton continues coming, stroking himself until he grows soft.

When he pulls away and sags against the wall, I push off the floor and walk into the bathroom to clean myself up. I grab a washcloth, wet it, and wipe myself down.

Then I clean my face and return to the bedroom to find Quinton stripped down to his boxers, lying on my bed. He can't seriously think he is going to have a sleepover.

I scurry across the room and grab a pair of panties and a shirt.

"I think you should leave," I say once I'm dressed.

The way he's lying on my bed, like he was meant to be there, makes me feel strange.

"I'm not done with you yet, so I'm not really sure why you

put clothes on. It's not like you'll be needing them for what we're going to do."

"Need I remind you, we only agreed to sex stuff one hour a week."

He rolls his eyes and pats the bed. "Rules were meant to be broken."

"You have your own room and I'm not comfortable with you being here. You can't sleep in here."

"I can sleep wherever I want, and just so you know, it's better if you don't let your enemy know the things that make you uncomfortable. They'll use it against you, every time."

"It's almost like you have experience in being someone's worst nightmare." I'm dragging my feet about crawling into bed with him. Quinton can't be trusted. He's a risk to my mind and body in more ways than one. I look around the room, trying to find a spot to sleep.

"Get in the bed and go to sleep, Aspen." Impatience drips off his lips.

"Thanks for giving me a choice."

"We're sleeping, nothing more. Now get in the bed, or I'll break the rules and fuck you right now."

"You know that doesn't make me feel any better."

"Aspen!" he growls, and against my better judgment, I walk across the room and climb onto the bed. Quinton moves over a bit, giving me enough room to lie down, but there is not enough room in a twin-sized bed to leave space between us. I grab the blanket from the end of the bed and pull it up over us.

"I just want you to know..."

Quinton interrupts me before I can finish my sentence. "Shut up, or I'll gag you."

I don't dare test that he'll do it. Instead, I press my head into my pillow a little harder and swallow my words. Silence settles around us. Even as anxious as I'm feeling right now, exhaustion wins out, and it doesn't take long for Quinton's body heat to envelop me, lulling me into darkness.

25

QUINTON

*B*efore I even open my eyes, I notice three things.

One, I'm warmer than normal in a cozy, comfortable way.

Two, I feel oddly rested as though I've slept longer than usual.

And three, everything hurts. There is a dull ache in my head, and my hand feels like I punched a concrete wall. Then I remember... I did.

Fuck.

I had no intention of drinking as much as I did or getting into a fight. Or coming here after. I didn't plan any of it, but I just couldn't take it any longer. The pain was too much, and I didn't care about the consequences. All I wanted was for the pain to stop.

One by one, memories from last night pop back into my head.

Nash passes me the bottle of bourbon that he, Ren, and I are drinking. My head is swimming with thoughts that refuse to go away. The weight of losing her is suffocating me. She's dead, and nothing will ever bring her back. I can't breathe or think. I'm barely functioning right now, and I don't know how to stop feeling everything I'm feeling. I want to shut it off. At the same time, I don't want to forget her. I don't want another day or minute to go by without her.

Nobody tells you that grief is like living two lives, one where you're forced to move on and go day by day living, and the other where your heart bleeds with every thump. A wound that will never heal.

"Let's play a game," Nash exclaims.

"Boo! Nobody likes your games," I slur, feeling the effects of the bourbon. The numbness that encompasses me is something I've craved for months.

"No, seriously, let's play. You get one hour alone with Anja or Aspen. Who you fucking?"

"That's easy. While Aspen is easy on the eyes and would probably be an easy lay. I bet she's a virgin. Plus, she's a rat. I'm not going to fuck the enemy, so I'm going with Anja," Ren explains.

Both Ren and Nash break out in laughter. My lips press into a firm line, and I decide I'm not even going to touch this one and instead take a huge gulp from the bottle of liquor. The brown liquid stopped burning a long time ago, but I can't tell if that's a good thing or a bad thing.

"What about you, Q, you fucking Aspen or Anja?" Nash questions.

Ren is smiling smugly from where he sits. He knows I'm a little infatuated with Aspen, but he has no idea how deep any of this goes.

"Neither," *I sneer and shove the bottle at Ren.*

The last thing I want to talk about is Aspen, not today, not when I should be remembering someone else, but again, maybe that's what I need. Maybe I need her right now, and I'm just too stubborn to admit it.

"What do you mean neither?" *Nash laughs.* "Rumor has it you've been seen near her dorm. Don't tell me you haven't fucked her yet."

"She's nobody."

"Really? That's not what I've heard."

I shove out of my chair, and it goes flying into the wall. My patience is gone, and the pain in my heart is making it hard for me to make rational choices.

Nash has a death wish. I'm sure of it.

"I don't care what you've heard."

He shrugs. "I mean, she's a rat, yes, but she is a hot piece. I'm not the only one who jerked off to her sucking your dick. I'm pretty sure every guy in this school has it by now. Let's be honest, a wet hole is a wet hole, am I right?"

I'm not sure what in that statement makes me snap, but like a rubber band being pulled tight, I sling across the table and grab Nash by the collar of his shirt.

"Dude, what the fuck," *he growls, and out of the corner of my eye, I see Ren standing, ready to break us up.*

"Shut up!" *I give him a shake, trying to restrain myself from punching him in the fucking face, but then he has to open his trap.*

"Calm down, man. If Aspen means nothing to you, why are you

acting like this?" After that, all hell breaks loose. I punch Nash in the face three times before he can get a jab in, and Ren is separating us, pushing me against the wall, telling me to calm down before I can really get him to shut his fucking mouth.

"This has nothing to do with Aspen. I just hate your fucking face. I want to drink in peace without you yapping in my fucking ear about some pussy!"

"Hurting other people won't bring her back, Q," Ren whispers into my ear.

My chest is heaving, and my heart is racing. I feel trapped, the numbness is receding, and I have to find another way to make the pain disappear.

Adela is gone. My sister is gone.

The events from last night make me groan internally. Slowly, I open my eyes, which are so dry my lids feel like sandpaper. I groan as the light from the bathroom hurts my eyeballs even though it's dim. I'm on my side, Aspen's back is flush to my front, and my arm is wrapped around her middle, holding her to me.

She tries to wiggle out of my hold, but I only pull her closer, not ready to let her go. "Where do you think you're going?"

"Away from you. You shouldn't be here."

"Who says?"

"Me, this is my room, and we said one hour a week. You've been here six hours."

"Six?" I look around the room and stop at the lit-up red numbers on Aspen's alarm clock. It reads 5:34 a.m., which means she is right. I've been here for about six hours, and what's even more surprising is that I've been asleep for most of that time. I don't remember the last time I slept for that many hours.

"Sleeping doesn't count. You sucked my dick for thirty minutes, so that's the only time that counts. I still have thirty minutes left for this week."

"That's not the deal we made, and you know it." She tries to shimmy out of my hold again. "Let me go."

"You're kind of cute when you think you're in charge. I told you last night that was your one and only veto. The only time I let you tap out. Stop me again, and the deal is off. You'll have to fend for yourself." It's an empty threat, but she doesn't know that.

Her body goes slack in my hold, and I know I have her right where I want. Like putty in my hand, she lets me turn her around to face me. I grab the hem of her shirt and pull it up her body, and she lifts her arms dutifully, letting me strip her bare.

I roll her onto her back and pull the flimsy panties down her slender legs before I chuck my boxers, getting rid of the last piece of fabric between us.

Lowering my body, I cover her like a blanket. My face is only inches from hers, and I take a moment to study her face. I'm so close, I can see every freckle on her nose, every variation of brown and green in her eyes, and every shade of pink spreading across her cheeks.

Her lips are pulled into a frown. She isn't happy, but she isn't scared like she was last night. Now more than ever do I thank the fucking universe I was able to stop myself.

I've done bad things, and I've taken a lot from Aspen, but nothing felt as bad as it did last night. Somehow, it felt different, worse, and something tells me if I had crossed that line, it would have broken her and etched a darkness into my soul I would have never been able to get rid of.

"Now spread your legs for me and keep them open. And don't look so miserable. If you behave, I'll make you come too." My offer only pours gas into the fire burning in her eyes.

The hazel color turns into a simmering ember, and I snake a hand between her legs and press two fingers inside her cunt. She isn't wet enough to make this a comfortable experience for the two of us, so I pull the digits out and focus my attention on her clit.

Staring into her eyes, I watch as her resistance to me crumbles while I stroke her clit, circling the bud over and over until I start to feel her arousal on my fingers. Straight white teeth sink into her bottom lip as she tries to stifle a moan of pleasure. Her lustful gaze clashes with my own.

Her body wants me even if her mind doesn't. Slipping a finger inside her, I find her wet and ready.

I can't help but smirk as I withdraw my finger once more and move to settle between her legs. My gaze moves between her thighs, and I almost growl while I line my cock up with her entrance. I can't wait to be inside her, to take her innocence and claim it as my own.

I work my way inside her slowly even though every fiber in my body screams for me to bottom out in one hard thrust, showing her who owns her and who she belongs to.

When I feel the resistance of her virginity giving way, her whole body tightens with a gasp, and her hands wrap around my biceps. I'm not sure if she's trying to push me away or pulling me in closer, but I don't mind the way her nails are digging into my skin. I welcome the pain because physical pain is always better than the alternative.

"Fuck, you're so tight," I hiss. "Relax a bit."

"You try to relax when something way too big is shoved up inside you," she snaps, making me chuckle.

"Is that your way of trying to tell me I have a big dick?"

"I hate you, and I hate this."

Dropping my head into the crook of her neck, I whisper into the shell of her ear, "Liar."

"Ugh," she grunts, digging her sharp nails deeper into my arms. "It fucking hurts."

"It will feel better next time." The reminder of the next time has all the different ways I'm going to fuck her running through my mind. Bent over the bed, taking her from behind, her riding my cock while I play with her tits, maybe while I finger her ass...

She whimpers, and I realize I've picked up speed in my excitement. I should probably slow down, but it feels so fucking good. How does she feel like this? Like she was made for me.

I could stay buried inside her forever, but I know she is actually hurting, and contrary to what she believes, I don't care for causing her physical pain. Luckily for her, it doesn't take long before I can feel the tingle at the base of my spine.

I thrust deep inside her a few more times before my balls

tighten, and I explode. My orgasm seems to go on forever, and by the time I come down from my high, I'm almost passed out again.

"Do you know how heavy you are?" Aspen's labored voice meets my ear, and only then do I realize I've let my entire weight settle on her small body.

I quickly push myself off the bed, slipping out of her cunt, making us both wince. Getting up from the bed a little too fast, I make a note to drink a shit load of water today when the room spins.

After the dizzy spell passes, I look down at the bed. Aspen hasn't moved. She is on her back with her legs spread, giving me a prime view of her swollen pussy that's leaking a mixture of my cum and her blood, both a reminder of what I just took from her and the fact that I didn't use a condom. Aspen must be reading my mind.

"Oh, god, you didn't use a condom!" She sits up, looking between her legs, then glaring up at me.

"Calm down. They tested everyone for diseases before we got here. We're both clean. Don't get up. I'm getting a washcloth." I turn to walk into her attached bathroom when she yells something at my back I wasn't prepared for.

"Quinton, I'm not on the pill!"

I stop dead in my tracks, my whole body freezing as her words slowly start to sink in. Fuck, how could I have been so careless?

"Did you hear me? I'm not on the pill. You can't come inside me. What if you get me pregnant?"

Pregnant...

That single word runs on an endless loop in the back of my mind as my limbs begin to unfreeze, and I'm able to make my way to the bathroom. Standing in front of the sink, I remember the thing is broken, but when I turn to the shower, there are a bunch of her clothes hanging out to dry. I slide some of the odd-smelling shirts to the side so I can reach into the shower stall and turn it on. I grab the washcloth and soak it in warm water before turning the shower off.

When I return to the room, Aspen hasn't moved. Her eyes follow every move I make. Carefully, I wipe between her legs with the wet washcloth, watching as the white fabric turns pink.

"Did you hear—"

"I heard you," I snap.

I don't know why I'm getting angry with her. This is on me. "Why is your stuff hung up in the bathroom, and why does it smell funny?" I ask, trying to change the subject.

She flops back down onto the bed, so she is flat on her back, and lets me clean her up. "The laundry people won't take my clothes, so I have to wash them in my shower, but I don't have laundry detergent, so I have been using hair shampoo. Until now at least, because I'm running out, and I would rather wash my hair than clothes."

"I'll get you more shampoo... maybe for an extra thirty minutes a week, I'll even have them do your laundry."

"Is that what you would do if you accidentally got me pregnant? Barter with me for everything? An extra hour for child support? Or would you just get rid of me altogether?"

"Shut up!" I bunch up the cloth in my hand and throw it across the room. She has no idea the nerve she just struck. I get back on the bed, and Aspen tries to jump out. I grab her and push her back onto the mattress.

Anger surges through me as my mind is running rampant. Is that how I came to be? Did my father sleep with the enemy? Did my father hate my birth mother, and did she hate him so much that she didn't want me?

"Quinton," she says like a prayer. A prayer for mercy.

I grab her throat with one hand, not squeezing but holding her firm enough to make her stop talking. Her hands come up, and her fingers wrap around my wrist. "I need you to listen carefully and do exactly what I say because right now, I'm on an edge you don't want me to go over. Do what I say, and I won't hurt you."

She nods slightly, fear pooling in the depth of her hazel eyes.

"I'm going to release you for a second, and you're to grab your ankles and spread your legs for me," I order.

She is hesitant, and I can feel her throat as she does her best to swallow down her fear. She slowly releases my arms, and a moment later, I release her throat and ease back, giving her room to move. Like a mouse that's afraid of getting caught in a trap, she moves hesitantly. When she has a firm grip on her ankles, I say, "Now, don't move."

Moving back into place, I wrap my hand around her delicate throat. My grip on her throat is loose, and I use my free hand to explore her body.

I trail my fingers down her breast and stomach slowly, drawing a shiver out of her when I get below her belly button. Gently, I run the tip of my fingers through her folds, drawing a whimper from her lips.

"Does this hurt?" I ask, my anger disappearing rapidly as she hands over control to me. When she shakes her head, I part her lips and press my thumb to her clit. Her eyes flutter closed, and her head tips back into the pillow.

I rub lazy circles over the small bundle of nerves until her back arches off the bed, and her breathing is labored. She keeps her eyes closed the whole time, probably not wanting to see who is bringing her pleasure like this. She still won't admit that part of her wants me.

Her face is flush, and a hue of red is spreading out across her chest and cheeks, the same beautiful shade of pink of her cunt at the moment.

Keeping pressure on her clit with my thumb, I use my finger to fuck her pussy with gentle strokes. I can still feel my cum inside her, which has my dick going hard all over again.

Leaning down, I take one of her nipples between my lips and suck on it. That's what drives her over the edge. Her whole body arches off the bed, pushing her tit into my mouth. Her pussy contracts around my finger as a strangled moan falls from her lips.

By the time she comes down from her high, her eyes are closed, and her body is slack. I'm half a second away from flopping down beside her and pulling her back into my hold, but I know that's a terrible idea. I can't stay here any longer. Ren is probably wondering where the hell I am, and I hate lying to him.

Spending the night in Aspen's room is going to raise enough questions as it is. Staying past breakfast is going to be unexplainable.

I pull my finger out of her and get off the bed. She immediately rolls to her side and tucks her legs up like she is going back to sleep. I take her bare, thoroughly fucked body in for another few minutes before I tear myself away. She murmurs something inaudible as I pull the blanket over her naked form.

I dress quickly and leave her room quietly. On my way to my room, I check my phone, which already has twelve messages from Ren.

Fuck me.

26

ASPEN

I hate everything and everyone today. Sunshine, puppies, butterflies, and rainbows. All of it can get tossed in a blender.

I'm ready to post a craigslist ad: **Uterus for sale.**

The only good thing about having my period is that I know I'm not pregnant with Quinton's child. Jesus, just the thought of the shitstorm that would set loose has a shiver running down my spine.

The things he's done to me and made me do are something that I want to forget, not something I want to build a life on, and it's definitely not anything I want to bring another innocent life into.

Even the people in the hallway seem to pick up on my murderous mood since no one *accidentally* runs into me on my way back to my room. I swipe my key card and push the door open, ready to curl up on my bed, when I find another bag sitting on my mattress.

This time I handle it less carefully, knowing that it's from Quinton and trusting him a tiny bit more now. Pulling it open, I find a bottle of shampoo as well as a bottle of conditioner inside. On the bottom, I discover a bunch of granola bars and even a few candy bars mixed between.

I'm not even that surprised he brought this. What is surprising is the note pinned at the top of the bag.

THIS ONE IS FOR FREE.
Don't get used to it.

-Q

FREE? Nothing is free. I know that better than anyone. My brain tells me not to touch any of this stuff, but my stomach tells me to eat everything in sight before someone takes it away from me.

My mouth waters just looking at the candy bars, and I already know there is no way I'm giving this back. Especially not today out of all days. Opening the bottle of water, I dig out some Advil from my nightstand drawer and swallow three pills. While I let them kick in, I curl up on my bed and unwrap one of the chocolate caramel bars.

The first bite is the best. Closing my eyes, I moan as the chocolate goodness hits my taste buds. The gooey caramel sticks to the roof of my mouth, and I want it to stay glued on there forever. I don't even chew. I just let it dissolve in my mouth, sucking on the chocolate, wanting to draw out the taste.

Mmm...

"That good, huh?"

My eyes fly open in shock as I realize someone is in the room. I sit up straight and hold on to the candy bar like I'm about to use it as a weapon.

"Calm down, killer." Quinton chuckles, flopping down on the bed beside me like he owns the place. "What's in that chocolate that makes you moan like that?"

My heart is still racing from the shock of him appearing out of nowhere when he grabs the bar from my hand and takes a bite.

He takes a fucking bite out of MY candy bar!

"What's the big deal? Tastes normal." He shrugs, inspecting the bar like he is trying to solve a puzzle.

I don't think. I simply act.

"You fucking asshole!" I scream at him seconds before I swing my fist into his upper arm as hard as I can manage. My hope was to hurt him, even if it's just a little bit. Instead, pain shoots from my knuckles all the way up my forearm. "Ow!" I yelp, cradling my hand.

What the hell is his arm made of? Fortified steel?

We both pause, staring at each other in shock.

"Did you just hit me?" he asks like he can't believe his eyes.

"You took my chocolate!" I defend.

His eyebrows pinch together, and his gaze bounces from me to the candy in his hand to the Advil on my nightstand.

"Ahhh, makes sense now. You're on your period." He hands me back the chocolate, and I snatch it from his hold. "I'll give you this one pass, but if you hit me again, I'll hit you back. I don't care if you're a girl. Don't fucking hit me."

I'm not even scared of his threat today. It's not that I don't believe him. I just don't care about anything right now. "Don't take my food, and I won't have a reason to use violence. Now, please leave. As you already guessed right, I'm on my period. I'm grumpy and in pain. I don't have a heating pad or a bathtub to soak in, and the Advil hasn't kicked in yet, so please, for the love of everything, get out and let me eat my chocolate in peace."

"No."

"No? I'm not having sex with you."

"I didn't say I was here for sex, did I?"

"That's literally the only reason you come to my room. Why else would you be here?"

"Okay, you've got a point there. I did come for sex, but I'm not interested in making a mess or hearing you whine the entire time."

"Could you be any more of an asshole?"

"Yes, I actually could. Do you want me to be?"

"Ugh..." I curl onto my side, facing away from him, and close my eyes. "Please, Q. Just leave me alone," I whine, not caring how pitiful I sound. I bring the chocolate to my mouth and start sucking on the end like it's a pacifier. Closing my eyes, I pretend Q isn't here and will the pain meds to work faster.

"I also came to give you this." I feel him throw something light on top of my blanket. When I open my eyes, I spot a small round pill dispenser.

"What the hell is this?"

"Birth control. You're gonna take one pill every day, starting today. Instructions are on the back."

"You can't be serious." I'm dumbfounded. "Wait, how did you even get this?"

"It doesn't matter how I got it. What matters is that you will be a good girl and take it every day. You were the one freaking out about pregnancy. You should thank me."

I almost snort. Shaking my head at him, I close my eyes again. I don't even have the energy to fight him on this. Plus, he is right. I don't want to get pregnant, and it's not likely he is going to stop fucking me.

"You know... I have a bathtub in my room."

"Great for you, and thanks for rubbing it in."

"What I meant was, I could let you use it," he offers, but I already know it's going to come with a catch. "For a price, of course." And there it is.

I don't answer right away, even though I know I should say no. But the thought of soaking in a hot bubble bath, soothing my back pain and stomach cramps, has my brain shutting off.

Against my better judgment, I ask, "What do you want?"

"I want you to tell me about your friend Brittney, the librarian." His question is one I did not expect. Why the hell does he want to know about Brittney?

"Why?"

"Because she clearly doesn't like me, which makes her my enemy, and I like to keep my enemies close. You might have already noticed that."

"So let me get this straight. The whole reason you and everybody else here hates me is because you think I'm a rat. Over and over again, you have told me to keep my mouth shut and not talk about anything and anyone, but now you want me to give you information on my friend?"

"I'm not asking you to give me any secret information or anything that could get her in trouble. I just like to know everything there is to know about my enemy just in case they ever attack me. And I don't know if you have noticed how Brittney looks at me, but if she's ever given the chance, she'll drive a knife into my back before I know it."

"Well, I can tell you something about her right now. I'm pretty sure she is the only decent person in this whole place. The only one who treats me like a human being, and the only reason she doesn't like you is because she knows you want to hurt me. She's a friend. I know the term might be foreign to you, so I'll explain it. A friend is a person who cares about your well-being, who protects and appreciates you, and who does all of it asking for nothing in return."

"I know what a friend is. I have many. I just don't wanna be yours."

I blame it on my period, but his comment hurts more than

it should. Of course, he doesn't want to be my friend. No one here does. It doesn't make it hurt any less, especially after giving him my virginity, and I'm using the term *give* here lightly since taken would be more appropriate. The need to lash out at him overwhelms me.

"I hate to burst your bubble, but you don't have any friends either. You have people who fear your father and who are nice to you because they want something. Do you really think any of these people here care about you as a person? Because I don't. At least I have one friend, a real friend. You have none, and knowing the way you are, I don't think you ever will."

In a flash, he is on me, his nose pressed against mine as he breathes through it like a bull ready to charge. The closeness of his body makes me dizzy.

"I'll let your mouthy-ass attitude slide since you're having a bad day but say one more thing that pisses me off, and I don't give a fuck if you have your period or not. I'll fuck your asshole and make that bleed too."

"I hate you," I growl directly into his face, though I'm grateful he takes a step back, putting some much-needed space between us. I can't think properly when he's around, and that terrifies me. He terrifies me.

"Good. At least you feel something for me." He grins, and I swear I could get whiplash from how fast his moods change sometimes.

"Where are you going?" I ask before I can stop the words from coming out.

He pauses, his hand on the doorknob. He doesn't look back

at me as he speaks. "Leaving. You don't want to fuck, and you aren't willing to share anything about Brittney, so I have no reason to be here."

I feel slimy, used, and when he opens the door a moment later, I let him walk out. I guess, in a way, it's better that he makes me feel like shit because if he didn't, I'd have this false sense of hope that things might work out differently. They won't; they never do. I'm a release to him, and he's a protector for me. Nothing else but those things matter, and I need to remember that. Good thing he's plenty good at reminding us both.

27

QUINTON

The cold Alaskan air whisks around us while we wait on the side of the helicopter pad for our families to arrive. Thank god, my busted lip healed up in time. I didn't want Scarlet to see it and think something bad had happened. Not that she hadn't seen a bruised lip or black and blue eye a time or two. I was more worried about explaining myself to her.

After being cooped up underground most of the time, I appreciate the sun on my skin even though the cold is seeping through my thick jacket and into my bones.

Ren is standing beside me, staring straight ahead into the vast forest surrounding us.

"You think someone could survive out there?" he asks, never taking his eyes off the forest.

I shrug. "Sure, with the right gear."

"What about right now? What if we were to be dropped off

dead in the center with nothing more than what's on us at the moment. You think we would survive?"

I make a quick check of what I'm wearing and what's in my pockets. A knife is tucked away in my boot, but besides that, I have nothing on me. My clothes are warm enough for now, but probably not to survive a night. I'd have to build a shelter, definitely a fire, plus hunt for food, but I think I could manage.

"We could make it, but I really hope that's just theoretical because I hate the cold."

"Same." Ren chuckles. "And yes, theoretical. Not planning on going on a survival trip any time soon."

We both look up simultaneously when the sound of an approaching helicopter fills the air. We hear them a few minutes before the helicopter breaks through the thick cloud, descending to where we are rapidly. The mirth that fills my chest cavity at the appearance of that helicopter is astounding. I'm more afraid now than I've ever been about losing Scarlet or my parents, and flying on a plane to Alaska would be the perfect opportunity for one of our enemies to swoop in.

Thankfully, my fears are just that, *fears,* and the helicopter lands smoothly at the center of the helipad. Not even a second later, the door opens. My father gets out first, his graying hair whipping around as he helps my mother out of the helicopter. As soon as her feet touch the ground, she looks up, her eyes darting around until they zero in on me.

Not many people are out here, waiting for their families to arrive, but there are enough for us to behave a certain way. We learned at a young age that we have to keep affection to a minimum in public, which is probably what my father is whispering into Scarlet's ear right now after she basically jumped out of the helicopter and into his arms. He sets her down in front of him and straightens her jacket, then waves her off like she is a perpetual child.

For all the hate I harbor for my father, this is one thing I can't hold against him. Even though he acts like this in public, he's always treated my sisters with nothing but love when we are inside the comfort of our home. Ren's family does the same, but I know for a fact, others are not that lucky.

Scarlet and my mother keep their heads bowed as they trail my father while walks toward us. Ren simply nods to them and makes his way toward the helicopter to greet his parents, Roman and Sophie, and his sister, Luna.

"Quinton," my father greets me, but I don't respond. All I want to do is hug the two women behind him, but I force myself not to and turn and start walking away from them.

"I'll show you where you will be staying."

I don't look back, knowing they are following me, and I feel my father's gaze at the back of my head. As we pass other students along the way, their eyes go wide. Some take a step back, cowering at my father's presence, while others simply stand in place frozen with fear. No one says anything. There are no greetings or pleasantries, and I'm fucking glad for it.

All families are staying at the top part of the university, in the castle part that has been rebuilt to house any guests the school might have as well as host large gatherings and parties. It's only a short walk from the helicopter pad to the castle. We use one of the partly underground tunnels that weaves through the mountain. The top is mostly glass, giving us a riveting view of our surroundings, though I can't enjoy any of it at the moment.

Silently, we walk through the entryway of the castle and up the staircase leading into a large hallway. I walk them to the end of the hall, where a set of double doors lead into the suite they will be staying in.

I unlock it with the key card I was given earlier and push open the heavy doors. "This is where you will be—"

I don't get the words out before a small body slams into my side, and thin arms wrap around my middle.

"I missed you," Scarlet murmurs into my jacket.

She's much smaller than me, the top of her head barely reaching my chest, but her grip on me is surprisingly strong, like a tiny monkey who can't be shaken off.

"I missed you too." I kiss the crown of her head and wrap my arms around her.

Out of the corner of my eye, I see my mom walking up to us, tears already forming, clinging to her long black lashes. I hold open one of my arms, and she falls into us.

We stay in our three-way hug for a few minutes. No one wants to let go. My father walks past us, scanning the suite like he's looking for anything that could harm us. Of course, that was already done, but nothing is good enough for him, especially when it comes to his family.

When we do finally break the hug, Scarlet jumps into a frenzy of questions immediately.

"Where do you sleep? Where are your classes? Are the dorms far from here, and can I look at them? Is there only the one cafeteria? What kind of food do they serve? Do they have the kind of tea I like? Did you make any friends?"

"Slow down. I'll give you a tour later. Yes, there is only one cafeteria, but they have pretty much everything you could want, including tea."

"Yeah, but is it the one I like?" She wrinkles her nose at me.

"Yes, they have all the food you like," I assure her.

"You look tired. Are you getting enough sleep?" My mom pipes in, concern etched into her voice. Lifting her head, she runs her fingers across my forehead and into my hair like she did when I was little. Only now, she has to reach up instead of down since I've been taller than her for a few years now.

"Yes, I sleep," I give her a washed-down answer.

The truth is the only time I slept well and through the night was when I was in Aspen's bed with my body wrapped around hers. I keep telling myself it's because I was drunk, but I've been drunk before and still didn't sleep.

She frowns at me, knowing that I'm not being truthful with her, but luckily, she lets it go... for now, at least. I'm sure this is not the last I'll hear of it.

"I'm also curious to see where you and Ren are staying. Will you show us the dorms now?"

The thought of me walking them through the dorms and possibly running into Aspen has my anxiety peaking. I need to stay as far away from her as I can with my father being here.

"Don't you want to rest first before I show you around?"

"Rest?" Scarlet asks as if I just proposed the most ridiculous thing in the world. "Do you have any idea how excited I have been and how long I've been waiting for today? Resting is the last thing on my mind. I want to see everything." Her excitement is almost infectious.

"Fine, I'll show you around. You won't need your jackets; everything is underground and heated."

Everyone, including me, gets rid of their outerwear, and we head back out. I show them the rest of the castle before leading them to the classrooms and the cafeteria.

The entire time I'm on edge, walking a very thin tight rope. Scarlet and Mom are too excited to notice, but of course, nothing slips past my father. The tension between us is even thicker than normal, and it only grows as the day goes on.

When we get to the dorms, Scarlet is beaming with excitement while I'm sweating bullets, having a small heart attack every time I see a blond girl come around the corner. I'm not sure what my dad is gonna do when he sees her, but I know it's not going to be good, and I won't be able to protect her from him.

I open my room with my key card, and we're immediately greeted with voices coming from inside. Ren, Roman, Sophie, and Luna are all piled on the large L-shaped couch.

"There you guys are," Roman greets and pushes off the couch.

He comes over to me and slaps a hand on my back in greeting. He is the only one in our extended family who is actually taller than me. As the story goes, he used to be an underground fighter, entering fights for money where only one person exits the ring. Even looking at him now, as his age is showing, it's no surprise that he won every time.

Luna and Sophie come over and greet me next, while Ren is greeted by Scarlet and my parents. The room suddenly starts to feel smaller.

"I love this apartment. Can I stay here tonight?" Scarlet asks.

I shrug, unsure if this is a good idea. I would like to have my sister here, but I don't know if my father will allow it. Seeing my apprehension, she turns to my parents.

"Please, it's been forever since I've seen Quinton, and you can't tell me there is a safer place than this apartment."

"I don't know," my father starts, but my mom cuts him off.

"Q and Ren will both be here, and in two years, she'll be here in her own apartment. I don't think it's a bad idea. Plus, then we'll have the suite to ourselves." She smiles, and Scarlet fake gags. My parents' love story is one for the books. If there has ever been a person to bring my father to his knees, it's my mother. However, that doesn't mean I want to hear them talk about fucking.

"Luna is staying here as well," Sophie chimes in, thankfully.

My father looks back and forth between Ren and me, his gaze penetrating. "You know the rules, and you also know if anything happens to your sister—"

"Nothing will happen to her, not here, not ever," I interrupt.

"Fine." He turns to Scarlet, who is ready to jump out of her skin. "You need to check in with me every few hours, and do not go anywhere without your brother."

Scarlet nods, her smile growing with every passing second.

"Then it's settled. You can stay." A smile breaks across my father's lips, and the tension in the air eases.

"Yay! I'm even more excited now. I can't wait for the ball, though. I want to meet all your friends." *Friends?* I don't have the heart to tell her I haven't made any friends, unless you count what Aspen and I are doing as being friends. Which I don't.

"Ren told me he has no date to the ball. What about you, Q? Are you taking someone?" Luna asks curiously.

"If it wasn't for you guys being here, I wouldn't go to the stupid ball in the first place. So no, I'm not planning on bringing anyone else just to bore them to death."

"Nonsense," my father interjects, and I can tell from the gleam in his eyes whatever he is going to say isn't going to be something I want to hear. "It will be good for business. I'll find someone for you to take."

Great. Just when I thought this couldn't get any worse, I've gone and stuck my fucking foot in my mouth.

"I'll sleep on the couch," Scarlet insists. "You can sleep in your bed."

"Okay." I smile, handing her a pillow and a blanket.

I watch as she makes her bed on the couch and crawls under the blanket, wearing pajamas covered in pink hearts and little owls. I already know she's gonna come and crawl into my bed, but I'll let her have her way. She hates sleeping in places she doesn't know, and every time we are someplace new, she ends up in my bed, not wanting to sleep alone.

I've told her many times just to come and sleep in my bed, but every time, she insists that it will be different now and that she is not a little girl anymore.

I'll believe it when I see it. "All right, good night. I'll see you in the morning."

"Good night." She smiles at me, pulling the blanket up to her chin.

Luna and Ren are already in bed, and Luna had no trouble admitting she wanted to sleep in her brother's room.

Walking into my room, I get ready for bed as well, brushing my teeth and stripping out of my clothes down to my boxers before I climb into bed.

Looking up at the ceiling, I lie awake in bed for so long I wonder if Scarlet actually did fall asleep on the couch. That idea is proven wrong when the door cracks open, and Scarlet tiptoes into my room.

I can't hide a grin when she climbs into my bed and slips under the blanket, settling on the other side of the bed.

"What if I wake up in the middle of the night and don't know where I am in my sleepy brain. It would probably freak me out."

"Yeah, probably."

"Then I would be screaming and waking up everyone. I just don't want to wake you guys up in the middle of the night."

"That's very considerate of you. Just don't snore so loud."

"I do not snore!" Scarlet whisper-yells.

We both chuckle, knowing that she does snore even though it's only a cute, quiet snore that I may have recorded on my phone before to tease her with. The room falls into silence after a while, and I close my eyes, trying to get at least a few hours of sleep.

"I miss her." Scarlet's small voice cuts through the quiet night.

"Me too," I admit.

I hardly think about Adela, let alone talk about her. It just hurts too badly, and it's easier to pretend she isn't dead. Like she's gone on a vacation and will return home when she's ready.

"This is the first time we're together somewhere without her, in public, I mean. Someone is going to ask questions, don't you think? What are we going to tell people when they ask why she's not here?"

"I don't know." I have no fucking clue. "We have to tell people at some point. I don't know why Dad is so adamant on keeping it a secret."

"Maybe because telling people will make it real..."

It's already real, I want to tell her, but I bite my tongue. I still don't know if that's my father's reason, but I do know Scarlet has a point. People will wonder where Adela is, and I am not sure how to answer that.

I'm not sure if I want to answer it either.

28

ASPEN

For the past week, everyone has been talking about the upcoming founders' ball. A few years ago, I would've shared their excitement, but now, I could throw up just thinking about it. Not that I don't like the idea of a party—dancing and food. It's the people I know will attend that have me curled up in a ball of nerves and anxiety.

As far as I know, most parents have flown in to see their kids and celebrate the tenth anniversary of opening the school. Of course, my mother has already emailed me about her regretfully declining the invite, which is not surprising at all. I didn't expect her to come.

Still, a part of me wishes she would. No matter how much she gets on my nerves. She is still my mom, and I want her to be there for me. I want her to want to see me. I want her to want me safe and happy.

Wishful thinking, I know.

More than ever, I hide out in my room, even skipping classes so I won't have to go out. I go to the cafeteria super early in the morning before most students make their way to breakfast. Then I go a second time between lunch and dinner. That way, I miss everyone, and so far, that includes the Rossis.

Today is the big day, the founders' ball is happening tonight, and the dorm halls are buzzing with people getting ready, even though it's still hours before it starts. I have to be the only one not excited about this event. I don't plan on going anywhere tonight. I've already stocked up on books, so I have plenty to read.

I've settled into my bed, snuggled beneath the covers, and halfway through the third chapter of the book Brittney told me I had to read when there's a knock on the door.

Startled, I drop the book into my lap and nearly jump out of the bed. I stare at the door like it's my enemy. Who knocks on my door? No one... at least, not usually. The only person who comes to my room has a key and wouldn't be caught dead knocking.

Something in the back of my mind tells me not to open the door, but curiosity killed the cat, and I'm the stupid cat getting up to open the door. My hand shakes as I grab the handle and twist it, opening the door.

All the air stills in my lungs when I see who is standing on the other side. My blood runs cold as I take in the large frame of the man, his black hair is graying, and his face looks weathered, somehow, ten years older than from the last time I saw him. But even his age doesn't take away how scary he looks. I know he could kill me in an instant, snap my neck like he was tying his shoe.

"Hello, Aspen. Are you going to invite me in?" Xander Rossi asks like we're old friends.

"I don't think that's a good idea."

"Stupid girl," he murmurs.

Of course, Xander Rossi doesn't need an invitation and pushes into my room, almost knocking me down to the ground in the process.

"What do you want?" I grit through my teeth.

"I just came to check on the daughter of an old friend," he explains casually, his eyes darting around the room inspecting the contents. "Are you settling into the university nicely?"

"Yes, this place is lovely," I reply sarcastically, "and everyone is so welcoming. It's very nice. Five stars, I would recommend it."

"I'm glad to hear you love it here. Lucas assured me that your accommodations here were adequate. I can see he was right. This place suits you."

Instead of giving him a witty remark, I grind my teeth together and dig my nails into my palm. Provoking him is only going to get me hurt.

"I heard you weren't coming to the ball tonight."

"I didn't think anyone would want me to attend," I say. "I wouldn't want to show up somewhere I'm not welcome."

"Of course, you are welcome there. I encourage all the students to come. And as luck would have it, I already have a date for you. He'll be here at seven to pick you up."

Dumbfounded, I stare at him, wondering where the hell this is going to go. Nothing Xander does is without a plan, and his plan, whatever it is, isn't going to be in my favor. Like I said, no matter what, I'm on the losing side, always.

"I can't," I object. "I don't have a dress." It's a lame excuse, but I hope it will be enough.

"I figured you wouldn't, which is why I already ordered you one. It should be here in time. So be ready at seven. I'll see you at dinner."

He stops at the door, looking at me over his shoulder. "Do not disappoint me, Aspen. You don't want to see me disappointed." He lets the threat hang in the air for a few seconds before adding, "I expect you to be there."

With that, Xander leaves my room, closing the door behind him without another word. I stand there for another moment with my mouth hanging open, trying to make sense of the whole situation. One thing is clear, the apple didn't fall far from the tree at all. Quinton definitely learned how to threaten people from his father.

The real question is, why the hell would he want me to go? And who is he sending as my date? Does Q know about this?

Ugh, I hate everything about this.

I know this is a trap. I just don't know how to get out of it.

While I still plot how not to make an appearance tonight, I look through my closet to see what I could wear. Xander said he'll send me a dress, but that is definitely not something I'm going to count on. I didn't even bring high heels. The fanciest shoes I own are black flats with a tiny bow on top. I guess that will have to do. The only dress I could possibly wear is an emerald-green sweater dress. Either way, I will stick out like a sore thumb at this party. Not that I need anything else to add to the giant bull's-eye on my back.

As I wait for the day to pass, my mind is too busy to get back into a book, no matter how much I wish I could escape reality. I spend the time on YouTube watching tutorials on how to curl up hair without a curling iron.

I end up using napkins and roll up my damp hair that way. Then I gather all the makeup I have, which is not a lot, and start applying it to my face until I look somewhat presentable.

Checking the time, I realize it's already six o'clock. I only have one hour left and still have no plan in place to get out of this. Another knock on the door almost has me falling out of my chair. Last time I opened the door, it turned out terrible, but Xander did say he was going to send a dress, so maybe that's who that is.

Hesitantly, I get up and walk to the door, opening it slowly. One of the maids is standing on the other side, holding a big box out in front of her.

"I'm supposed to drop this off here." She gives me a nervous smile, shoving the box closer to me. I open the door all the way and hold out my hands. The maid briefly glances at my napkin-rolled-up hair but doesn't comment. I'm sure I look quite ridiculous with this hairdo.

"Oh. Okay, thank you." As soon as the box is in my hands, the maid spins around and walks away from me like she can't get away fast enough.

I close the door and carry the box to my bed, where I open the lid slowly to peek inside. I'm still not fully convinced that this isn't a joke, and something won't be jumping out at me any moment. At first glimpse, all I see is a silky red fabric.

I drop the lid onto the floor so I can inspect the entire contents of the box. I pick up the corners of the red fabric and lift the dress up, finding a pair of stilettos on the bottom of the box. It's a little bit more flashy and revealing than what I would normally wear, but other than that, it's actually a pretty dress.

I strip out of the sweater dress I'm wearing and slip on the red dress Xander sent. Surprisingly, it fits perfectly. The only problem I have is that the bra is showing since the dress itself is completely backless. I'm not really comfortable going without a bra, but I don't think there's going to be a way around it.

Stepping into the shoes that came with the dress, I notice how they match perfectly, and I can't help but wonder who actually picked this out.

I doubt Xander has this kind of fashion sense.

All dolled up and ready to go, I sit on the edge of the bed and wait for the clock to turn to seven. With every passing minute, the feeling in my gut that something terribly bad is happening tonight grows. The worst part of it all is that I'm actually hoping for Quinton to walk in. I could never get so lucky.

A part of me waits for the familiar clicking of the lock when he swipes his key card and walks into my dorm room. It never comes. Instead, another knock fills the room, and my stomach sinks even lower.

I open my door for the third time today, even though I want to do anything but that. This time, I find someone on the other side I did not expect—someone I loathe. Someone I wouldn't touch if he was the last person on the planet.

"Well, hello, Aspen. I see you dressed up for me." Matteo gives me a mischievous smile. "Are you ready to go, or do you need help with the dress?"

"One, I didn't dress up for you. Two, I'm only going because I'm forced to. Three, if you even think about touching me with your slimy fingers, I will cut your dick off in your sleep."

"That's a bold threat for a rat like you. You hide out in your room all day, too scared of your own shadow, but you expect me to believe that you will come and find me at night to break into my room?"

I hate that he is right almost as much as I hate him.

Shoving past him, I walk into the hallway on shaky legs. I'm used to walking in high heels, but the anger and fear I'm feeling right now leave me on shaky ground. Matteo holds his arm out as if there is a world where I would actually take it.

I glare at him, and he shakes his head. "Suit yourself. I hope you trip and fall on your face."

"I hope you trip and fall onto a sharp knife."

"Oh, that mouth of yours, it's just begging to be stuffed with my cock."

I walk away from him, hoping that he's not going to follow closely, but of course, that would be too much to ask. He catches up to me with ease, walking beside me the entire way to the ballroom of the castle.

A tiny part of me had hoped that I could somehow blend in tonight and not be the center of attention. When we enter the lavishly decorated ballroom, I know right away that blending in won't be possible.

"I guess no one told you that this was a black and white ball." Matteo chuckles, amused with himself.

"I like being different," I lie, trying to play off my ever-growing distress.

Every pair of eyes is on me as we enter the large space. All the men wear black tuxedos while most of the women wear white dresses. You would think I would be used to the sneers and glares by now. But the truth is, I'm more uncomfortable now than I have ever been.

Just when I thought it couldn't get any worse, Matteo grabs me by the hand and leads us to a table. It's one of the larger tables that seats about fifteen people. At the very head of the table sits Xander, his wife, Ella, next to him, and Quinton on the other side. I glance at the blond girl sitting beside Quinton, expecting Adela or Scarlet to have that spot, but instead, I find Anja from PE class smiling back at me like she just won the lottery. Another man sits beside Anja, and I consider the fact he might be her father, but then Matteo speaks beside me.

"Hello, Father," he greets. The man looks up from his phone, and the first thing I notice about him is his pointed nose and the gleam of hate in his eyes.

He brushes a few strands of gray hair from his face. His frame and features are intimidating.

"Please, have a seat." Xander waves at the empty chairs,

dragging my attention back to the dinner. "I'm so glad you could make it. Though that's a very interesting choice of dress, Aspen."

"Sorry, I missed the memo that it was a black and white ball."

"I'm shocked they allowed her here. She should be locked up just like her father." Matteo's father speaks like I'm not sitting right here. I stop myself from rolling my eyes and purposely take the chair not next to Ella, leaving a space between us.

As I take a seat, I make sure the dress doesn't show my boobs as I move around.

The only person wearing something more revealing is Anja, who might as well have come naked. Her see-through white dress isn't leaving much to the imagination. I look around, wondering where Anja's parents are since it seems Matteo's father came.

Maybe they couldn't make the trip from Russia. That seems like a stupid excuse, but I'm not about to ask her where they are. Maybe hers are as shitty as mine?

Matteo takes the seat beside me and attempts to slide his hand up the apex of my thigh. I slap it away without looking, scanning the table for a knife that I can stab him with.

"I didn't think you would be here," Quinton whispers, demanding my full attention.

I haven't dared to look at him, and when I do, I know exactly why. His penetrating stare has a shiver running down my spine, and tonight there is an edge to him. He is angry, but I don't know if he's angry with me or the situation. I'm sure I will find out later.

Looking away from him, I finally notice who else is sitting at the table. On the other end, Roman Petrov sits at the head, his wife, Sophie, on one side, and Ren and his sister, Luna, on the other side. Scarlet is next to Luna, but I don't see Adela anywhere.

That's weird. Where would she be? Maybe she decided not to come, but that's unlikely. Unless she knew Matteo would be here. Maybe she knew and made an excuse not to come. I doubt she ever told her father or Quinton about that night. Or maybe she did, and they just didn't care.

Appearances are everything when you're in the mob. I'm so curious about where she is that I almost ask but stop myself at the last second, knowing better.

Once I'm settled, everyone starts to chat about random stuff. Anja is telling Ella about class while Xander stands up, along with Matteo's father, and greets some arriving guests.

Ren talks to his father about some fighting techniques while Luna and Scarlet chat about coming to school here in a few years.

The only person who remains quiet is Quinton, who ping-pongs his murderous glare between Matteo and me. If looks could kill, both of us would be dead by now. Anja leans over to whisper into his ear a few times, her hand running casually over his upper arm.

Unwanted jealousy weasels its way into my gut, and only then does it dawn on me that Quinton could possibly feel the same. Is that why he's so angry? Is he jealous? As soon as the idea enters my mind, it floats away like a cloud on a stormy day. There's no way he would be jealous, not of Matteo, not of anyone. He doesn't care about me in any sense of the word. If anything, he is jealous that someone else is touching his toy.

To him, I am a physical object—nothing more or less.

Lost in thought, I almost don't notice the gentle touch on my leg. When I look down, I find Matteo's hand once more, inching to the inside of my thigh. It's official; he really wants me to kill him. Furious anger ripples through me, and I slap his hand away, ready to land a slap to his face as well. Matteo smiles, literally smiles, like a fucking psychopath. Slowly, he leans into my side, and I inch away until it feels like I'm going to fall off my chair.

His voice is so low only I can hear it. "Mark my words, Aspen, by the end of the night, I will fill all three of your holes, one by one."

Not if I can help it.

"You can try but *mark my words.* If your dick comes anywhere near one of my holes tonight, you will not have one in the morning."

"Good thing I brought a gag and some rope to keep you in place." He chuckles and straightens in his seat.

More determined than ever, I promise myself that I will find a way out of this. I'm smart and should've known better than to depend on Q for my protection. The only person I can depend on is me. The only person who can protect me is myself. After tonight, everyone will see that, even Quinton.

29

QUINTON

I don't remember the last time I was this irritated. Every little sound from Anja makes me want to grab a fork and jab it into my ear. Then there's her not-so-subtle glances and touches. I swear if she touches the sleeve of my tux one more time, I'll be tempted to rip off each one of her long, red-painted nails.

At this point, her screams would be more pleasant than the stupid giggly sounds she makes every time my mother says something. I'm so fucking irritable, I don't even like myself right now. I can't even enjoy Scarlet being here. Not when we are in public, and I have to treat her like shit, and definitely not when Aspen and fucking Matteo are sitting across the table from me.

Even worse, Matteo's father, Michael, is here as well, and the dark gleam in his eyes and the way he's watching Aspen make me uneasy.

Why the hell is she here and with Matteo, of all people? Is this all a game to her? I doubt it. She would rather run through fire than be stuck anywhere with him, let alone voluntarily come as his date. I recall my father's reaction, and suddenly, it becomes clear that he knew she was coming. I wouldn't be surprised if he was the one who invited her.

The question is, why?

I'm vaguely aware of the music being lowered and someone announcing that dinner will be served momentarily. A few minutes later, servers arrive at our table, setting large platters with an array of food in the center of the table. My eyes catch on Lucas approaching our table with his brother, Nic, and his wife, Celia. I know enough about the Diavolo family that it's better to have them as your ally than an enemy. My father, of course, pushes out of his chair and greets them, giving Nic and Lucas a handshake. My mother gives Celia a little wave and smile, which she politely returns.

"I hope everyone is enjoying the festivities?" Lucas asks, his eyes gliding over the table. I notice the way his gaze hones in on Aspen, and my skin crawls. I hate the way everyone is looking at her, but what the hell am I to do? The dress she's wearing alone puts an X on her back.

"Yes, everything is great. Thank you for inviting us. I hope Quinton isn't causing too much trouble," my mother jokes, but no one laughs, least of all me.

"Of course not. Quinton is a star student." Lucas and my father let out a chuckle, almost like there's a hidden meaning behind their words.

Nic and Celia take a seat at the table next to us, and Lucas and my father exchange words that I can't hear. I drag my attention back to the table. As soon as my father returns to his seat, the servers start asking everyone what they would like, then proceed to pile food onto the plates.

Aspen stares wide-eyed, inspecting the food carefully as if she is trying to figure out if it's poisoned or not. Only when she sees everyone around her start to dig in does she pick up her fork and start eating herself.

I watch as she cuts into the steak, spearing a generous piece and bringing it to her lips. Once the large chunk of meat is inside her mouth, she closes her eyes and starts chewing with a low moan that has my cock twitching in my pants.

She catches herself a moment too late, and her eyes fly open. Luckily, I seem to be the only one who noticed. She clears her throat and continues eating. Her restraint doesn't last long because a moment later, she is shoveling potatoes and carrots into her mouth like she hasn't eaten in years. This time, everyone at the table takes notice.

"Jesus, slow down, pig." Matteo laughs, and I'm one second away from throwing the steak knife at him. In my mind, I see it landing in his right eye, blood running down his face, soiling the crisp white tablecloth. I can hear his scream and see myself smiling like a sadist.

"Are you not going to eat, Quinton?" My mom's voice drags me from my bloody fantasy.

"I'm not hungry," I reply, leaning back in my chair. "Some people at this table spoiled my appetite." I'm talking about

Matteo, but I'm sure everyone else here assumes I'm talking about Aspen. I look at Matteo to drive home my statement, but he doesn't seem to notice, or maybe he just doesn't care.

I stare at Aspen, admiring her beauty. Her long blond hair is falling off her shoulders in soft curls. She's wearing a red dress, revealing much more than it should. Her makeup is fresh and not overly done. She is beautiful, and I kind of hate it because now that I see it, I don't think I'll be able to unsee it.

"Yeah, I don't know how long Aspen and I are going to stay. I know they're doing the auction after this, but I think we might just go back to the dorms and chill."

My molars grind together, and I reach for the knife without thinking. It takes all my willpower not to respond to that statement. Why the hell did Matteo and her come together?

"I didn't know you two were a thing. I'm so happy for you," Anja chirps in a sarcastic tone that belongs in a soap opera.

"Oh." Aspen clears her throat, her eyes darting around the table self-consciously. "We aren't together."

The anger in my veins becomes a low simmer at the sound of her voice. For whatever reason, Aspen is a healing balm to my rage. She is the control when I'm spiraling, and she doesn't even have the slightest fucking clue.

"Don't be like that, Aspen. You know it's deeper than that." Matteo grins, and my rage is back to boiling again.

Using the napkin, she wipes her mouth, and when I see Matteo's arms move like he is touching Aspen under the table, I almost lose it.

She jerks away, confirming what I saw, but she doesn't need

a knight to save her. Not that I'm a knight. Lifting her arm, she elbows him in the side, but he doesn't move his hand.

My already boiling anger reaches new heights, and I'm half a second away from lunging across this table, tackling Matteo to the ground, and driving my fist into his smug face until he is nothing more than a bloody mess.

She is mine to touch, mine to torment, only mine.

"Excuse me," Aspen grits through her clenched teeth and shoves to her feet. "I need to use the ladies' room," she announces before turning around and walking away from the table.

From behind, her dress is even more revealing. Her entire back is bare, making it obvious that she is not wearing a bra.

As I watch Aspen disappear from the room, my head spins. Everything is so out of control. My father being here is fucking everything up.

I had just found a fix for my pain, a small calm to the raging storm, and now he's taken that away from me. Once again, I feel lost, unhinged, and this time, I'm not sure if I can ever get back to sanity again.

"Are you okay, Quinton?" My father's voice booms in my ears, and I sit up a little straighter. Either I can sit here and deal with what's happening in front of me, swallowing it down and forcing myself to digest it later, or I can do something about it right now.

Looking over at my father is like looking at myself in the future. "I'm fine. I just need to use the restroom."

It's a lie. All of it. That's all I've been doing is lying. Lying to myself, lying to my parents. I'm far from okay, but in my life, there is not room for anything else. It's either be okay or pretend to be okay, which is where Aspen comes in.

30

ASPEN

I can't take this anymore. I feel like I'm suffocating, a rope wrapped around my throat, tightening with each breath I take.

Making my way through the crowd, I ignore the hateful expressions and hope that no one is going to attack me while I'm in the bathroom. It's a risk I'm willing to take. I know being anywhere by myself up here is not wise, but right now, I'll do anything for a few moments of alone time.

The bathroom is empty when I walk inside, and I've never been more glad about anything in my life. I catch my reflection in the mirror, and I'm not surprised by how pale I look even with the makeup. I'm exhausted, and all I want to do is go back to my dorm and spend the night like I had planned.

Tearing my eyes away from the girl I barely recognize anymore, I step into one of the bathroom stalls. I hear a sound behind me, but before I can turn around, someone grabs me.

With a shriek, I spin around and start fighting immediately, but my wrists are captured with ease, and I'm pinned to the bathroom stall.

"Why the fuck are you here with him?" Quinton growls, inches away from my face. His hot minty breath fans over my cheek, and I sigh in relief.

"Do you think I want to be here? With him, of all people? I hate him. I asked you to get him off my back. I wanted to stay in my room and read, and I definitely didn't want to wear this dress."

"Then why the fuck did you?"

"Because your father made me! He sent me this dress and told me not to disappoint him and come to this ball. He even arranged a date for me."

I can tell Quinton believes me, his anger simmering down a tiny bit, but the murderous gleam in his eyes remains. He seems unhinged, his arm shaking like he is trying not to punch the wall. He looks like he is barely holding on but trying to regain control. Then it dawns on me... *control*. That's what he is craving, what he needs from me.

"Are you wearing any panties? I know you're not wearing a fucking bra." He grabs the strap of my dress and pulls it down, exposing my breasts to him.

"I couldn't wear a bra in this dress, and yes, I am wearing panties."

"Take them off," he orders.

"Are you serious?"

"Very. Now take off your panties before I rip them to

shreds." Getting impatient, he starts pulling up my dress until it's bundled around my hips. I pull off my panties, letting them slide down my legs so I can step out of them altogether.

While Quinton watches me, he takes off his tux jacket and hangs it over the stall door before he starts undoing his pants.

"Quinton, we can't. People will know, and what if someone comes in?"

"The door is locked, and I don't give a shit who knows what we're doing."

He frees his already hard cock and starts stroking it while I stand there with my dress bunched up around my stomach, my naked ass pressed against the stall.

Without warning, he lets go of his dick and grabs me by the hips, lifting me and pushing me against the wall. "Wrap your legs around me and hold my shoulders."

I barely have time to follow his directions before he lines himself up with my entrance and impales me in one hard thrust. The air swishes out of my lungs, and a sting of pain follows as he gives me only a moment to adjust to his length before he starts fucking me. My nails dig into the fabric of his dress shirt, and I yearn for that connection, that chance to hurt him back.

"Your pussy is mine. Mine to fuck. Mine to tease," Quinton growls, nipping at my earlobe. Each thrust of his hips is punishing and straddles the line of pain, but there is a niggling of something more. Something warm moves through my core, and I'm growing wetter with each stroke.

Holding me in place with his body, he easily finds my hardened nipple, pinching the nub between two fingers, and a delicious zing of pleasure makes its way through my body.

"Pretend you don't want me. In fact, pretend for both of us because now that I've had a taste of you, I don't know if I can ever go back."

His touch becomes rougher, and my thoughts become hazy as he moves inside me, using me as an outlet for his rage. I let my head fall back against the wall, and Quinton swoops in, his mouth on the pulse at my throat in an instant. His woodsy scent surrounds me, filling my lungs with every breath I take.

I never thought I would be the type to crave darkness, but something about him when he's unhinged and owning me, knowing he holds all the power, excites me.

What is wrong with me?

"I should mark you. Put hickeys all over your neck so everyone knows that you've been claimed. What do you think?" His voice is smoke swirling around my head, seeping into my pores. I open my mouth to object, to ask him why he would do something like that, but before I can, his mouth is on my skin, and all that comes out is a moan.

My chest heaves, and that low rolling boil of pleasure in my gut moves outward. Quinton's mouth is vicious, and he alternates between biting me and soothing the bites with his tongue. That, combined with his deep thrusts, sends me careening toward my climax.

"Shit. I can feel your muscles quivering. You're going to come soon, aren't you?" Quinton pulls away from my throat, his cheeks flush, his chest rising and falling as rapidly as my own.

"Yes," I whimper, gripping him a little harder.

"Look at me. I want you to see who gave you that orgasm, who owns your body, and who controls every move you make."

The fire in my belly explodes, and a warmth works through my limbs as my eyes roll to the back of my head. I've made myself come many times before, but it's never felt like this.

My orgasm sparks Quinton's, and he rests his head in the crook of my neck, fucking me harder and faster than he had been before, chasing his release. I let him use me, let him take what he needs too. When he finally comes, it's inside me *again*, and I make a mental note to remind myself to keep taking the pill. I refuse to get pregnant, especially with his baby.

After a moment, Quinton slowly eases out of me and places me back down on my feet. My legs are shaky, and I'm a little dizzy, but I place a hand against the door to steady myself.

The post-orgasm haze has left my mind, and now I'm back to being focused on myself.

"Clean yourself up. You look like a hooker right now."

"God, you're an asshole."

"Yeah, well, you just came on this asshole's cock, so I'm obviously not that bad." He's looking at me like he might come back for seconds.

I turn, shaking my head, and walk out of the stall. It's then that I catch a glimpse of myself in the mirror. My curls are in disarray, my eyes are hazy, and my cheeks are flushed. We won't even talk about my dress. As I take a step closer to the mirror, my gaze catches on my throat, where Quinton was teasing me with his tongue and teeth.

Right there for the world to see are his love bites. The ten tiny red marks will fade over time, but definitely not by the end of the evening.

"What the hell?" I whirl around when I see Quinton watching me in the mirror. Again, he is smirking.

"You weren't complaining as you creamed all over my cock."

Something inside me snaps. "Why would you do that? You know others are going to be able to see it, right?"

He shrugs. "That's the point. I want him to see it."

I grit my teeth and shove at his chest. "I'm not a trophy to be fought over. Marking me is only going to stir the pot and cause problems for me."

I don't know why I didn't stop him. Why I even let him fuck me in this bathroom stall, knowing everyone out in that ballroom knows what we were doing.

"Marking you will show him you're mine. It will show others you're unavailable."

"It will show nothing besides me being mauled by an animal," I murmur, adjusting my hair quickly to cover the bites as best as I can. I let Quinton leave the bathroom first, and I follow a few minutes later, my knees damn near knocking together with each step I take.

As soon as I reach the table, all eyes are on me. I pretend I can't feel their stares on my skin. Dropping down into my chair, I shield my face behind my hair and look anywhere but in Quinton's direction. The servers take our plates from dinner and serve dessert next. My stomach is too twisted for me to eat anything else, so I pass on it.

Matteo is staring at me, his angry glare hot on my skin. Does he know what we did? Do they all know? Of course, they do. Why wouldn't they? Matteo leans into my side, and even as I try to lean away, he wraps an arm around my shoulder, tugging me into his side.

Hot breath fans against my face. "Do you think I don't know what you just did in there? That we all don't know." He pauses, and my fingers itch to grab a fork and stab him in the eye. "I mean, if your face doesn't say it, your neck will, right?"

I can feel my cheeks heating with embarrassment. The asshole calls me out right in front of everyone at the table. I'm tempted to look over at Quinton just to see his reaction, but I let my hair continue to act as a curtain of protection.

"Touch me again, and I swear I will stab you in the eye with a fork."

Matteo lets out a soft laugh. "Damn, you're feisty. I like it. Can't wait to see what you do in bed tonight."

"We are doing nothing!" I snarl and scoot away from him with my chair. My low whispering yell draws the attention of Quinton's mom. I can see her concerned gaze on me out of the corner of my eye. How did such a kind, quiet woman end up with a man like Xander Rossi? Now that I think about it, I don't want to know.

Matteo thankfully takes the hint and leaves me alone as the night goes on. The main event of the evening is the auction. Xander gives a grand speech that I try my best not to roll my eyes at. Scarlet and Ella, and even Quinton, watch him with an awestruck look in their eyes.

I hate to admit it, but I'm a little jealous. Jealous of the love they have for each other and jealous of the fact that they're all together, well, minus Adela. Her disappearance is still a mystery to me.

As the auction comes to an end, I've never been happier to escape a room. I'm the first person out of my chair and heading for the door. My exit isn't as sneaky as I would like it to be since I excuse myself to go to the restroom, which they all know is a lie. I remind myself that all I have to do is make it back to my room, and I'll be okay.

As soon as I'm out of sight, I dart down the hallway and head back the way I came. Since most of the guests remain at the auction to socialize, I shouldn't have to worry about running into anyone else. I only make it to a set of stairs when a hand lands on my shoulder.

Whirling around, I see Matteo grinning down at me. "Were you going somewhere?"

I've put myself in a bad situation here, and I'm not sure how I'm going to get out of it. Matteo is huge, twice my size and weight. I have no weapon and no way to protect myself.

"Don't fuck with me, Matteo."

"But that's what I plan to do."

"I swear you won't like what happens if you don't leave me alone," I warn, still trying to come up with a plan in my mind. I attempt to evade him, but he grabs me by the shoulder, fisting the material of my dress. The sound of ripping fabric fills my ears, and I look down at my shoulder to find the dress half clinging to life. It's in that split second that Matteo invades my space further, his eyes gleam with resentment, and instead of responding, he pulls his fist back and punches me in the eye.

Pain spears the side of my face, and for half a second, I'm too shocked to even react.

Then something inside me snaps, and I remember that I have to save myself. Matteo grabs me by the arm and starts tugging me down the hall.

"If you had just laid down and taken my cock like the slut you are, maybe you wouldn't have gotten hit."

There is no justification for what he just did, and I'm not going to lie down and be stepped on. I'm not a doormat. I'm a fucking queen. I let him drag me down the hall for a few steps before I swing my body around and knee him in his balls as hard as I can. His grip on my arm disappears as he moves to cradle his junk. I don't wait. I spin around and run away from him as fast as I can.

"You fucking bitch. I'm gonna kill you for this," he groans behind me.

My chest is heaving, and my heart thunders against my ribs as I rush down the hall, wanting to put as much distance between us as I can. In my haste to return to the dorms, with one eye half swollen shut, I fail to notice a looming figure ahead and run headfirst into him. God, no, I do not need any more problems tonight.

"I'm glad I ran into you. Your date for the evening isn't over yet." Xander Rossi's voice implodes around me, and I take a shuddering step backward. He looks at my face but doesn't even blink or acknowledge my swelling eye. He doesn't care. I'm a means to an end for him. The enemy's daughter.

But I made the choice tonight to save myself, to fight back, even just a little. The words my father spoke to me the other day enter my mind.

I put as much conviction as I can muster into my next sentence. "I know it was you, and if you don't let me go, I'll tell Q." I have no idea what I am referring to, but the shocked expression Xander gives me is enough to keep me from admitting that out loud.

Xander stands a little taller, and I do the same, meeting his gaze head-on. I pray he doesn't realize I'm bluffing and have no idea what I am talking about.

"Good evening, Aspen. I'll be seeing you soon."

I shiver at the meaning behind those words, but I don't say anything. Like a mouse, I scurry past him, only stopping once I reach my room. Once inside, I kick my shoes off, fall to my knees, and start sobbing.

*A*spen excuses herself, claiming she needs to use the restroom. I know it's nothing but a shit excuse to escape the party. Matteo leaves a few minutes later, and I have to forcefully restrain myself from going after the fucker. I'm tempted to go back to my dorm and crash for the night, but there's this niggling in the back of my mind that tells me to check on Aspen first.

I'm still in my tux, but I've made a habit of keeping Aspen's room key on me at all times, even today. I pull the card out of my pocket and swipe it at her door. It unlocks with a low beep, and I push into her room.

Aspen is on the bed, curled up in a fetal position, facing away from me. She is still wearing the red dress, her back mostly exposed with her blanket only partly covering her body. Her shoulders are shaking, and quiet sobs meet my ears. She is crying, which has me worried. She hardly ever cries. As a matter of fact, I've only seen her cry once.

Closing the door behind me, I walk into the room and sit down on the edge of her bed. When I reach out to touch her shoulder, I notice that her dress is ripped on the side, like someone tried to tear it off her. Rage spreads through my veins like a wildfire.

"Aspen." I place my hand on her back, but she just shrugs away. "Aspen, tell me what happened."

"Go away." She sniffles. "You broke your side of the deal."

"What are you talking about?"

"You said you would keep Matteo away from me. You didn't. Our deal is off."

"Aspen, look at me," I order, getting more and more irritated with her. "What do you mean by that? Did he touch you?"

Grabbing her by the hips, I roll her toward me. She struggles, trying to push me away, but I don't budge until her face is turned toward me, and I see how swollen and bruised her eye is. *Motherfucker*.

"What else did he do?" I ask through clenched teeth. If he raped her, I'll kill him no matter the fucking rules.

"I got away before he could do more. I protected myself since you didn't hold up your end of the bargain. Now, please leave." She turns away from me again, and this time, I'll let her. Mostly because I can't stand seeing her this weak and vulnerable. The darkest part of me calls out to hurt her, exploit her weakness and use that vulnerability against her. I know if I don't walk away now, I will do just that. I will hurt her when she is already down, and that would probably break her.

Getting up, I head for the door, ready to get far away from her before I change my mind.

"Quinton..." she says so softly I almost miss it. My hand freezes inches before the doorknob.

"Yes." I look at her over my shoulder.

"Are you really the only person who has a key to my room?" Her voice is shaky and raw with emotions. She's scared, and though part of me likes her scared, I want to be the one who controls her fears. If she is going to be afraid of a monster, it will be me, and only me.

"I promise, no one is going to come into your room besides me. I'm the only one with a key, and I have it on me at all times."

"Okay..." She curls deeper into herself, and the urge to curl up next to her is tugging on my chest, pulling me toward her like an invisible force. I know if I get into that bed right now, I won't leave until the morning, and I can't stay here another night, but I also don't want to leave right this second.

I shrug out of my tux jacket and hang it over the desk chair. Rolling up my sleeves and unbuttoning the top of my shirt, I try to get a bit more comfortable as I sit down on the ground next to her bed. I lean my back against the side and tip my head back against the mattress.

She doesn't say anything, but she doesn't have to. I know she is glad I'm staying, no matter what she says out loud. I know she wants me to protect her. I know she is scared, and she turns to me for comfort. I also know that she shouldn't, just like I shouldn't feel the need to defend her.

Yet, here we are, needing each other in some weird fucked-up way that should have never happened. One thing is clear. This... whatever *this* is, it's not going to end well.

It's the only thing I can think about while I sit here staring off into space. Time ticks by, and I feel my own eyes growing heavy. It's tempting to stay here, but I can't.

I need to be back at my apartment. Scarlet is there, and every minute I'm here is time I'm wasting not spending with her. It doesn't take long for Aspen to fall asleep, not with the comfort of my protection surrounding her. I hate seeing her eye black and blue. It makes me feel things I shouldn't, a rage that has nothing to do with anger but with the need to claim, and that's terrifying.

Once I'm sure Aspen isn't going to wake up, I push off the floor and grab my jacket. I give her one last parting glance before I leave the room, shutting the door quietly behind me.

The corridor is deserted, and thankfully so. I don't need to have a run-in with anyone right now. My temper is already on edge, and to start a fight with my father here is asking to get my ass beat.

The apartment is quiet when I walk inside. I'm not surprised everyone went to bed after the excitement of the ball. There's no Scarlet on the couch, so I assume she's in my bedroom. As soon as I step inside the room and flick on the light, I see her squirming on the bed. She's pretending to be asleep, I'm sure of it, but who sleeps with their legs moving on the mattress.

"I know you're awake, and I know you're going to ask me a million and one questions, so get to it, so we can go to bed before the sun starts to rise."

Not even a second after I've started to speak does the blanket get tossed to the floor, and Scarlet sits up on the bed, her legs crossed, her eyes filled with wonder.

"Who is she? How long have you been friends with her? Why didn't you take her on a date since you clearly like her?" The questions all come out at once like word vomit.

"Aspen is a friend," I lie. I'm not about to tell her what she really is to me. "And I wouldn't say I like her. I tolerate her, more or less."

Scarlet gives me a look, the kind that says: I know more than you think. "You don't have to lie to me, brother. I know you like her."

I almost laugh. If Scarlet knew the things I've done to Aspen, she would change her mind. "You think I like her?"

Scarlet nods her head, a smile on her lips. "Yes, and I think she likes you too. I don't know why you and Matteo didn't just switch dates. Neither of you seemed happy with your selections." Sometimes, I forget how intuitive she is to her surroundings.

"Even if I wanted to, I can't like her. Aspen is Clyde Mather's daughter. The same guy who snitched on Dad and caused our house to be raided," I explain.

"Oh." Scarlet's smile falters, and sadness flickers through her eyes as she remembers that day.

A spark of curiosity ignites in my brain. "You wouldn't be mad if I liked Aspen?"

"What happened wasn't her fault, and I can't blame her for something her parents did." She looks away for a long moment, and sadness creeps onto her face. I toss my jacket onto the desk and cross the room, ready to console her, when she lifts a hand and looks back at me.

"What is it?"

"It's just, I haven't seen you interested in anything as much as it seems you're interested in her, not since Adela's death."

Suddenly, the air feels heavier, and every breath I take is weighted. "What she and I share. It's not like that..."

"No, stop. I'm happy to see you like this, and believe it or not, I like her too. She's sweet and pretty." A smile lights up her face once more, and my heart starts to beat normally again. Scarlet is all I have left, and to hurt her in any way would wound me beyond repair.

"I'm glad you like her, and I agree, she's very pretty." I smile.

Scarlet's smile becomes a fully-fledged grin. "I knew you liked her. You can't lie to me, Q. I know you better than you think!" She punches the air with her fist like she won some unknown victory, and I roll my eyes, gathering up my pajamas for bed.

"Sure, you do. When I get back in here, you better be ready to go to sleep."

"What are you talking about? I was already sleeping, but then you came in and rudely woke me up."

"Right, sure you were, with snakes for legs."

"Shut up!" She laughs and tosses a pillow at me.

These are the things I miss. I need these moments because without them, without the little glimpses of light, I'm afraid I might be eaten by the darkness that continually grows like a cancer that can't be beat. Aspen helps keep the monsters at bay, but what happens when that's not enough? What happens when the need for control overpowers me? I don't allow myself to dwell on the thought longer, not when it hits me that if Scarlet realized I showed an interest in Aspen, then our parents definitely did as well.

32

ASPEN

*T*he next morning, my head is pounding, and before I even head to the cafeteria for breakfast, I pop some Advil into my mouth and swallow it down with some bottled water. I give the medicine a few minutes to work and get dressed.

Things go from bad to worse when I build up the courage to look in the mirror and discover that my black eye has gotten blacker and even more swollen.

"Just my luck!" I growl to no one but myself.

The black eye forces me to go through my clothing once more, and I find a hoodie in the mess of clothes. Staring at my reflection, I try to conjure up some type of plan. If I leave my hair down and put the hood up, I should be able to hide the black eye, that's if I don't have to look at anyone. Doubt starts to flicker in my mind. The idea is going to backfire on me. I just know it, but it's the only option I have. I can't stay in my room and not eat.

Once my stomach starts to growl angrily, I know I can't hide any longer and slip out of my room and into the hall. I was exhausted last night and ended up sleeping a little longer than usual, so the corridor is congested with people.

Things are no better once I get to the cafeteria. I'm not looking forward to my smoothie, but it's better than eating nothing. Normally, I'm the only person waiting for food, but there is already a line of students, so I get in line with everyone else.

I try to ignore the looks I'm getting or at least the looks I think I'm getting. I'm doing my best to keep my head down and my face shielded by my hair, so I don't have to explain the black eye, or better yet, be mocked and told I deserved it.

The line is moving slowly, and the tiny hairs on the back of my neck are standing on end as if to warn me of something coming. Looking over my shoulder, I spot Q, Ren, Luna, and Scarlet walking into the cafeteria.

"Shit!" I mutter under my breath.

The line moves, and I go along with it. At least a few people are behind me, which means they probably won't even see me. When I get to the front, I scan my card like I always do.

"Your shake is not ready yet. You'll have to wait."

"Ugh, can't you just give me some eggs or something? Please, I don't want to wait."

"Too bad, princess. Wait, or you'll get nothing."

"I'll take nothing then." I'm already halfway spun around

and ready to walk back to my room, no matter how hungry I am, when the guy behind the counter stops me.

"Wait! You already scanned your card."

"So? Just hit cancel, or let it go through. I don't care if it comes off my account." I shrug.

"You scanned, so you'll have to get your food."

"I don't want it anymore. Hit cancel," I repeat. I know damn well this guy is only trying to make things difficult for me, so I cross my arms in front of my chest and stare him down.

"Are you trying to tell me how to do my job now? I told you to fucking wait. It shouldn't be that hard to understand, even for you."

"God, who pissed in your cereal this morning?" The staff here has been less than friendly to me, but they never treated me this badly.

"Can you go anywhere without causing trouble?" Ren's voice cuts in.

I want to give him a snide response, but I'll keep the 'Don't you go anywhere without being a dick' to myself. Turning away from everyone, I lean against the wall and look away from them, but of course, even that is not enough for Ren.

"Come on, Luna. We'll eat up at the castle with Mom and Dad. I don't want you around her. Q, are you coming?"

"I really want to eat here," Scarlet whines, and I'm a little shocked by her speaking up at all. "I want the full school experience."

"You do what you want; we're leaving."

I watch them go out of the corner of my eye but don't turn

back around, not until someone taps me on the shoulder. I turn around carefully, half expecting someone to mess with me. Instead, I find Scarlet's smiling face. "Here, you can have this. I'm a vegetarian," she lies and gives me her plate. I know she is lying because I watched her eat last night, and that steak she ate wasn't very vegetarian-like.

I glance over at Q, whose facial expression doesn't give anything away. It's like he is just watching his sister and me from the outside but not wanting to interfere or react.

"Thank you," I say honestly and take the plate from her.

"What happened to your eye?" Her eyebrows draw together in concern.

"Oh... I fell. Not used to walking in those heels."

She clearly doesn't buy it but doesn't ask any more questions either. She turns back to the guy behind the counter. "I need another plate, veggie omelet, please."

While she is momentarily distracted, I use the opportunity to slip away. I find a seat in the corner of the cafeteria, where no one else is sitting, and start eating my food. I clear my plate in record time and return my tray to the kitchen before heading for the door.

I almost make it out the door when my eyes catch on Quinton's table. It's only him and Scarlet sitting and eating breakfast. His sister is laughing at something he says, and for some reason, that makes me smile. I'm happy for them, truly I am, but beneath that happiness lies jealousy.

I don't want to be jealous, but I can't help how I feel about it. I am jealous, yearning for that same sense of happiness only family can give you. I'm jealous that they can sit out here and don't have to worry about someone attacking them, and I'm sad that Quinton would never publicly eat a meal with me.

Those thoughts stay with me as I rush back to my room. Even when I'm closing the door behind me and turning the lock, I don't feel safe anymore. Not that I ever really felt safe in my dorm room, but now even less so. As long as Xander Rossi is here, no room in the school will be safe for me.

Slipping out of my shoes, I fall into my bed and curl up in a ball. The events of last night and this morning keep replaying in my mind. I still don't know what Xander did, but it must be bad if he doesn't want Quinton to know. I play with the idea of telling him the whole thing, but that'll probably backfire. Like Quinton always says, my mouth is going to get me in trouble.

I decide to take my mind off reality and grab a book off my nightstand. I'll try to get lost in the pages, but after two chapters, my eyes keep falling shut, and I finally give in and put the book aside.

Of course, I slept terribly last night. I'm not even sure how many hours; I just know it wasn't much. Grabbing the blanket, I pull it over myself and close my eyes.

Just when I start to doze off a little, I hear the clicking of the lock. The door is pushed open, and I sit up in my bed so fast my head spins.

"You're already going back to bed?" Quinton's voice fills the room, and I relax back down onto the mattress.

"This might come as a surprise to you, but I didn't get much sleep last night. Something about being in the same place as people trying to kill you will do that to you."

"Don't be so dramatic. No one is trying to kill you."

"You're right. Matteo only wanted to rape and beat me. Nothing to be dramatic about."

He doesn't have an answer to that, probably because he knows I'm right. If Matteo had gotten his way, last night would have ended much worse for me.

Quinton sits down on the edge of my bed, the mattress giving way under his weight, making me roll toward him. "He won't bother you again—"

I hold up my hand, making him stop talking. "You've said that before, and how did that work out for me?"

"Yesterday happened because of my father, but he is gone now. My family just left."

"Oh... I'm sorry."

Quinton tilts his head, inspecting me. "Are you really?"

"I mean, I'm sorry you had to say goodbye to your family. I'm not sorry your father is gone. If it was up to me, I would never be in the same zip code as your dad."

"That's understandable."

"Why are you here?" I ask. Though I can guess why.

"I want to fuck you, of course."

"Of course," I echo his words. "Did you miss the part where our deal is off? You didn't hold up your end of the bargain."

"My father is gone. Our deal is back on."

"No." I shake my head.

"Fine. No deal then. I'll just come and go as I please, use

your body wherever I feel like it, and while I'm at it, I'll give Matteo a spare key."

I flinch at his words and the coldness of the voice delivering them. He holds all the power here, and he doesn't miss the opportunity to let me know it.

"I'd like to think you wouldn't do that to me, but then I remember who you are and what we are to each other. I guess our deal is back on. Unfortunately, you have already had your hour of fun, and my head hurts anyway. So, I'll see you next week."

I turn away from him, hoping he'll simply leave, but like everything involving Quinton, nothing is easy.

"You can't really count the bathroom sex as an hour. That was a quickie, ten minutes at best. You still owe me most of that hour."

I roll back over onto my back to look at him. "My head really does hurt, okay? Have you seen my face?" I point at my eye. "Please, just let me sleep. I'll give you a full hour tomorrow night, okay?" I'm probably going to regret this later, but right now, I just want to sleep.

"Fine. I'll be back tomorrow to collect."

"Great..." I pull my blanket closer to my chest.

Quinton gets up from my bed and walks out of my room without another word.

Yeah, I definitely will regret giving him another hour tomorrow.

33

QUINTON

he time on my phone stares back at me in an almost mocking way. I can't sleep, and I'm going fucking crazy lying here in bed. Ever since my parents and Scarlet left a few days ago, it's been harder than ever for me to get decent sleep. The time ticks to four, and I decide I need to do something before I end up ripping this room to shreds.

Pulling on a pair of shorts and a hoodie, I slip my feet into my Nikes and grab my wallet, which contains the key card to Aspen's room. I remember her telling me about her broken sink and decide now is the perfect time to fix it.

I'm bored out of my mind and can't sleep. What better time to fix something? I'm not much of a handyman, but I'll do anything to stay busy this morning. Plus, it's something I can hold against her later to squeeze out an extra hour.

The corridor is empty when I step out into it. There's a janitor's closet down the hall where they keep extra linens and towels for students. Not that I'm telling Aspen that. I slide my key card into the door and step inside the small space, flicking the light on.

There is a mop and bucket, broom, and numerous cleaning products. In the corner is a black duffel bag, and I unzip it to check the contents. My eyes drift over the various tools, and I pick it up, carrying it over my shoulder. Exiting the room, I close the door behind me and head to Aspen's room.

Any normal human would consider their actions before entering another person's dwelling without being invited, especially at four in the morning, but I've never considered myself normal.

When I reach Aspen's door, I've barely broken a sweat. I pull the key card out of my wallet and enter the room without warning. I step inside, and the first thing I notice is Aspen spread out across her bed. She's wearing panties and a T-shirt. The blanket is kicked away and at her feet, giving me a perfect view of her ass.

My cock starts to grow in my shorts, and the temptation is too much for me. If I wanted to fuck her right now, I could, but I came here to fix her fucking sink, so I'm going to do that instead. Stomping into the bathroom, I drop the bag and look at the damn thing like it's a foreign object. I'm not even sure how to approach the problem, much less what the problem itself is.

I pull out a pipe wrench and start twisting to loosen the pipes, so I can figure out what the hell is going on, but the wrench slips out of my hands, and my fist slams into the wall.

"Motherfucker!" I yell as pain ricochets up my arm.

"What the hell?" Aspen's sleepy but confused voice carries into the bathroom. "Do you have any idea what time it is?" she yells a second later. "What in the world are you even doing?"

I grit my teeth and ignore her, focusing my attention on the sink. It's too damn early to be arguing anyway.

"Seriously, what the hell are you doing?" she asks again, her voice closer this time.

I try to block her pestering voice out, but this pipe is annoying me, and it's probably not even the pipe that's the problem. It's the whole fucking sink.

"Go back to bed, Aspen," I growl and twist the wrench again. My muscles bulge as I twist the wrench, but the pipe doesn't budge.

Angrily, I toss the wrench at the wall and stare at the sink. I'm ready to rip it right out of the damn wall and toss it out the bathroom door, but then Aspen appears in the doorway, her sleep-filled eyes find mine, and she takes in the scene before her.

"You didn't have to fix the sink, Quinton," she states, all matter-of-factly.

"I know. I don't have to do a damn thing when it comes to you, but I do it anyway."

Aspen isn't affected by my shit mood, or maybe she is, but she doesn't say anything. I grab the wrench and start trying to rip the pipe off the sink again while she takes a seat on the closed toilet, obviously wanting to watch me.

Her presence isn't annoying to me, though. If anything, I've come to enjoy the lull of calm that rushes through my veins when we're in the same room. A strange, invisible string tethers us to each other, a connection I don't understand. It's almost like *friends*.

Which reminds me. "So, tell me more about Brittney. What do you guys talk about or do in the library?"

A long moment of silence passes, and I peer over my shoulder to find Aspen staring daggers at me.

"It's a library. We read books, and I help her categorize them and stuff. Nothing that other students don't also do."

She's a liar—a bad one, but I won't let on that I know she's hiding something. She might use the library as a form of escapism, but something more is going on there.

"You just seem close, and I can't help but wonder with your bartering if there is something more going on."

"No, Quinton, there's nothing going on. Is it a crime for me to want to escape all the snide comments and hateful looks by going there?"

"Not really." I can tell this is going nowhere fast. Aspen is a vault right now, her emotions and secrets bottled up tight, and unfortunately, I don't have the damn unlock code yet. I stare at the wrench in my hand. I guess I'll have to resort to something a little more drastic to get the answers I want.

"I'm not hiding anything. I'm just using the library for what it's supposed to be used for, studying."

I toss the wrench down, my frustration toward the damn sink mounting. That, combined with Aspen's attitude this morning, has my temper flaring. I'm wasting my damn time with her right now by trying to fix this thing.

"I can't fix it."

"Okay, but I really do need a sink."

"I know. I'll have someone fix it for you." I push off the floor, the bathroom suddenly smaller with both of us in it. My gaze sweeps the space, and I see the clothes she must've washed last night hanging off the side of the tub. *Bingo.* "I'll take your clothes and wash them with mine. No one will know the difference."

"They're going to know the difference, Quinton. My clothes are for a woman, and yours are not."

I pin her with a glare. "Clothes are clothes. Now, do you want me to wash them for you, or would you like to continue washing them in the shower?"

"No. I'd appreciate you doing this. What do you want in return? I'm sure this comes with a price."

I nod and smirk. "I want my hour now."

"Seriously? It's five in the morning."

I shrug. "I don't care. I'm hungry, and you're on the menu. Now hurry up before I change my mind."

She gives me a wary look before reluctantly agreeing. "Fine, but I want my sink fixed too."

She needs me, probably more than I need her, but I'm not going to tell her that. I don't want to rub it in her face. At least not today.

"I'll get it fixed. Now, go get on the bed. On all fours."

With a huff, she scurries out of the bathroom, stripping out of her clothing when she reaches the bed. I watch like a lion stalking its prey as her creamy-white ass jiggles when she climbs up onto the bed. Once on her knees, she spreads her legs ever so slightly, and I catch a glimpse of her pretty pink pussy.

"You act like you don't want me, but we both know you do. You want me even when you hate me, and that's okay because I feel the same way about you."

Like always, when it comes to Aspen, my cock grows to steel, and I'm hard as hell in a second.

Pushing my shorts down my legs, I slip out of my shoes and crawl up onto the bed, which squeaks with our combined weight. I take another moment to gaze at her in this position. It really is perfect.

"Are you going to fuck me or just stare at me?" Her sassy tone makes me want her more. It makes me want to fuck her hard enough that she can't get a single word out of that troubled mouth of hers.

Pulling my hand back, I land a slap against her ass cheek, my tongue darting out over my bottom lip as I watch it jiggle.

"I'm going to do whatever the fuck I want because, for one hour, you're mine. Mine to fuck, torment, and tease... Do you understand?" I slap her ass again, a little harder, and she lets out a groan instead of a response.

I massage each globe and then slap them both, enjoying the way her ass sways every time I slap it. She presses her forehead into the mattress, opening her legs a little wider. My finger trails down her ass, and I delve into her pussy, sinking two digits inside her channel. She's already wet and presses back against my fingers, chasing her own release.

"Fuck yourself on my hand," I order.

Her entire body freezes for a moment, and then she does exactly what I told her to do. Moving back and forth, she fucks my hand with slow strokes, almost teasing herself. Mesmerized, I watch as my fingers disappear and reappear as she goes back and forth.

My cock leaks precum from the tip, and I'm so turned on, I want to pull my fingers free and sink inside her right now, but I let her continue, watching as she works herself on my fingers. Her breath becomes ragged, and she starts to move, bouncing against my hand.

"As badly as I want to watch you bring yourself to orgasm, I want to feel you squeezing my cock instead of my fingers."

Aspen lets out a frustrated whimper as I pull my fingers from her drenched pussy. Her arousal glistens on my fingers, and I bring them to my lips, lapping up her intoxicating juices. My eyes drift closed, and I let out a growl.

Fuck, I want to taste her, eat her until she's writhing and her legs are shaking. Until she has to beg me to stop because she's afraid she might die from the pleasure itself.

When I open my eyes again, I find Aspen staring at me over her shoulder; her eyes are hazy, her cheeks pink, and she has a death grip on the sheets.

I drop my hand and grab her by both hips, centering myself directly behind her. I look down and see her puckered asshole. That virgin hole will be mine as well someday.

Guiding the head of my cock to her entrance, I push inside, filling her cunt in one thrust.

"Jesus..." she mumbles, and I smirk, loving the way her pussy wraps snugly around my dick. As fucked up as it is, she is my missing piece. The calm to my storm, the virtue to my wickedness.

Holding her hips with bruising force, I waste no time fucking her, and soon, the only sounds that can be heard are our labored breaths and the slap of our skin.

Something is different in the way we fuck. It's slow and leisurely, like we have all the time in the world. I tease Aspen to the edge of an orgasm, over and over again until her arousal is coating both our thighs.

Her puckered hole stares back at me, and I release her hip and bring my thumb to my lips. I suck the digit, getting it nice and wet before I bring it to her asshole. I'm not satisfied with the wetness and build a little saliva in my mouth before spitting against her asshole. Her entire body tightens up as I trace the hole, pressing gently against it while I continue fucking her pussy with my cock.

"Your puckered asshole is a little jealous that I've given your pussy all the attention. I think next time, I'll take your ass." I dip my thumb into her asshole gently, each stroke shallow, the tight ring of muscles giving way as I push my finger inside.

"Quinton." She lets out a strangled moan, and I can't tell if it's because I've mentioned taking her ass or because I've upped my pace, angling my cock in a way that makes it certain I'm hitting the very tender tissue at the top of her pussy.

My own control starts to unravel, and it won't be long till I come, the ache in my balls becoming painful.

"Who does this pussy belong to?" I ask through my teeth, moving my thumb in her ass a little faster.

"You." Aspen moans, pressing back against my cock, seeking out her pleasure like the little minx she is.

"That's right!" I pull my thumb from her ass and use the same hand to slap the creamy flesh. Then I start to fuck her even harder, setting a grueling pace, pressing her into the mattress as I use her body to bring us both the relief we seek.

"Oh, god, oh, god..." Aspen starts to pant, her face turned, with her cheek pressed against the mattress. Leaning forward, I thread my fingers through her hair and grab a fistful, pulling her back toward me. She doesn't object to the action even though I'm certain her scalp is screaming at her.

I rail into her faster, and when her pussy starts to contract, the muscles twitching and pulsing, I let myself go.

As she falls apart, I do too, and we both come at once, her wet pussy squeezing every drop of cum right out of me. I release her hair and slip out of her warm heat, sighing as I lean forward and fall onto the mattress.

I let my eyes fall closed and immerse myself in the post-orgasmic waves of pleasure. A sheen of sweat covers my body, and I feel rejuvenated.

"Fuck, that was good." My voice cuts through the silence, and I sit up on the bed, looking down at a very thoroughly fucked Aspen. My cock twitches to life, and I wonder if I could get away with a second round.

I notice then that Aspen is staring at me. "Don't even think about it. You had your hour. I'm going back to bed."

"You don't have to pretend you hate me, not here inside this room."

She shakes her head, her blue eyes shining with some unsaid emotion. "Yes, I do because any other emotions would lead us down a road neither one of us is going to survive." The seriousness in her tone reminds me of how right she is. It also spurs me to get dressed and leave. If I allow us to think we aren't enemies inside this bedroom, then who's to say those feelings won't follow us outside of it.

When I step out of the bedroom, the realization hits me. I can't forget that I'm the one in control and that no matter what we share or do together, nothing will change the fact that we're still enemies.

a week passes without any interaction from Quinton. He makes good on his end of the bargain, having the laundry services deliver my clean clothes right to my door. Then someone, probably the janitor, comes by and fixes the sink one day while I'm at class.

All these things make being here a little more bearable.

There was no way for me to lie to myself. He was helping me, and I hated it, but more than anything, I hated that I needed his help. Without him, I wasn't sure how much longer I could stay here, and with my mom's warning of how unsafe it was outside of Corium looming over my head, I couldn't exactly leave. It was to endure hell here or risk death out there. Sometimes, death looked like a better option.

A loud knocking drags me from my thoughts, and I look up from the book in my hand. The knocking means it's not Quinton, and as wary of that as I should be, I decide to climb off the bed and answer the door anyway.

As soon as I pull the door open and see who is on the other side, I consider slamming the door in his face.

"You going to let me in?" Quinton questions, waving a bottle of wine in my face and holding two paper cups in his other hand.

"Why did you knock when you have a key to get in?" My defenses are up, especially with his surprise knocking and the bottle of wine in his hand. He's insane if he thinks I'm going to take one sip of that alcohol in his presence.

His lips tip up at the sides. "I like to keep things interesting."

I try to ignore the way he looks, just standing there leaning against the doorjamb so casually in his jeans and black T-shirt. The smell of cedar and lemon fills my lungs as I breathe him in, and a warmth settles deep in my belly. *No.* Do not fall into his web.

"No," I reply and shake my head as if I'm trying to wake myself up from this never-ending nightmare.

"No, what?"

"No, you cannot come in."

The smirk vanishes from his face, and something dark and sinister takes over his features. "That'd be a fine response if I was asking, but it's a new week, and a new week means I'm allowed one hour of your time, where you do as I say, no matter what."

I cross my arms over my chest. "And what is it that you want?"

"For us to have a glass of wine together." His reply is dry, honest, and I don't like it. Not even a little bit, but what can I do? Deny him? No. We have a deal, and as badly as I want to tell him he can shove that bottle of wine up his ass, I don't.

"Fine, but one drink, and that's it."

Quinton shoves past me and into the bedroom while I shut the door, closing us inside. We've been alone inside this room many times, but tonight feels different. I can't pinpoint in what way, but I feel it in my bones. Something bad is going to happen.

Placing the two paper cups on my desk, Quinton pours us each a glass and passes me a cup. His fingers briefly touch mine, and a bolt of lightning zings through me.

"Cheers." He smirks and brings the class to his lips, taking a gulp of the red liquid.

I peer down into my cup, trying to build the courage up to take a drink. Quinton's piercing stare doesn't help matters.

"Drink it. Or the deal is off, and you can go back to fending for yourself." His spiteful words cause me to bring the cup to my lips, and I gulp the red liquid down, the bitter tang hits my taste buds, and my lips pucker.

"Good, isn't it?"

I wipe my mouth with the back of my hand. "Actually, no. It's terrible."

"Too bad, keep drinking."

"I agreed to one drink."

He takes a threatening step toward me, and I can feel his body heat rolling off him and slamming into me. "If I were you,

I would just keep drinking. You never know what I have in store for you tonight."

The warning is clear. He has something planned, something that I'm going to need alcohol to get through. I try not to let the dreadful thoughts take root, but it's harder than you think when you're trapped in a room with your worst nightmare.

My fear of what might happen next causes me to take another gulp of wine, and I empty the glass, setting it back down on my desk.

"For someone so adamant on only having one glass, you sure did drink that fast."

"Shut up," I growl.

Quinton doesn't say anything and instead fills my glass once more. I take the cup and sit on the edge of the bed, trying to block out his presence. Then it occurs to me. What if he's going to try to do something I don't like, something like... anal? He mentioned it the last night we fucked, that my ass was next, and we won't even mention the fact that he fucked me there with his thumb. The mere thought makes me drink more, and I find myself guzzling the wine in my glass down like it's water and I've just run a mile in Death Valley.

"Slow down, captain, or you'll get yourself drunk."

I don't dare tell him that's what I want, what I need if he thinks he's going to put his cock in my ass. I'll let him do a lot of things, but I'm not letting him do that, at least without me being incoherent in some way.

"I'm an adult, not a kid. This isn't my first time drinking alcohol."

"You're really fucking feisty tonight." Quinton slams down onto the bed, sitting beside me. His paper cup is long forgotten, though the bottle of wine is still in his hand. My thoughts drift, and warmth settles deep in my gut, working its way outward and into my limbs.

Is the wine already taking effect on me? God, I hope so.

Q leans into my side, and I swear I can feel his feral rage. "Keep up the attitude, and I'll have you on your knees again, my cock jammed into your pussy so far you won't know where I start, and you stop."

I shiver and take another drink. Quinton smirks and fills my glass once more. With each drink I take, my body starts to feel heavier, and after a while, my brain becomes foggy. Without realizing it, I lean into Quinton's side, my head resting on his shoulder. Suddenly, I can't keep myself sitting up straight, which isn't a bad thing if he still plans to have sex with me.

"How are you feeling?" Q's deep voice rumbles in my ears.

A hiccup slips past my lips, and I wish I could stop myself from saying what I do next. "You have a really nice voice. Has anyone ever told you that?"

Steadying me, he replies, "No, I don't believe anyone ever has. They've told me I have a really nice cock, though."

"You're so full of yourself." I shove off the bed and stumble forward. I've been drunk before, but this feels different.

"I bet you wish you were full of something," Quinton murmurs.

He snakes an arm around my waist and tugs me back toward the bed. I fall backward, my flailing limbs and body landing on top of him in a heap. Oh, god, this is where he tells me he wants to fuck my ass—the entire reason I've drunk as much as I have.

My stomach churns, and my skin feels flush. "What do you want?" The words come out in a slur, and I don't recognize my own voice. The room is spinning, and I lean into Quinton's body to make it stop.

"Everything, but right now, I want to know more about Brittney. Who is she? Why are you such good friends?"

"I already told you why. She's nice to me. She lets me stay in the library and hide out from everyone. She also has books in the library."

"Books in the library? You don't say?" Quinton mocks, making me giggle. "So, you hide out in the library with your books."

He dips his head, burying his face in the crook of my neck, and starts nibbling on my skin there.

"Mm-hmm, we hide out together. I hide from you, and she hides from Phoenix," I mumble, rubbing my back against Q's chest as his arms tighten around my body.

"You don't have to hide from me," Q whispers into my hair.

"Just from everyone else then?" He doesn't have a response for that. We both know it's true.

Time ticks by slowly, and Quinton holds me in his arms for a bit before moving us around and placing me on the mattress. I lay immobile, staring up at him. Watching and waiting for him to do something even though all he does is pull the blankets back and cover me up.

He's pulling away from me, and I need something to tether us together, something to bring him back.

"What happened to her... your sister...Adela." The words pass my dry lips with ease.

He stops and drops the covers onto my stomach. The look on his face is a mixture of both pain and sadness.

"What do you mean, what happened?"

I yawn, the wine having obviously made me tired as well. "Where was she at the founders' ball? I didn't see her."

There is a long moment of silence, and even in my drunken state, I can tell he's contemplating something.

Lifting my hand, I reach for his. "You can tell me. I won't tell anyone."

For some reason, I feel that whatever he is hiding is the primary reason for his rage. It's the reason for his lack of control.

His expression changes, and he takes a step back. Our connection snaps, and all that's left is a vacant spot in front of me.

"Go to sleep, Aspen. I think you've shared enough with me for the night, and I'm not in the mood to share anything with you. We aren't friends. We aren't even acquaintances. We're enemies, and nothing that ever happens in this room will change that."

His words cut me deep but don't surprise me. He would never admit to me if I meant something to him, just like I would never admit if I was falling for him.

"Good night, Q," I whisper, unwilling to touch what he's just said.

Clenching his jaw tightly, he storms out of the room, slamming the door closed behind him. With the wine circulating through my veins still, I let my heavy lids fall closed. Sleep invades the edges of my mind, but even as I drift to sleep, the question at the back of my mind still lingers. *What happened to his sister?*

35

QUINTON

*T*he following morning, before I even have breakfast or coffee, I go to the library. The halls are quiet, and it's not until I reach the library that I think maybe it might be closed this early. Thankfully, the doors are open, beckoning me forward. I catch a glimpse of the morning sunrise peeking up through the mountains as I enter, and I pause in the doorway to stare at the majestic beauty of nature. Strange how its beauty can become your worst nightmare in a split second. The mountains, while a sight to see, are more than dangerous.

"Can I help you?" A low voice grabs my attention, and I swivel in its direction. My gaze lands on Brittney, standing before me, a blank expression on her face.

Oh, this is going to be good.

"Yes, yes, you can. In fact, you were just the person I was looking for." I take a step toward her, and her brows jump up, a look of almost shock overtaking her features.

She should know that while she is a teacher here, and I have no real interest in her besides what she can offer me in terms of finding my birth mother, she should still be scared of what I can do to her. What will I do if she doesn't give me what I want?

"Do you need help finding a book?" she questions almost innocently, and I cross my arms over my chest, making myself appear bigger, scarier.

"No, no. Let's just say I know the little secret you told Aspen. I know what you are hiding from, or better, who you are hiding from. But don't worry, I want you to know that I won't tell Phoenix where you are... under one condition."

Brittney's nose wrinkles and creases appear on her forehead. I can see the anxiety building, feel it as it rolls off her and fills the room.

"You do understand that blackmailing a teacher could get you kicked out of Corium?" There is a bite to her tone that I don't like, so I drive my point home.

"And you do realize who my father is, right? I could make it so you can't get a job anywhere. I can make it so that you're poor, without a job or home, living on the streets, begging for your next meal." A visible shiver works its way through her body, and her jaw tightens.

"What do you want from me?"

"I'm glad you decided to help me."

"I didn't. I decided I value my job and food on the table more. Now tell me what you want or get the hell out of the library."

I decide to pause the asshole attitude and get to the point. "I need you to find something, actually, someone, if you can."

"Who?"

"My birth mother. I need whatever information you can find, and if you happen to discover where she is living, that's even better. Whatever you find, I want it."

"Okay, tell me everything you know about her, and I'll do my best to see what I can dig up." I rattle off all the info I know, which isn't much.

"Give me two days. Meet me here at the same time. I'll warn you, though, I'm not sure how much information I'll get with what you've given me."

"Whatever you find, I want to know. I don't care what it is."

Brittney nods, and the weight on my chest becomes heavier. What will I do when I find out who she is? Better yet, what if she tells me things about my father that I'm not ready to hear?

When I leave the library, I'm a mess, confused by my own emotions. What if my father was trying to protect me from her? What if she didn't want me? I shove all the lingering questions to the back of my mind. Until I have a logical answer to them, there is no point in dwelling on them.

I meet Ren for breakfast as usual and ignore the festering in my gut. Something bad is about to happen. I can feel it.

TWO DAYS PASS, and they're as anxiety-riddled as ever. I do my best to keep a safe distance from Aspen, even if it's hell to do. I can feel my need for control rising up. It won't be long till I have to make a trip to her room and find something to barter her with.

I drag myself out of bed and walk to the library to meet Brittney. As soon as our gazes connect, the tiny hairs on the back of my neck stand on end. She pushes her glasses up the bridge of her nose, staring at me almost nervously.

"I get the feeling whatever you're going to tell me isn't something I'll like.

"It didn't take me long to find a name, but her name doesn't matter, not now."

"What do you mean?"

"Tia was her name, and she's dead."

Dead? Why did I never think that was a possibility? "What happened, and when?" The wheels in my head start turning again; maybe she died in childbirth, or maybe one of my father's enemies killed her.

"I don't know what happened. I just know she is dead."

My jaw aches, and my teeth crack with the pressure of my grinding teeth. "Dig deeper, find out who killed her and why."

Brittney gives me an apprehensive look. "Sometimes, when you start digging for things, you move dirt and uncover secrets you were never meant to discover."

"What the fuck is that supposed to mean?" I growl, angry that my birth mother is dead. Any chance of finding out what happened between my father and her is gone.

"It means you might be better off not knowing what happened."

I shake my head at her stupidity. "I don't care what you have to do. Find out what happened, or else I'll end your career here and make you wish there was a place you could hide from us."

Brittney doesn't reply, and I'm thankful for that. I can feel my rage boiling up to the surface. It's only six o'clock, and I've shot my entire day in the ass with this little piece of information. Working out isn't going to make this energy go away. Nothing but control will help me. When I can't control the pieces of my forever moving chessboard, I move to control someone else's.

Each step I take toward Aspen's room sends a spike of adrenaline through my veins. She is a drug I can't shake, forbidden fruit dangling at the top of the street, and I'm starving. When I reach the door to her room, I've already got the key card out. I let myself in, opening the door slowly, and with one deep inhale of her sweet scent, it's like I can think a little clearer.

I close the door behind me, and my cock hardens to steel when I turn around and drink her in. She's sleeping on her stomach, one arm under the pillow, and her blond hair frames her head like a halo.

She's not wearing panties, and the blanket is kicked away, leaving her completely exposed. My mouth waters, like a fucking steak has been set before me. Every day, I learn she is a temptation I cannot afford to want, yet I'm not strong enough to deny either of us what we crave. Crossing the room, I lick my lips and reach for the button on my jeans.

I'm just about to strip out of my clothes and sink nine

inches deep into her tight pussy, fucking her until we're both spent, when my eyes catch on something glittery.

My lungs deflate like a balloon, and I stare at the bracelet Aspen is wearing, willing myself to unsee it clinging to her delicate wrist.

I'd know that bracelet anywhere as it was a piece of jewelry my sister Adela was very fond of. A thin rose gold bracelet with a heart-shaped diamond pendant. It looked beautiful on her, but on Aspen, it looks...

The room spins, and my hands become fists.

Something inside me snaps. The control I often seek out in Aspen is out of reach. I'm spiraling. As if God knew what would happen next, Aspen woke, her head lifting off the pillow and the bracelet moving as she sits up. I can't look away from that bracelet. How had she gotten it, and when?

"Quinton, what are you—"

I cut her off before she has the chance to speak. My hand wrapping tightly around her throat as I slam her naked body against the wall. My body is pressed against hers, trapping her.

Like prey, she stares at me, her eyes pleading. I squeeze her throat a little tighter and watch as the fear trickles into her blue eyes.

"Where did you get that bracelet?" I sneer, wanting to rip the answer right out of her.

Her eyes dart down to her wrist, and I can see her piecing the puzzle together. The only way she got that bracelet was to steal it from my sister.

"It's not... it's not what you think." The words slip past her trembling lips, but I'm too far gone to give a shit. My thoughts shift, swarming like bees, and I want to destroy her, break her.

I could kill her. I should. My grip on her throat tightens, and I watch through the haze of destruction as her lips become blue, and fear, like I've never seen, overtakes her features.

She claws at my hand, her nails digging into my skin, her feet kicking at my body but never fazing me. I watch as tears slip from her eyes and slide down the apples of her cheeks.

She's so fucking pretty when she cries. Too bad it's all fake. I grit my teeth and smile, smile at her, and watch as the light in her eyes fizzles out.

The stupid dangling of the bracelet causes me to lose focus, and at the last second, I release Aspen. She falls to the floor, landing in a heap. Her heavy pants for oxygen fill the room, and I ignore her existence as I angrily grab her hand to take the bracelet off. She doesn't fight, lift her head, or say a single word as I undo the bracelet and take a step back. The rage inside me is more powerful than it's ever been in my entire life, and I'm glad she keeps her mouth shut because today, I might just kill her.

"Stay the fuck out of my way. Next time I get you alone, there will be bloodshed." My booted feet slap against the floor as I leave the room, uncaring of what happens next.

Aspen is no longer my solution. She is the enemy, and I'll make her pay for stealing from my sister.

36

ASPEN

ear immobilizes you. It consumes you even when you don't want it to. Every day I stay here, I become more afraid of what will happen next. Quinton is on a warpath, and he won't stop until he's destroyed me. I stay hidden in my room, too afraid that if I leave, I may run into him in the corridor. His parting words linger in my mind, and every time I close my eyes, I see him standing there, hovering over my bed, staring at the bracelet.

I wish I could explain how I got it. I know he thought I stole it, but I didn't, and blind with rage, he couldn't see past that.

Lying in bed, I stare at the door, waiting for something bad to happen. It's only a matter of time. I can't eat, sleep, or even shower. I'm looking over my shoulder even when I know there is no one else inside the room with me.

I'm freaking myself out, and I don't know how to make it stop. More than that, my heart is aching because stupidly, I thought we were becoming something else. Not lovers, or even boyfriend and girlfriend, but maybe equals.

I know I should eat something, but I ignore my rumbling stomach. I've eaten very little, and hunger is finally catching up with me. Pressing my head into the pillow, I let my eyes fall closed and try not to think about Quinton rushing into the room to choke me.

The reminder of what he did sticks with me. I can still feel his fingers around my throat, still feel his boiling rage threatening to consume me.

He almost killed me. He could've, but for some reason, he didn't. Probably so he could elongate my pain and fear.

The sound of a key card entering the door has my eyes opening and my body on high alert. My heart thunders in my chest, and I look for the nearest item that I can use as a weapon, but there is nothing. The door squeaks as it opens, and my heart sinks into my stomach when Matteo appears on the other side.

"Get out!" I order, my voice unrecognizable.

"Really? That's the greeting you offer me after ditching me after the founders' ball? I'd expect better from you."

"How did you get in here?" I try to hide my fear and straighten my shoulders to make myself appear taller and stronger.

He smirks. "A key."

"How did you get the key to my room?" I press, unable to hide the trembling of my lips. I know the answer. I don't even have to ask, but I want him to speak the truth out loud. I need him to say it, so I can force myself to believe it.

"Quinton gave it to me. In fact…" He slides a hand into his pocket and pulls out his phone. My stomach knots, my eyes darting toward the door, which surprisingly has been left cracked open.

If I scream, would anyone come for me? Doubtful. I have to get out of this room and save myself. I have to find a way to leave this place for good.

Whatever monsters are out there cannot be worse than what is hidden behind the walls of Corium. Matteo types something into his phone and then turns the device toward me.

"Remember when he fucked your face?" When he hits play, vomit claws up my throat, and I look away, unable to watch the video. That day still haunts me, and to know that it's been recorded… "Unfortunately, I have more bad news. Quinton sent me a message saying he wants me to share it with the entire school. Told me he doesn't care who sees it."

My heart splinters, and while I expected something to happen, I never could've anticipated it would be this. I was stupid to have ever thought I could trust Quinton.

All it took was for one misunderstanding to occur, and he and I were on opposing sides again. There was no equal ground between us, and I was too blind not to realize it.

"Poor, Aspen, got her tiny little heart broken," Matteo taunts. He rushes toward me, and I dart away, but he's bigger and faster and manages to grip me by the wrist, tugging me back toward him. My lungs heave in my chest, and my only thought is to escape. I have to get away.

"You can't leave, not yet. I haven't gotten what I came here for." The hand at my wrist tightens, and his other hand comes up to my head, his fingers sink into my hair, and he yanks hard. Fire burns across my scalp, and I let out a yelp as he tosses me toward the bed.

"You owe me a blow job, bitch," he sneers.

"I owe you shit. Let me go." I try to shove him away, but he just tightens his grip.

Why did Quinton not show me a move out of this?

"Or what? What are you going to do?" He laughs, the sound only reminding me of that night. I squeeze my eyes shut, wishing that this wasn't real. Why do I keep ending up in these situations? Why can't people just leave me the hell alone?

"Let her go, Matteo." A voice cuts through my haze of fear, and my eyes fly open, just in time to see waves of anger flash over Matteo's face. I glance past him to the door, and to my utter amazement, I find Ren standing in the doorway of my room.

"What is wrong with you and your cousin? Since when do you care about scum like this, especially this one? You should be cheering me on, holding her down while we take turns fucking her. Did you and your family go soft—"

Ren moves as fast as lightning and grabs Matteo by the neck, pulling him off me with one hand. In the same movement, he slams his fist into Matteo's face so hard, his head snaps to the side, and his eyes roll back, the single punch knocking him out cold. He falls to the floor like a bag of sand with a loud thud. I would feel sorry for him if he was anyone else, but since he is who he is, I feel like a tiny bit of justice has been served.

Ren turns his icy glare on me, and I shiver at the darkness there. "I still hate your guts, but lucky for you, I hate this guy more."

I move off the bed, not wanting to stay in this vulnerable position, but then I'm at a loss as to where to go? Matteo is on the ground in my room, and when he wakes up, he is going to come after me regardless.

"You look scared," Ren states the obvious.

My lip trembles, and a response sits on the edge of my tongue.

Do I tell him how scared I am or keep pretending? Fuck it.

"Of course, I'm fucking scared. Everywhere I go, people have it out for me. I can't even hide out in my own room without people coming in, trying to hurt me. What am I supposed to do? Where am I supposed to go?"

"You're gonna be okay," His voice is almost soothing.

Frenzied, I shake my head. "No. I'm not okay. I'm... I have to get out of here. I can't be here anymore. It's not safe."

I don't know why I'm telling him any of this. It's not like he cares, and I know he would never help me do something like that, not without there being a price.

"Look." Ren runs a hand through his hair, and his eyebrows pinch together almost like he's contemplating something. "Let me help you."

I'm shocked. Confused. Everything is upside down, and I

don't know which way is up or down. How do you escape a box of torment when you can't find the door?

"Help me?" I croak.

"Yes, let me help you get out of here." He pauses and takes a deep breath before continuing. "I have a helicopter that I can get you on. It'll fly you to the airport. After that, you're on your own, but it's better than nothing."

He's giving me a way out, an exit. I'd be stupid not to take it, but what if it's a trap?

What if it isn't, and you pass up the opportunity?

Knowing that Quinton won't protect me any longer and that I'm nothing to him gives me the push I need.

I can't stay here. Not anymore. Not without his protection.

"You would do that?"

"Don't get any ideas. I'm not doing it for you, but yeah, I would do it."

I nod. "Okay, take me to the helicopter." I swallow around the knot of fear in my throat. I can't believe I'm doing this.

"Are you sure?" Ren asks earnestly.

"Yes. Please, help me. I can't stay here any longer. I'm not safe."

With a nod, he takes a step back and walks around me. I quickly grab a bag from under my bed and stuff the essentials inside. While Ren is on the phone with someone telling them to get the helicopter ready, I put on my boots and jacket. When I'm finished, I stop and stand in front of Ren. I give him a nod, signaling that I'm ready.

He surprises me by reaching for my bag and offering to

carry it without words. I hand it to him, grateful for his kindness.

Matteo groans on the floor as he starts to come back to, and the need to get out of here reaches a new peak.

"Follow me," Ren orders, and like a mouse, I follow him. I wrap my arms around myself, trying to keep all my broken pieces together.

Ren doesn't look at me, not when we step into the elevator or even when we reach the double doors that lead outside. The cold air pricks my lungs, and for a moment, I can't breathe. I'm chilled to the bone, the cold air seeping into every pore on my body.

Ahead a helicopter sits, its propellers slicing through the air. *It's now or never*, I tell myself. Ren hands me my bag and gestures toward the helicopter. I look back at the elevator doors, almost willing Quinton to appear, but he won't. He doesn't care about me.

"Thank you!" I yell, hoping he can hear me over the propellers as I climb into the helicopter, where a pilot is sitting in the seat. He doesn't look back at me, and I don't say anything. My hands shake as I buckle myself, and I blink back tears, trying to stop myself from crying. He doesn't deserve my tears or pain, but they belong to him anyway.

Ren gives me a wave, a smirk on his lips, and then the helicopter is rising into the air, the engine roaring in my ears.

Why is he smirking, and why do I get the feeling that something bad is about to happen?

37

QUINTON

The ringing of my phone startles me awake, and for a moment, I'm disoriented with the lingering sleep. Patting the bed next to me, I search for my phone. When I find it, I squint while looking at the screen and see Scarlet is trying to FaceTime me.

I sit up and use the back of my hand to rub the sleep from my eyes before I answer the call.

"Hey." Her smiling face comes into view. "Sorry, did I wake you up?"

"It's fine. I was just resting my eyes."

"What's wrong?"

"Nothing. Why do you think something is wrong?"

"Because you are not even fake smiling. You look sad," Scarlet points out. Dammit, why does she have to be so attentive?

"I'm fine. Just tired," I lie. Well, it's half of a lie. I am fucking tired, but I'm also upset.

"Is it about Aspen? Did you guys have a fight?"

I huff out a breath. I don't particularly want to talk to Scarlet about this, but I also know she's not going to let it go, and it's not like I can talk to anyone else.

"I wouldn't call it a fight. I just found something out about her, something that proved to me that everyone was right. She's just like her father, someone who can't be trusted."

"What happened?"

"I found Adela's bracelet in her room. She stole it from her. Probably to use it as blackmail or whatever was going on in her slimy mind."

"Wait. Aspen has Adela's bracelet?"

"Had," I corrected her. "I took it from her."

"Did she not explain how she got it?"

"Explain?" I ask, dumbfounded. "What is there to explain? She stole it. She stole from us, from her. I didn't give her a chance to say anything after I found it. I don't want to hear another word out of her mouth. Ever."

"Quinton, I don't think it's what you think. The bracelet wasn't stolen. That was just a story Adela came up with."

"What the hell are you talking about?"

"Adela told me that someone attacked her that night at the fundraiser. Some guy cornered her when she went to the bathroom. She said there was a girl her age who came to her rescue. Adela gave her the bracelet as a thank you, begging her not to say anything. I had no idea that it was Aspen."

"What? No, no, that can't be right. You are making this up. We would've known about that. Adela would have told me." I keep shaking my head, trying to pull the memories from that night from my brain.

"Adela didn't want to tell anyone. It was the first time she was allowed to go out with you guys. Dad was already so worried about her all the time, hovering over her. She thought if she told you or Dad, it would only get worse. That's why she kept it from you."

"Fuck!" I'm so stupid. Why didn't I give her a chance to explain? "I gotta go, okay? I'll call you back tomorrow." I hang up the phone before Scarlet gets the chance to say goodbye. Shit, I feel like a fucking douchebag.

I made a mistake, and I'm man enough to admit that, but am I ready to tell Aspen? I can still see her eyes brimming with fear, my warning lingering in the air between us. I just saw red that day.

Between the bracelet and the memory of Adela, coupled with what Brittney told me, it was too much to handle.

Now I'm agonizing over doing the right thing and apologizing, something I never do, not for anyone. Apologizing means admitting you were wrong, which is something I normally avoid at all costs.

Fuck it. I don't give myself time to think it through. All I know is I need to be near her. Getting out of bed, I get dressed quickly and head out.

On my walk to her room, I think about what I said again. I

wouldn't be surprised if she hadn't left her room. I'm sure she's been too afraid to even risk being seen.

As I get closer to her room, I reach into my pocket to grab her key, just to find it empty. What the hell? I must have dropped it in my hurry to get dressed. At least that's what I keep telling myself, but with each step, there's this strange awareness that pricks my senses.

I look up and find Ren standing at the end of the corridor. That's when I know something is really wrong.

"She's gone," he says. I'm not sure I'm hearing him, so I rush toward him.

"What?" I ask, my tongue feeling heavy.

"She left. Got on the helicopter and left."

Nothing that he's saying makes sense. Why would she leave? She wouldn't, would she? There is no place safer than Corium for her. The second she leaves, she becomes fair game to every single one of her father's enemies.

"Why? What do you mean? When?" The questions come out in a haze. Ren just stares at me blankly, like he's shut down his emotions.

When he doesn't answer me, I start toward the elevator, pressing the button, willing it to move faster. I can feel Ren behind me, his movements mirror my own, but he doesn't seem to care. It's almost like...

"What's going on, Ren? Why did she leave? What did she say to you?" The questions come out in a roar this time, the elevator dings, and the doors open.

I rush out into the cold, the wind whipping past me. The

organ in my chest skips a beat, and something I haven't ever felt before cuts through me. It's an emotion I can't quite pinpoint, and I imagine it's what they call heartache. I look up into the sky and see the helicopter heading away from us. Fuck. I have to figure out how to get it to circle around and come back.

"Make them turn around! She can't leave here, or she'll fucking die," I yell. Ren still appears to be in a trance.

"She got on the helicopter by herself. Obviously, she'd rather die than be here."

I don't believe that for a second. The reason she got on that helicopter at all has everything to do with me.

I did this to her. I pushed her to leave.

Heartache becomes horror when the helicopter starts to descend toward the forest. What is the pilot doing? Why is he... the question doesn't even finish forming in my mind. Not when the helicopter disappears into the forest, and a plume of fire and smoke appears a moment later.

My hands start to tremble, and I take a step forward like I might be able to help in some way.

"I'm sorry," Ren whispers. "I'm sorry it had to be this way." It takes me a moment to digest what he's said, and I turn to face him, staring into his vacant eyes, which are focused on the fire off in the distance.

"What did you do?" My voice cracks, all my emotions giving way. I don't even have to think about it. She's dead. There is no way she survived a crash like that, yet I somehow hold on to the hope that she did because the thought of her dying because of me kills me.

When Ren finally looks at me and replies, my entire world flips upside down. "What you couldn't."

First of all, **Thank you for reading King of Corium!**
Second, we are deeply, deeply sorry about this cliffhanger.
Please, we beg you for your forgiveness and promise we will deliver a worthy continuation in book two of Corium University Drop Dead Queen.

Did you know Quinton's parents, Xander and Ella have their own book?
Check out Keep Me now!

ABOUT THE AUTHORS

J.L. BECK AND C. HALLMAN ARE
USA TODAY AND INTERNATIONAL
BESTSELLING AUTHOR DUO WHO
WRITE CONTEMPORARY AND
DARK ROMANCE.

FIND US ON FACEBOOK AND
CHECK OUT OUR WEBSITE FOR
SALES AND FREEBIES!

WWW.BLEEDINGHEARTROMANCE.COM

ALSO BY THE AUTHORS

CONTEMPORAY ROMANCE

North Woods University
The Bet
The Dare
The Secret
The Vow
The Promise
The Jock

Bayshore Rivals
When Rivals Fall
When Rivals Lose
When Rivals Love

Breaking the Rules
Kissing & Telling
Babies & Promises
Roommates & Thieves

***

DARK ROMANCE

The Blackthorn Elite
Hating You
Breaking You
Hurting You
Regretting You

The Obsession Duet
Cruel Obsession
Deadly Obsession

The Rossi Crime Family
Protect Me
Keep Me
Guard Me
Tame Me
Remember Me

The Moretti Crime Family

Savage Beginnings
Violent Beginnings
Broken Beginnings

The King Crime Family
Indebted
Inevitable

The Diabolo Crime Family
Devil You Hate
Devil You Know

Corium University

King of Corium
Drop Dead Queen
Broken Kingdom

***

<u>STANDALONES</u>

Convict Me

Runaway Bride

His Gift

Also by the Authors

Two Strangers

This Christmas